Dear Reader:

If no one has told you that you are loved and appreciated today, I love and appreciate you. Whether you have read all of my books or this is your first one, whether you purchased this book or borrowed it from a library or a friend, whether you received it as a gift or found it lying on a park bench or a subway seat, I appreciate your placing your faith in me to entertain you for a little while.

Writing is my passion, but the catalyst for it was my love of reading as a small child. Thus, I realize the responsibility that an author has to take their readers to another place, to spark discussion and thought, and to create characters that seemingly walk right out of the pages and become a best friend, a relative, a lover, or a twin.

Total Eclipse of the Heart is extremely special to me, not only because it is a milestone—my 25th book—but because I have long wanted to tackle the topics within it: loving with disabilities, remaining in toxic relationships, and maturing to the point where you understand that there is a significant difference between what you want in a mate and what you need.

A NOVEL

Thank you for reading this and, again, you are loved.

Blessings,

Zane

"Are you a good man?"

She was picking at her food and I got the feeling that she was self-conscious about her weight.

"I like to think so. My wife's opinion fluctuates from day to day though."

"You have an extremely big heart, Damon Johnson. Extremely big."

I found myself blushing. It was not every day that I had a woman like Brooke compliment me. I take that back. Women had complimented me before the accident, but most of them were trying to get into my pants, especially Carleigh's friends. Now I would hear them whispering about my "injury" like it was the end of the world as they knew it.

A little while later we parted with a big hug and a smile. As I watched her walk away, I marveled at what a wonderful woman she was and hoped that our lunch would be the beginning of a wonderful friendship. . . .

Praise for Zane and her unforgettable erotic novels

"A legend among her fellow authors."

—*Today's Black Woman*

"The woman does incredible, erotic things with words. Read with a lover nearby."

—*Eric Jerome Dickey*

"Sweaty, grab-the-back-of-his-head-and-make-him-scream sex."

—*Entertainment Weekly*

**This title is also available from
Simon & Schuster Audio and as an ebook.**

TOTAL ECLIPSE
of
THE HEART

ZANE

New York Times bestselling author

ATRIA PAPERBACK

New York   London   Toronto   Sydney

AP\

ATRIA PAPERBACK
A Division of Simon & Schuster, Inc.
1230 Avenue of the Americas
New York, NY 10020

First Atria Paperback edition July 2010

ATRIA PAPERBACK and colophon are trademarks of Simon & Schuster, Inc.

For information about special discounts for bulk purchases, please contact Simon & Schuster Special Sales at 1-866-506-1949 or business@simonandschuster.com.

The Simon & Schuster Speakers Bureau can bring authors to your live event. For more information or to book an event contact the Simon & Schuster Speakers Bureau at 1-866-248-3049 or visit our website at www.simonspeakers.com.

Designed by Rhea Braunstein

Manufactured in the United States of America

10 9 8 7 6 5 4 3

The Library of Congress has cataloged the hardcover edition as follows:

Zane.
   Total eclipse of the heart : a novel / Zane.—1st Atria Books hardcover ed.
     p. cm.
   1. African Americans—Fiction.   2. Man-woman relationships—
Fiction. I. Title.
   PS3626.A63T67   2009
   813'.6—dc22   2009039838

ISBN 978-0-7434-9929-3
ISBN 978-0-7434-9930-9 (pbk)
ISBN 978-1-4391-8330-4 (ebook)

FOR JAE

Throughout the centuries, love has been defined in many ways. In today's society, most people relate love to a deep feeling of sexual desire and attraction. They believe that as long as the sex is incredible, then love is definitely blooming in the air. Too many people confuse lust and sex and end up trapped in toxic relationships. The world is full of people who remain in relationships that they realize they have no business in. Yet, they stay, hoping and praying for change, believing that the other person will eventually appreciate them and recognize their value. This cycle leads to regret, despair, and oftentimes depression.

Every once in a while, two people meet by pure chance; not while they are out on the hunt for a new lover. With no expectations between them, nature takes its course . . . the right way. They get to know each other, never realizing that their interaction might lead to the ultimate experience; the one thing that most of us crave our entire lives.

What results can be "a total eclipse of the heart."

CONTENTS

TOTAL ECLIPSE

of

THE HEART

PART ONE

SOLAR ECLIPSE

Solar eclipse—the obscuration of the light
of the sun by the interposition of the
moon between it and a point on Earth

Brooke Alexander

July 3, 2007
Washington, D.C.

Oh, that's it, baby.

"Yeah, that's the spot.

"Lick it slow.

"No, lick it faster.

"Now slower.

"Damn!

"Oh, shit!

"I'm cumming, baby!

"Aw, damn!"

I glanced up at the expression on Patrick's face as he tried to regain some of his composure. Remnants of his semen were still trickling down my throat. In the beginning of our relationship, I would take his dick out of my mouth seconds before he came. He insisted that I swallow, even though I used to find the taste repulsive and had never done that for a man before him. At one time Patrick was so special to me that I would have walked over hot coals for him, so I did it. Now it had become mechanical.

My best friend, Destiny, told me that men want women to swallow because it makes them feel "powerful" and "special." It makes a man feel like a woman is somehow being submissive to him if she "drinks from his fountain." I felt like Destiny was being way too overdramatic. Men like it because the shit feels good, just like women like it when men go down on them. After all, when we cum, they sop up all of our juices. Still, I hadn't acquired a taste for semen and that was the bottom fucking line.

Patrick was still shaking and whispering something that I couldn't quite make out as I got up from the bed and began my usual "post-dick-sucking" routine. I always made a beeline for the bathroom to brush my teeth and gargle like my life depended on it. At first, Patrick was offended, but after I explained to him that I was making certain allowances to pleasure him, so he shouldn't give a rat's ass what I do after the act is over, we reached amicable terms. Patrick got his head regularly and I got to rinse the taste out within a few minutes afterward.

"Come back to bed!" Patrick yelled out to me as I stood there glancing at my reflection in the mirror. "We're not done yet."

Yes, we are fuckin' done, I thought to myself. I *did not* want to go back out there and let him stick his dick in me. Giving head had become my way of avoiding the actual act of fucking. I'd suck him off real good, in hopes that he'd be too exhausted to do anything else. Going down on him had become an impersonal act; a *chore,* so to speak, to avoid hearing him complain. Actual lovemaking was something different altogether. That meant that he expected me to show him a lot of affection, to gaze into his eyes as he pumped his dick in and out of me, and to whisper sweet nothings into his ear. I couldn't even stomach the thought of it.

If someone had asked me even two years earlier which of my friends or family members was most likely to be involved in an abusive relationship, the last person that would have come to mind would have been me. Now, don't get me wrong. There weren't any late-night trips to the emergency room for broken bones, black eyes, or cracked ribs. Patrick never struck me with his fists; he simply battered the hell out of me with his words.

We'd been together for a little over a year, and in that significantly small amount of time compared to a lifetime, Patrick had managed to destroy my self-esteem, stress me out to the point that I'd gained nearly forty pounds, and cause me to alienate most of the people in my inner circle. Even though I'd been involved with a wide array of men with issues, Patrick took the cake. I tried to convince myself that he had a stressful job, and he did. But that wasn't an excuse for calling me out of my name, being demeaning to me, and often acting like I was not "worthy" of him.

It was a sick, toxic situation, but I felt trapped. More like *entrapped* because he was the perfect man for the first few months after we met. They always say that people should give relationships time to develop. That sooner or later a person's real traits will be exposed. I should have listened to "they."

I barely recognized the woman staring back at me in the mirror. She had worry lines under her eyes. There were numerous gray hairs, even though she'd yet to turn thirty, and she looked completely drained. I had to make a change—somehow, some way.

"Brooke, what's taking you so long?" Patrick asked, walking into the bathroom with his half-limp dick in his hand. He walked up behind me and started slapping the head of it on my bare ass. "You going to wake Magnum back up? He's ready for a good workout."

I clamped my eyes shut. I used to think it was cute that he called his dick Magnum. Patrick had an average-size dick at best, but you couldn't tell him that he wasn't hung like a mule. He'd always say things like "You know you want this big dick." "Tell Daddy you want this big dick." And "Yeah, I'm going to fill you up with *all this* big dick."

"Patrick, I don't feel too good." I opened my eyes and stared at his reflection behind me in the mirror. "I think my period is coming."

"Humph! Bullshit! Your period ended less than ten days ago, *bitch*!" He spewed the word *bitch* at me; spittle flew out of his mouth and onto my shoulder. He backed away from me. "Just remember, what you won't do, some other whore will."

He stormed out, and for a few minutes after he left, I weighed my options. I could get dressed and leave. I could give in to him like I always did, go out there, spread my legs, and be nauseous while he did his dirty deed. Or I could retrieve a butcher knife from the kitchen and bury it in his chest while he was sleeping. The final choice stood out the most.

When I finally emerged, Patrick had vanished. I hadn't heard a door open or close, so I assumed that he was in the guest room or on the sofa. Either way, I was relieved that he wasn't in bed waiting to jump my bones.

I locked the bedroom door, propping a chair up underneath the handle for good measure. I didn't think that Patrick would graduate to physical violence, but I was no dressmaker's dummy nor blind to the possibilities. I wasn't cut out to slaughter someone, but the thoughts were constantly filling my head. I wasn't cut out to be someone's slave, either, but I felt like one. The chair was placed there just as much for his protection as mine. If Patrick ever did haul off and hit me, one of us was going to the fuckin' boneyard, pure and simple.

I fell asleep that night with tears streaming from my eyes. The next day, we were scheduled to attend a Fourth of July party at his parents' house, where I'd have to pretend that everything was great . . . once again. I'd always felt that putting on pretenses was unnecessary after a certain age. As children, we have no choice but to conform to the wishes of our parents. We pretend to like school, even if we hate it. We pretend to *love* church, even if we don't really feel like attending. We pretend to enjoy food that we can't stand to appease our mothers. Pretend. Pretend. Pretend. Well, I couldn't do it anymore. I adored Patrick—some things about him—but a change was going to come or I was going to have to leave.

Damon Johnson

Carleigh, I'm telling you. That motherfucker is too fine for words. I bet he blows your back out every damn night."

"You ain't never lied, Jordan. Do you see that rocket in those shorts? I can see that *damn thing* all the way over here."

"Do I see it? Girl, it's making me hungry. I'm starving and I'm not talking about those ribs on the grill."

"Yeah, forget about him cooking out here. I wouldn't mind heating up some shit in the bedroom."

"Carleigh, tell us the truth. Can you even handle all that man? He looks like he needs at least four or five women to keep him satisfied."

"Ya'll crazy. I keep my shit on point. Damon is well taken care of, thank you very much."

"Well, if you ever need some backup pussy, give a sister a call. You can call me twenty-four/seven."

"I know that's right. Call me, too. Shit, I'll settle for simply watching him go to work. Give me a bowl of buttered popcorn, a Pepsi, and a front-row seat."

"You all better find you a man on Damon's website and leave mine to me."

"Please, those men on that website are full of crap. Last few good men, my ass."

"What about Bobby and Steve? They're cute, in an old-fashioned sort of way."

"Carleigh, you need glasses. Those suckers aren't cute by any stretch of the imagination."

"You hear those pigeons over there?" Steve asked, as I threw another slab of baby back ribs onto the grill.

"How can I not hear them?" I replied. "Carleigh's friends are a trip."

Bobby grabbed a barbecued chicken leg out of the pan and started gnawing it down to the bone. "Have any of them ever actually tried to get busy?"

I smirked. "They have no shame in their game. I'll leave it at that."

"Oh, come on," Steve said. "Spill the beans. You know women aren't the only ones who gossip."

"Don't I know it," I said. "You and Bobby are worse than any women that I've ever seen. All you chatter about is your sex lives, or lack thereof."

"Rub that shit in, why don't you?" Bobby popped the tab on his third beer. "I'm *this close* to finding the lady of my dreams." With his free hand he pressed his thumb and index fingers together. "I'm simply taking my time. I only plan on getting married once."

"Everybody only plans to get married once," Steve said.

"True," Bobby admitted. "But I'm not going to end up like a lot of these peeps. I have zero intention of being on my third or fourth marriage by the time I'm forty. I want to settle down, father some legacies to carry on my name, and have readily available pussy in my bed every night."

I laughed. "Seems like you have it all figured out."

Steve looked at me. "When are you and Carleigh going to have some kids? You've been married for going on four years."

"Damn, you sound like my mother. Everything happens in due time." I flipped the ribs over and took another sip of my orange juice. I don't know why I felt like I had to defend my manhood, since neither of them were getting sex on the regular. Yet, I felt compelled to add, "It's not from lack of sex that we don't have a child. I can tell you that much."

Bobby glanced at my cup of juice and shook his head. "Damon, I don't see how you do it."

"Do what?"

"Refrain from drinking alcohol."

"Is liquor a requirement these days?" I asked.

"No, but, shit, it helps take the edge off," Bobby replied.

I glanced down at Bobby's beer gut and chuckled.

"Preach!" Steve said, cosigning as he poured himself some whiskey—his drink of choice—into a cup. "Life is stressful and I need to be able to relax."

"Well, I work out to relax."

They both smirked, hating on me because of my body.

Bobby looked over at the women sitting around the table on the deck still talking trash, and then back at me. "Damon, I have to admit. You have it all. A fine wife."

"Amen," Steve said.

"A nice crib."

"Amen."

"A good job."

"Amen again."

"One of the hottest up-and-coming websites."

"Amen four times."

"And you're cut like a statue."

Steve said, "I'm not commenting on another man's body. There I draw the line; but amen to all that other shit."

We all laughed as I finished up the grilling so we could eat before the fireworks started later on that evening.

As we sat around the deck eating, Carleigh's friends continued on their tirade about how fine I was. They loved scoping out men in general, but they especially loved checking me out. Most women would feel uncomfortable if their girlfriends acted like they wanted to fuck their husband on sight, but not my Carleigh. She had me hooked and she knew it. In her mind, there was zero chance of me cheating on her. She was right.

While Steve and Bobby were both single and looking, I will be the first to admit that most of my other buddies had a problem with being devoted to one woman, even if they had exchanged marriage vows. I'd taken mine seriously. Carleigh and I had been married for four glorious years and I wouldn't have traded her for all the women in the world. Men tend to be egotistical creatures, and some of my married friends had the nerve to get pissed if their mistress or mistresses stepped out on them. That defied logic, but it made perfect sense to them.

There are some decent men, but the silly, immature men make it hard for women to differentiate. On the other hand, so many women play games that men have to be damn near as cautious, or they'll be somewhere feeling dejected or used. That was one reason why I was glad that I'd settled down early in life. Well, early for this day and age. During the last century, people married young—such as fifteen or sixteen—and had four or five kids by the time they were twenty-five. I got married at twenty-five; Carleigh was twenty-three; and while some of our friends had jumped the broom, most of them had not.

Carleigh and I met at the Essence Music Festival in New Orleans. She was there with her best friends Jordan and Sharon, and I was there with my ex-girlfriend. I know, I know. It makes me out to seem *doggish*, but I really am not. Fran and I were on our way downhill long before then. In fact, that trip was our last-ditch effort to make love out of nothing at all. We simply were not compatible, and it showed daily. Too many people stay, waiting for the other person to break it off. A lot of men start searching for their next woman so they won't have a dry spell once the shit does hit the fan. I'll admit that I was somewhere in limbo between those two things when I boarded that flight to Louisiana.

Fran got down there and started flirting with men every chance that she got. I found her cuddled up in a corner with a man in the hotel lounge the very night we arrived. She claimed that they had known each other for years, but the lie was obvious. I could tell by the expression on his face that he had no clue what the fuck she was talking about. He was trolling for sex and thought he had got lucky. If I hadn't come down to see what was taking Fran so long—she was supposed to be getting one drink "to knock the edge off" and then coming back up—she would probably have ventured back to his room and got her freak on.

I had suspected Fran of cheating for a while. The clues were there. Late nights at the office. Girlfriends with constant weekend emergencies. Her mother always needing a ride to a doctor's appointment or the grocery store. Returning home looking guilty, every single time. Even though I suspected that she was disrespecting me, I still did the right thing.

When I met Carleigh outside the Superdome on our last night, the magnetism was instant. She bumped into me while Fran was in the long-ass line for the ladies' room. She had on a Washington Redskins T-shirt, so I asked where she was from. I was pleasantly surprised when we realized that we were *homies*. People from the Washington, D.C., area say that they are from D.C. even if they live an hour out in the suburbs. Carleigh was from Largo, and I was currently living in Silver Spring.

We exchanged business cards for purely innocent reasons. She was a Realtor and I was looking to purchase a new home. It was all legitimate, I swear. Fran didn't see it that way. When she returned from the ladies' room, she looked like she wanted to wring Carleigh's neck. I introduced them, but Fran wouldn't even shake Carleigh's hand. Damn shame how some women act so catty.

To make an extremely long-ass story short, when we returned home, I informed Fran that it was time for her to hit the road and make other living arrangements. She threatened to sue me or to keep it simple and sever my dick. That didn't make me stay with her. For the life of me, I don't understand the latest trend of people suing one another when they break up. If you are not married, what the hell should someone owe you? You both took a chance and the situation didn't work out. Why should someone have to pay you to move your ass on? I have noticed the trait even more with men than women. Brothers demanding that a woman help pay their bills if they get kicked out of the woman's home. First off, they should be the main provider and not be living off her in the first place. Second, if it is time to move the fuck on, just do it. Fran couldn't grasp that reality.

The situation was unhealthy for both of us and needed to end sooner as opposed to later. Fran accused me of fucking Carleigh in New Orleans. That was absurd, I informed her. I met Carleigh the last night of our trip, and Fran and I left the concert together, went to a late dinner, then hit the sack. There was zero space and even less opportunity for me to fuck anybody but her. Fran was determined to make that hypothesis work for her. She suggested that I may have drugged her, then snuck out of the room. That did it, because any woman who thought that I was that hard up or insane over getting pussy was a complete nut. I helped Fran pack and dropped her off at her sister's condo in Rockville, then told her to misplace my number.

Carleigh and I hooked up the following Saturday—not for sex but to check out offered properties. I will confess that I was checking out her body more than the houses, but it all worked itself out. I was the perfect gentleman the entire three months that she helped me to locate the idyllic home. It was even more crucial that I find a new house by then. I was trying to get absolute closure from my dealings with Fran, and we had shacked up together for over a year. While her name was never on the deed, her memory was still there, and I believed in starting anew.

Fran thought that she would be moving with me when I found my new spot. That was another reason for the timing of our breakup. I didn't want to give her the delusion that we would be setting up another home as a couple. For a minute, she had become a stalker, parking down the street and setting up overnight surveillance to see what I was doing. Yeah, I had to get the hell out of there.

After I moved into my four-bedroom, three-and-a-half-bathroom, all-brick home in Wheaton, I decided to sever the business association with Carleigh and ask her out on an official date. We had been out to eat numerous times, but never as a prelude to the possibilities. I didn't want her to feel any pressure to hook up with me based on making a real estate commission. Too many men make women feel uncomfortable with the "what I can do for you" bullshit.

We dated for about six months and realized that we were true soul mates. Carleigh made me feel comfortable, and women don't realize how important something so simple can mean to a man. I could be myself around her, and she would often express the same to me. I asked her father for her hand in marriage, and four years later, it was still all good. She was the yin to my yang, and we seemed to complement each other in every way.

The fireworks that night were unremarkable. In our backyard, we could view those set off from a large, nearby park. Granted, we could have headed down to the National Mall in D.C. or to the Baltimore Harbor, but we were too full and preferred to chill out.

Carleigh curled up beside me on a blanket on our back lawn. Some of our neighbors were shooting off little rockets and running around with sparklers. I remember doing that shit as a child. My boys and I thought we were pyrotechnic experts until Chris got burned on the arm. The next year, and every year after that, we didn't touch anything hazardous. Instead, we watched other little knuckleheads get hurt and laughed at them.

After the fireworks show was over, I went into the house to put my digital camera away in my home office. Jordan came in right behind me and shut the door. I hadn't even seen the snake get up off the lawn, rather less slither behind me with her fangs exposed.

"Yes?" I asked.

"What are you doing?"

"Putting my camera away. That should be obvious." I knew where this was headed, so I asked, "Where's Carleigh?"

"In her skin." She laughed, teasing her hair with her index finger like she had invented an original line instead of repeating a tired-ass one. "Why don't you put the camera away and take something else out?"

Yup, it was definitely headed there.

"How many times do I have to tell you? I'm not fooling around with you. I don't want you. I love Carleigh, and I have no intention of cheating. You need to get some of that built-up wax out your damn ears."

"Speaking of wax, I got a Brazilian the other day."

"I'm thrilled. Now, can you please step off?!" I waved her away like a wasp since that's what she reminded me of. The female wasps can paralyze their prey with their sting. She was not about to reel me in. "You need to find a man someplace other than in this house."

"You're beginning to sound like a broken record."

"And you're beginning to act like a broken woman." I plopped down in my leather desk chair. "Jordan, you're an eye-catching woman. There are tons of single guys in the D.C. area. You need to stop harping on this shit with me. It's nonsense and it's not happening. Not today, not tomorrow, and not even when cars start flying."

She came closer and sat on top of my desk, lowering her tube top so I could see her breasts. "Do you like what you see?"

"No, I don't." I sighed. "Every woman has a pair of tits; I'm not overwhelmed."

"What if I show you my pussy?"

"Every woman has one of those, too. If you don't stop harassing me every time you come over here, I *will* tell Carleigh."

"No, you won't." She pulled her top back up. "If you were going to tell, you would've done it already."

"The only reason that I haven't said anything is because Carleigh will be harmed. She cares for you and thinks you're her friend and—"

"I *am* her friend. We go way back."

I have no clue why I continued the conversation, but the nature of a woman has always amazed me.

"Since you go way back, why would you try to fuck me? I mean, what if I did it? Then what? You would be content to share me with her, or is your intention to take me away from her?"

"Why don't you give me a serious dick-down and find out?"

That did it. "I don't have time for this." I got up from my chair and headed for the door. She tried to grab my wrist. "You really need to find a different ambition in life. You and I will never happen."

"Never say never," Jordan whispered as I opened the door and left.

When I got back into the yard, everyone was up dancing to "Milkshake" by Kelis.

"Damn, did you all catch a second wind blowing through here or something?" I asked, pushing up on Carleigh, who was doing a poor rendition of the chicken-noodle-soup dance.

"Dance with me, baby," Carleigh said, pulling me to her and giving me one of those wet, sloppy kisses that I so adored.

Carleigh was drunk, and even though I didn't drink, when she got toasted, it meant that she would be ready to fuck me until I was damn near comatose once everyone else left.

I glanced over at Steve, who was now grinding up against Jordan. She looked bored to tears. I hadn't even noticed her slither back outside.

"Steve, didn't you say you have an early day tomorrow?"

Steve smirked at me; he knew what was up. "No, I can hang out all night, if you all want to. I have a spare suit in my car."

I wanted to smack him. "Well, we're not partying all night."

I was about to walk over and cut off the iPod when Casper's "Cha Cha Slide" came on next. That was all she wrote; they all started clapping, hopping, and stomping, doing the popular line dance.

I have to admit that something about women doing a line dance is sensual, whether it's a country-music one, the electric slide, the booty call, or anything else. Seeing all those hips moving at the same time can make a man's dick hard; imagining those same hips propped up on his lap and working over his dick. It is amazing how so many women can shake their asses on a dance floor but freeze in place if you ask them to get on top during sex. I gave in to the moment, sat down on a deck chair, and watched them to see how low they could go.

Everyone finally left around 2:00 a.m. Carleigh was drunk as she walked Jordan to her car. Jordan had *implied* that I should be a gentleman and see her out, but I smirked and walked in the opposite direction instead. By the time Jordan and Carleigh finished running their mouths in the driveway, I had taken a hot shower and climbed into bed. Carleigh came in the room and collapsed beside me on the bed. By that point, I was exhausted and prepared to fall asleep without sex, but she made her move within seconds.

"Damon, I'm horny," she whispered, flinging the comforter off me and reaching into my pajama bottoms to caress my dick. "I need some of that good good."

Carleigh always referred to our sex as "that good good," implying that it was so hot that she had to double up on the compliments.

"You can have all the good good you want," I said, reaching over and pulling up her top, exposing her breasts. "Why don't you go take a shower first?"

"I'm too drained to take a shower. I want you to put me to sleep with that dick."

After being outside all day, I was appalled that Carleigh would climb onto clean sheets with a dirty body. I was even more appalled at the thought of making love that way. The only place funk belongs is in the bass line of a Parliament song. I was about to insist that Carleigh bathe first, but before I could go there, she was already devouring my dick with her mouth.

She definitely got a rise out of me so I put her to sleep in that good good way. I refused to eat her pussy without her bathing, but I did slide my dick in and out of her until she moaned, her toes curled, and her eyes rolled up into the back of her head. Even though I was tired, it still took me damn near an hour to climax. I have never been able to cum quick, which could be a blessing and a curse. Women love that I am not a two-minute man, but sometimes a man wants to be able to bust a nut and fall asleep. That has never been the case with me. Carleigh got what she wanted and then dozed off. I lay beside her, glanced out the window, and thought about Jordan. Not in a sexual manner—never that—but I wondered that if Jordan was capable of fucking Carleigh's husband, what else was she capable of? I really needed to tell my wife that her friend was not a friend at all, but, ultimately, it would have devastated Carleigh. No matter what, I couldn't be the one to take the light out of her eyes. I loved her way too much for that.

Brooke

July 4, 2007
Springfield, Virginia

B rooke, you look great in that dress!" Mrs. Sterling, holding true to form, was passing out insincere compliments. "Where did you get it?"

"I got it from a designer sale at T.J.Maxx," I replied, intentionally irritating her by mentioning a discount store. "You can get some great deals there, if you look hard enough."

She gasped like I'd shot somebody. "Thank goodness Nicholas and I don't have to worry about prices. I could never be seen in such a *bargain-basement* establishment."

"For most of the working class, designer clothing costs are too extravagant, so we have to do the best we can."

"The operative words are *working class*. That is a category that I have never fit in."

Mrs. Sterling always made it a point to jog the memory of anyone who would listen that she and her husband were affluent. Standing there on the ten-acre estate made it obvious enough. They lived by the shore and Mr. Sterling's yacht was docked so all the guests could eyeball it.

"How many people are you expecting today?" I asked, trying to change the subject before she started talking bank-account balances.

"Oh, about fifty or sixty. It's a small gathering."

"In my entire life, my parents never had fifty people over to our house."

"That's because your parents reside in a shack compared to this house, dear."

That was a nice stab. I had to give it to her. The gloves came off.

"My parents may not reside in the lap of luxury, but they're extremely happy and don't hide their dirty little secrets behind stock portfolios and security bonds."

She grimaced at me and I smirked.

Nice one, Brooke, I thought as I walked away from her to find Patrick. I could feel her eyes throwing daggers at my back.

Mrs. Sterling hated my guts. I was not of the "social material" that she felt was worthy of her son. The first time he brought me to their home for dinner, she wanted to know my "lineage." I quickly informed her that my father was a plumber and my mother was a schoolteacher, that I was born and raised in Washington, D.C., and that I had an older brother in the navy. She wanted to know if I was "world-traveled." I told her that the only time that I'd been out of the metropolitan area was on a field trip to New York City when I was a senior in high school.

She looked like someone had shoved a full enema bottle up her crusty old ass and squeezed. Mr. Sterling was kinder to me. For several months afterward I actually thought that he approved of me and Patrick. Then Patrick got angry one night and burst that bubble, informing me that his father "thought I was a fine piece of ass but not wife material." Patrick said that his father suggested that he should fuck me for no more than six months, then find a high-class socialite to show off on his arm.

Even though Patrick agreed with them—that became painfully obvious—he still kept me around. When I was evicted from my studio apartment in Adams Morgan, he insisted that I move into his Capitol Hill penthouse. I was reluctant but caught up in feelings at that time, so I agreed. My parents were cramped up in their three-bedroom with doodads and miscellaneous crap they had collected during their nearly thirty years of marriage. Moving back with them seemed like taking a step backward in my life. My reality check was discovering that I'd taken *five* steps back by being with Patrick.

Patrick was a prominent attorney and was even voted one of the hottest bachelors in the area by *Washingtonian* magazine. I thought he was the moon, the sun, and the stars when we met at the restaurant where I was waiting tables. Patrick had what we women call swagger, and he was articulate and convincing. He charmed my pants—and my drawers—right off of me, even though he had been on a date when we met.

He slipped me his cell number when she excused herself to the ladies' room to powder her nose. I actually overheard her say that shit: "I'll be right back. I'm excusing myself to go powder my nose." That was some uppity nonsense right there. Women go to the ladies' room to piss and shit, hopefully wash their hands, and possibly take a quick glance in the mirror. The only nose powdering done is when they snort blow.

I called Patrick the next morning. He picked me up in a black Bentley, took me to his place, and fucked me like I'd never been fucked before. I didn't realize that my body could be so flexible. The man could write a manual on sex positions. Over time, he convinced me to do some things sexually, swallowing his semen and engaging in anal sex, that I would never have fathomed before then. He had only insisted that I do anal a few times, unsuccessfully trying to convince me that I would develop a love for it. A couple of my friends swore by it, claiming that anal sex gave them more intense orgasms than vaginal sex. I refused to cosign on any of it. My ass started hurting at the mere thought of it.

As the party went on that Fourth of July, more and more people showed up to feast on the lobsters, shrimp, and oysters. The Sterlings had a live band perform with the lakefront in the background, and all their stuck-up friends looked ridiculous trying to dance. I wanted some ribs, chicken, and hot dogs with chili and coleslaw. No such luck. I wanted to hear some Jay-Z, Prince, and Mariah Carey. No such luck. I wanted a rum and Coke, but settled for a French Connection—Grand Marnier and Hennessy cognac.

Patrick was holding court on the side among a bunch of young socialites who wanted to take my spot. Shit, I was hoping one of them would make him dump me. I know what you're thinking. Why didn't Brooke simply walk away? Like the saying goes, some things are easier said than done. I could have left Patrick, but there was no place better to go. I didn't get involved with him because of his money. His wealth was an extension of his charm. I did love Patrick, but he didn't appreciate my devotion. I believed that he loved me as well, but didn't truly comprehend the definition of it. I was delusional enough to believe that he could, and would, change his ways for me . . . eventually.

Patrick beckoned me to him as he moved away from all the designer-clad hoochies and over to the overpriced patio table where his parents were seated. It looked like something you would find in someone's dining room instead of outside, but it was typical for them. I downed the rest of my drink, desperately needing another, and went to him.

Mrs. Sterling was still determined to humiliate me, and now she had an audience. Two other couples were sitting with them. As I walked up, she said, "Here comes Patrick's, um . . . play toy. Her name is Brooke."

I strained a smile and sat down next to Patrick. The people introduced themselves, and then, one lady, who had endured way too much plastic surgery and had been damn near *botoxed* to death, asked, "So, Brooke, are you a lawyer like Patrick?"

Mrs. Sterling let out this hideous cackle, and Mr. Sterling gave her an evil glare. I think he had become torn between his personal outlook on me and the reality that his son had developed true feelings.

"Actually, I'm in the food industry," I replied uneasily.

"Oh . . . ," the woman said, playing with a string of luxurious pearls around her neck. "You're a restaurateur. What's the name of your establishment, and do you have more than one location?"

"Ernestine, the girl is *not* on our level," Mrs. Sterling said. "She's a waitress—in a dump at that. She used to work in a nicer place, where Patrick picked her up along with his doggie bag, but she lost that job. She wasn't quite up to their standards."

I pinched Patrick's leg as hard as I could. He gave me a "You're on your own" gaze and went back to drinking his top-shelf whiskey.

"Are you really going to sit here and let your mother talk about me like that?" I asked bluntly. When he didn't respond, I tried to get up, but he pulled me back down. I wrestled with him to get my wrist free. "Let me go. I'm ready to leave."

"Thank heaven," his mother said.

Mr. Sterling cleared his throat. "Brooke, I apologize for anything the missus might have said to offend you, but please stay and enjoy the fireworks. They're set to begin in less than ten minutes."

My mouth flew open; then I gulped. "Anything she might have said to offend me? Are you for real?"

Mrs. Sterling glared at me. "Look, dear, I was only speaking the truth. You had a halfway civilized job, even if it was still beneath anything my son had any business dealing with. You gained a bunch of weight and they got rid of you. And—"

"You think I got fired because of my weight?"

She didn't reply but she and her friends shared comical glances.

"The reason I gained so much weight is because your son has me stressed the fuck out!"

"Brooke!" Patrick exclaimed. "Watch it!"

"Oh, now you have a fucking tongue?" He finally let go of my wrist. I rose from the table. "All of you can kiss my monkey!"

"Did she say 'monkey'?" I heard the woman with the pearls ask.

"Yeah, monkey, as in my pussy, my twat, my coochie!"

The woman's mouth flew open in shock as I turned my back on them.

I stomped off in the direction of the front driveway, where cars were being valet-parked. I walked up to the three young men standing around in red jackets. "I don't have the ticket but can you bring up Patrick Sterling's Bentley?"

"Sure thing," one of them said, then took off running.

"Where do you think you're going?" Patrick asked, approaching me.

"I'm getting the hell away from here."

He spotted his car pulling up. "Not in my car, you're not. I can't believe you told them to kiss your monkey."

I glared at him. "Patrick, I'm taking your car. You can either call the police and report it stolen or try to physically stop me in front of all these witnesses so I can file assault-and-battery charges."

The two young men standing there looked on while the third one was getting out of the driver's side.

Patrick shook his head. "I would never hit you, Brooke."

I shrugged. "At this point, I don't know what you're truly capable of. Until five minutes ago, I never thought that you'd sit there and let your mother talk shit about me in front of her friends. Granted, I realize she doesn't like me and she takes potshots at me every chance she gets, but that's in private. I can handle that, but she's gone too far and you allowed it. You sat there and watched her humiliate me and did nothing."

Patrick's eyes glassed over. "She's my mother."

"And I'm your . . ." I paused. "I don't know what the hell I am to you. Maybe you need to figure that shit out before you come home."

I went over to get in the car, tossing my purse on the passenger seat. "He'll tip you," I told the valet. "He has plenty of damn money."

"How am I supposed to get home?" Patrick asked.

I snickered. "Patrick, you're at your parents' house. They have a dozen cars and a chauffeur. Give me a break."

I got settled in the car and floored it, having no clue where I was headed. I didn't want to go home. I'd distanced myself from the majority of my friends and had no clue what they were doing for the Fourth. I decided to go see my parents. I sat there with them, on their balcony, watching the fireworks at the National Mall. Daddy had half a slab of ribs and two barbecued drumsticks left over. I gobbled them down with one of his Coronas. They were elated to see me and I them.

"You can always come back home," Mommy whispered to me later that night as I laid my head on her lap in my old bedroom.

"I don't know what's wrong with him. I thought he loved me."

"He probably does love you, but he's trying to satisfy everyone in his life, and no one's ever accomplished that . . . not even Jesus himself."

Mommy always had a way to make sense out of things. She was right. Patrick was trying to please everyone, and it was stressing him out. In turn, he was taking his anxiety out on me. I was determined that we would smooth things out.

"I'm going to make him happy, Mommy. No matter what it takes."

"Only if you're happy, sweetheart. Don't surrender your needs for someone else's."

I fell asleep as she continued to play with my hair and sing softly to me. Patrick didn't report his car stolen, but he blew up my cell phone a hundred times between midnight and noon the next day. My voice mail was full of messages from him pleading for me to call or come home. I had to work the three-to-eleven shift at the diner and decided to let him sweat. He was lying in wait when I pulled into the parking lot.

I didn't speak when I got out of his Bentley, determined to walk right past him. He was standing beside his father's Porsche 911 and clinched me into his arms . . . into a loving embrace.

"I'm sorry, baby. I had words with my mother."

"*Had words?* What does that mean?"

"She promised that she'll never do anything like that again."

I could feel his heart beating in his chest as he held me. I pulled away and gazed into his eyes. "Life is full of empty promises."

"Just give her a chance. Give *me* another chance."

"I'll be home tonight. Wait up so we can talk."

He glanced at the dilapidated diner where I worked. "You know, you don't have to work here. You don't have to exert yourself at all. We can get married . . . tomorrow . . . even tonight, and—"

I pressed my index finger to his lips. "We have way too many issues that need to be resolved before we can go there."

"And I'm prepared to resolve them."

He seemed genuine enough, but he always did after we had a blowup. After every time he called me out of my name and attacked my self-esteem, I kept telling myself that this time would be the last time, that he would see the light of day and somehow be the man that I needed.

"I'll see you later," I said.

We shared a brief kiss, then walked away from each other in silence.

Damon

July 12, 2007

"Honey, when are you coming to bed?" Carleigh asked from the doorway to my home office. She was wearing nothing but a turquoise thong and a matching lace bra.

"I'll be there soon." I stared at her for a moment.

She blushed. "What?"

"You sure know how to seduce a man." I grinned at her. "That's some sexy lingerie. Where'd you get it?"

"Aw, I have a secret spot."

I chuckled. "Is it the same secret spot that most of the other women have that's located in half the malls in the country?"

"Maybe."

"When's their annual fashion show?"

Carleigh frowned. "You don't need to see it. Men watch that fashion show on television like it's the Super Bowl, when you need to be checking out the action in your own bedrooms."

I didn't respond; she was right. Every year, when the *Victoria's Secret Fashion Show* aired on CBS, men were burning up cell-phone lines and shooting emails and text messages all over the place to remind their friends to watch. It was July and I already knew that it was coming on December 4. When I asked, I was joking. I loved Carleigh and would never forsake her for another, but, hell, all men look. If they aren't looking, then cheating with another female is the last thing that their women need to be concerned about.

Carleigh approached the desk. "What are you up to?"

"Uploading profiles to the site. They flooded in this week. The word must be spreading like wildfire because we're damn sure blazing."

I heard the smirk without even glancing up.

"Why can't you support my efforts?" I asked as I finished uploading the information for GoodBlkMan4U from St. Louis.

"It's not that I don't support your efforts, Damon, but be for real!"

"I am for real. This is something I set out to accomplish, and I plan to see it through. It would be nice to have my wife cosign on it."

"That website is no different than all the other dating sites—full of men sweating pussy over the internet."

"Humph!" I kept typing.

"All you're doing is providing additional means for imbeciles to line up naive women from coast to coast so they can run game, obliterate their self-esteem, and then pull a disappearing act and leave them pregnant, penniless, and infected with diseases."

I shook my head. I wanted to ask Carleigh why, if she had such a low opinion of men, she had even given me an opportunity to get next to her.

"You don't have to respond, Damon, because there's nothing you can say."

"Oh, there's a lot I *could* say."

"Then say it."

"Trust me, Carleigh; you don't want me to go there! Not right now!"

I was so tempted to tell Carleigh about her triflin'-ass friends, all of whom had tried to bed me at one time or another. It was hard as hell to keep my lips sealed, but I couldn't hurt her like that, not even to prove a point.

I did say, "You might think the world is full of canines, but who are they pumping from behind in the doghouses? Women who don't care about sharing dick, or taking another woman's man, that's who. Some women thrive on that shit."

"Well, none of my friends would *ever* go there. They're like me. One dick per person."

I smirked. "If you say so."

"I know so."

Carleigh was distracting me too much for me to finish updating the site. I logged out of the administration section and shut the system down. She stood there, eyes blazing, the entire time.

"So, are you ready for bed?" Carleigh finally asked.

I chuckled. "You go ahead. I'm going to see if I can catch some late-night episodes of *Law & Order.*"

"Oh, so now you have an attitude?"

"No, I need to unwind. I'll be in later."

Carleigh sucked her teeth, turned around, and stomped down the hallway toward the bedroom in her black, five-inch, marabou-puff mules. Her ass cheeks looked succulent in that thong and my dick was hard. I wasn't going to make love to her that night though, come what may. Carleigh was under the impression that she could mouth a bunch of gibberish, then pounce on my dick and put it out of my mind. She had damn near perfected it over the years, but I was learning to retain the upper hand.

Thelastgoodmen.com was my brainchild. From day one, my wife had been critical of it. The ironic part is, in a roundabout way, she had planted the suggestion in my head. Our conversations during our house-hunting days had often turned to past relationships. Carleigh had been pulled through the wringer a few times, and it was hard for her to grasp that she would ever find a decent man. I was *that man*.

After reading a lot of blogs, comments online, and visiting websites that shone a negative light on men, I wanted to provide some insight on men who fit the other end of the spectrum. Through my unofficial research, I realized that a lot of people—both men and women—seemed to believe that they should wound a person before that person wounded them. People carry so many emotional scars that if they wore them on the outside, we'd be living in a world full of disfigured souls.

I'll admit that a lot of men, especially since the evolution of the internet, are nothing more than predators trying to see how many notches they can get on their belt. I was on one site and men in their forties, fifties, sixties, and even seventies were on there acting like immature, adolescent boys who'd never been inside a woman. Requesting half-naked women as friends. Posting lewd or desperate comments on their profile pages. Asking when they could get inside their drawers. Sure, the women in question were putting themselves out there like that, believing that their only asset was in between their legs. Yet, when a man used them for sex, they were heartbroken. They assumed that they'd break the men off so much better than any other woman that those men would be ready to settle down. Not!

Men view women exactly the way they present themselves. If a woman portrays herself as a whore, the man is going to make her a whore. If a woman portrays herself as a lady, he's going to make her a lady. If she portrays herself as weak-minded and undemanding, he's going to run all over and through her, and then she'll never hear from his ass again.

Thelastgoodmen.com was started to transform all that. It was for men who had sown all their wild oats and were ready for the bona fide thing: a reciprocal, loving relationship with one woman, for life. Men couldn't automatically add themselves, a process that would've made life ten times easier for me. Instead, they had to fill out a sequence of forms and go through a screening. The screening had its limitations, as does anything in life, but at least they had to hold up to some form of scrutiny. First, they had to fill out a lot of personal information, most of which remained confidential. They had to describe their past dating history, upload at least three photos of the same person to prevent fake pictures, and provide two references from women they'd dated within the last five years, unless they were recently divorced.

Carleigh had all kinds of observations when I first described the procedure to her. Her exact words were "Are you stuck on stupid?"

She took my "brilliant" concept and made a mockery of it. She threw her entire arsenal at me.

"How do you know they didn't write those references themselves?

"What do you plan to do? Call the women up, or email them to confirm?

"Even if they have three pictures, how do you know it's them? It might be some dude they know.

"How do you know the pictures aren't ten or twenty years old?

"They could make up a ton of bullshit in their profile.

"You need to fact-check *everything*! Their profession; their income; *every damn thing*!

"I bet half of those men on there are married, engaged, or shacking up.

"What if a chick meets someone on your site and he chops her into fifty pieces and throws her ass on the grill?

"This widow I sold a house to met a man online. He took her for everything. The insurance money, her house, and the low-down, dirty bastard gave her herpes!

"Are these men going to fax in a recent HIV test?

"To top it all off, you let them rate their own looks. Surprise! Surprise! All of them check off 'extremely good-looking,' even the trolls who crawled out from under their bridges.

"I can't believe you wasted even five dollars on that domain! The last good men! What a crock of shit!

"You are such a Neanderthal!"

Carleigh went on and on. I'd rushed home to share the news with her—the site was up and running and several men had signed up the first day. I thought we'd pop the cork from a bottle of champagne and rejoice. Instead, she'd crushed me. Then she wanted some dick.

That was a year ago and I'd fallen for the okeydoke. Ten minutes after she called me a Neanderthal, she was sucking me off and had me eating her pussy. But times had changed, and as I sat there watching *Law & Order*, I wondered if our marriage could last. I loved Carleigh and I believed she loved me, but was love worth compromising my dreams?

Sometimes I felt like a trophy husband, a prize for her friends and associates to salivate over. I had ideas, and goals, and while I made a low six-figure income as human resources manager for a Fortune 500 corporation, I wanted to assemble my own empire.

Dealing with disgruntled employees and their complaints day in and day out had given me the crystal clear insight that most people are not passionate about their profession. It was all about a paycheck and a comfort level, without taking any serious risks. I was a risk-taker and knew that I could accomplish something better.

I ended up falling asleep on the sofa that night—on purpose—and was startled awake at 6:00 a.m. by Carleigh slamming pots and pans around in the kitchen. I could envision her, hair all over her head, wrapped in a terry-cloth robe since the thong and bra didn't work, waiting for me to storm in and confront her. Instead, I grinned, turned over to face the back of the sofa, and went back to sleep until I had to get up an hour later.

Brooke

'M determined to get this weight off," I told Destiny as I tried to short-circuit the treadmill that I was jogging on.

"Well, my diet starts tomorrow." She was standing beside me, eating a Snickers bar.

"You ought to be ashamed of yourself, eating candy in a gym."

"And you ought to be ashamed of yourself for not calling me for four damn months," Destiny came back at me. "Then you have the audacity to tell me to meet you here, instead of someplace where I can chow down on something deep-fried in trans fat. You know good and damn well the only workout my ass ever gets is in somebody's bedroom."

I laughed. "You still seeing Harold exclusively?"

"I'm still exclusive with him, but I doubt it works both ways. That's the way love goes."

I slowed down my pace and adjusted the settings on the treadmill. "Why would you accept that? When did Sharing Dick 101 become a prerequisite for dating?"

"That's cold, Brooke."

"It's the truth. Harold's been cheating on you from day one and you think it's copacetic."

Destiny glared at me. "Hold up, Miss High-and-Mighty. Didn't you meet Patrick when he was in the middle of a date and fuck him the very next night? Odds are that he tapped that chick's ass the night before he tapped yours, and you know it."

I got off the treadmill altogether. "That was different. He was seeing her before me and—"

Destiny smacked her lips. "An entire day before you? Whoop-dee-fucking-doo."

"My point is that, to my knowledge at least, Patrick didn't see her again after we hooked up. I don't even know her name, never did, so she must not have been too significant."

Destiny and I stared at each other, then burst out laughing. "Why is it that when women get together, trifling-ass men always dominate the conversation?" I asked.

"Because we rely too much on men to define us," Destiny replied with a shrug. "A woman without a man is like a light socket without a bulb. We need someone to turn us on."

"And off." I giggled. "You sure have a way with words." I eyed this fine man walking into the workout area in black shorts and a wifebeater. "Speaking of being turned on, look at that."

Destiny looked at him, all six foot five of him, and sighed. "See now, if I had a man like that in my boudoir, I'd beam to work every day, hopefully with a limp and a sore back."

"We shouldn't diminish a man's value to his looks. We get mad when they do that same shit to us."

"True, but he does look like he has some high-quality ding-a-ling in those shorts. Besides, it never hurts to look."

I watched him begin working out with the free weights. His

arms seemed strong enough to lift a bus. "I've never seen him around here before."

Destiny play-slapped me on the arm. "When was the last time your fat ass came here to work out?"

"Point taken." I checked myself out in the large mirror on the wall. I had on loose sweats because I didn't want people seeing my "real physique" until I dropped some of the weight. "At least I'm trying. You need to work out with me. I'm going to try to come at least twice a week, for starters, and move my way up."

Destiny directed her eyes to Mr. Fine. "You should see if he needs a sweat partner."

"Girl, I can see his wedding band from here. Besides, I have a wonderful man at home."

"Patrick is handsome; I will give his ass that. I'm still not feeling him."

"Why not?"

Destiny's mood turned solemn. "Look, Brooke, it doesn't take a paleontologist to figure out that we hardly hang out anymore since you've been with him. I damn near fainted when you called this morning."

"We've been spending a lot of quality time together. Between my shitty work hours and the amount of time Patrick has to spend inside courtrooms and preparing his cases, we have to do what we can do."

"I'm not knocking all that, but you're here with me now. It's not like the dude is riding shotgun up your ass twenty-four/seven. I could meet you at the diner and chat during your breaks. I could—"

"Breaks? My boss can't even spell that word, rather less practice it."

"See, excuses, excuses. We all have hectic lives in today's society, but we make time for what we truly want to make accommodations for. I miss taking in a movie from time to time, hanging out at a club, or at least talking on the damn phone. You don't even have time to engage in a *conversation*?" Destiny stood there, tapping her foot, anticipating another bullshit excuse to fly out of my mouth.

"Okay, you got me. How about this? From now on, we're going to make it a point to talk at least once a day, even if it's for five minutes. I promise."

"Empty promises."

I felt it sting deep down in my heart. *Had I just made an empty promise to her when I was always accusing Patrick of doing the same?*

"You'll see," I said. "We're going to be as close as we used to be; closer even."

Destiny glanced at her watch. "I've got to run . . . but I'll speak to you tomorrow. Right?"

"Come hell or high water."

Destiny glanced at the sexy man in the wifebeater. "Or come big, juicy dicks and low-hanging, fruity balls."

We both laughed, traded quick kisses on our cheeks, and then she left. I endured the treadmill for another thirty minutes, determined to meet my goal. I watched Mr. Fine as I picked up my pace and lost myself in an incredible sexual fantasy involving him, me, and a bottle of whipped cream, as my iPod carried me through to the finish line.

Damon

July 19, 2007

WHAT a difference a week makes. Carleigh had gone from snarling at me the week before to dropping by my office with a picnic basket full of wine, fruit, and chicken-Caesar wraps—one of my favorites.

"Did we have lunch plans?" I asked as she barged in my office door, wearing a tight, floral sundress and high-heeled sandals.

"No, honey, but I missed you." She set the basket down, came around my desk, leaned over, and planted a fat, juicy kiss on my lips. "I don't have another showing until seven, so I might miss dinner. I didn't want to wait that long to see you."

"Well, that's very considerate of you." I watched her go back and close the door, alerting my secretary, Jane, not to disturb us. I glanced at the crystal clock on my desk. "I have a departmental meeting in an hour."

"I'll take whatever I can get." She started pulling the items out of the basket and setting them up on my desk. "We really need to spend more quality time together."

"I come home every night. I'm in here at nine, out at five, and home by six."

Carleigh giggled. "I know your schedule, sweetie. I could set my watch by you. But since this real estate market has gone from roses to thorns, I'm busting my ass to make sales."

I shook my head. The mortgage crisis had more houses in fore-closure than anyone had ever imagined. There had been a boom in the market for years, with developers throwing up million-dollar homes right and left in the metropolitan area. Mortgage companies and banks were shelling out low-interest, adjustable-rate mortgages like pediatricians handed out lollipops and smiley-face stickers. People were able to move in, sometimes by putting up less than five grand, and bought into the illusion that the world was their oyster.

When the two-, three-, or four-year ARMs matured and their monthly payments jumped from $2,000 to $6,000, reality hit. Some people were training their kids to eat tuna fish and crackers for dinner. Others simply said, "Fuck it all," and moved in with rela-tives or rented, abandoning their high debts. Refinancing at lower rates was damned near impossible due to the backlash. New regu-lations and criteria were added, and even those with credit ratings of 700 or higher were being scrutinized and required to provide more substantial proof of eligibility before even having a prayer for approval.

Carleigh was feeling the crunch and had been taking a lot of her frustrations out on me. I meant every single word of my vows and I was going to stick by her, for better or for worse, even if she be-came a stay-at-home wife. To be honest, that was one of the reasons I'd hoped she would grow excited about my website. We could've been partners and grown closer through the process. Instead, I'd sit in my home office, updating the site, while Carleigh burned up phone lines with her friends with nonsense and gossip. Or they'd commandeer the house, make a bunch of noise, and hire buff dudes to come over and pamper them with pedicures and massages. I didn't take issue with it; Carleigh was all about me when it came to meeting her sexual needs. I was her "boy toy" and she relished it. Even when I withheld the dick because I was mad at her about something, she wasn't about to stray. She would've never risked leaving me for highly unlikely greener pastures. Everyone knows— or at least should know—that the other side of grass is dirt.

So many people fall victim to the game—lured away from the person who has loved them unconditionally, supported them through the terrible times, celebrated with them through the good times, for a mere pipe dream. I didn't believe thelastgoodmen.com was contributing to the degradation of females—at least not really. I was simply capitalizing on an exploding trend that was going to flourish, with or without me. In a way, I felt that I was improving the odds for women seeking men on the internet. On those other sites, they could wind up with anything, which was true of life itself. There were no guarantees that the best men could be found in church, and definitely not by hanging out in clubs. There were no guarantees with my site either. That had become clear lately, and I was glad that Carleigh expressed no interest in it. I would never have heard the end of it.

"So, how are things with the site?" Carleigh asked, as if she were reading my mind.

I cleared my throat between bites of my wrap. "Everything's going great. Why do you ask?"

"Just trying to show some interest. After all, I realize it's a significant part of your life."

She was definitely reading my mind!

"Well, it's appreciated."

She took a sip of wine and waited for me to say more. Finally, she threw a grape at me. "So?"

I played dumb. "So?"

"How many profiles are up now?"

"Thirteen hundred; give or take a few."

"Wow, you'll be catching up to MySpace and eHarmony any day now." The sarcasm dripped from her words and she had this devilish grin on her face.

"Carleigh, I thought you came here to have a pleasant lunch."

"I did. I was merely asking about the site. I'm not allowed to do that?"

"You're obviously trying to belittle me and I don't appreciate it." I tossed my wrap down and stood up. "In fact, if you came to give me a verbal beatdown, we can do this shit at home."

Carleigh laughed. "You're too damn sensitive, Damon. Sit down and finish your food."

I took a seat but refused to eat. "I'm full, but thanks for bringing lunch over. It was a *pleasant* surprise."

Carleigh smirked and shook her head. "Mama was right."

I sat there patiently, waiting for her to elaborate. After a full minute of watching her eat in her prissy sort of way—where she was so determined to keep her mouth sealed while she was chewing that it was almost comical—I lost my composure.

"What was your mother right about?"

"It's nothing."

"Carleigh, you know I hate it when you do that. Start to say something and then refuse to finish. I'm not a psychic and never professed to be."

"That's for damn sure."

I took a deep breath and looked at my clock. Fifteen more minutes of hell before the meeting.

"What the fuck did your mother say?" I asked irately.

Carleigh's mother never fully approved of our marriage. She

expected Carleigh to marry a millionaire—a pro baller or cosmetic surgeon who made a mint from injecting youth-seeking women full of Botox. By anyone's standards, I made a good living, and I owned my own home—one that Carleigh had banked the commission from. Still, I failed to meet Carleigh's mother's expectations for her one and only darling child, her princess. Ninety percent of me didn't give a rat's ass what her mother had said, but the remaining 10 percent wanted to see how creative the old battle-ax could get.

Carleigh was gawking at me after I cursed at her. Her mouth was open and I could see half-chewed food. I couldn't help but comment.

"Wow, I can't believe you're chewing with your mouth open!"

Carleigh clamped her mouth shut quickly and swallowed. "It wasn't anything about you, in particular. Mama simply warned me about men period."

"And what would your mother know about men?"

"That does it!" Carleigh stood up and gathered her purse. "You can clean this shit up and bring the basket home. I'm out of here!"

I watched her leave and thought, *A week didn't make a damn difference after all.*

Every time I thought Carleigh and I were working toward a more civil union, drama ensued. I pictured her huffing and puffing on the elevator down to the garage, cursing me underneath her breath. She didn't like my saying anything about her mother, who hadn't been able to snag a man in more than two decades, and it was not for lack of trying. Carleigh's mother flung herself at every man over fifty that she could find—eligible bachelor or not. She never had any takers. No amount of liquor, senility, or desperation would reduce a man to what she yearned for: a puppet.

I cleaned up the lunch items and headed to my meeting. It was hard to concentrate during the two or so hours that it lasted. Never would I have imagined entering into such an unhealthy relationship—rather less a marriage. I felt like Carleigh and I had taken enough time to become acclimated to each other before we took the plunge. We were friends first and didn't become intimate until much later. In my mind, we had followed all the rules, but yet, we didn't seem much better off than two people who met at a club, went home and fucked and sucked the same night, and headed to a chapel in Vegas the next week.

I had a coworker, Kim, who had married twice and twice divorced. The first time, she married someone she'd known since she was ten. After the marriage, he totally changed up on her, and it almost ruined her emotionally. He was extremely abusive. Then she turned around and married a man she'd only known for a few months, after he had swept her off her feet. Within two years, she was filing for divorce again, after discovering him cheating. He was one of those fools who thought sweating other pussy on the internet was cool, until it cost him his marriage. Kim was childless and planned to stay that way. She said that there was no way she would bring children into the world to watch their father—or fathers—disrespect her.

Unfortunately, Kim's opinion of men was becoming the norm in society. While tons of women were still desiring to be loved and looking for dick in all the wrong places, many others had resorted to gaining their pleasure from sex toys—or other women—because they were sick of being mistreated by men and feared catching a deadly disease.

I felt like I'd mistreated Carleigh earlier by taking a stab at her mother, but we were really mistreating each other by making mountains out of molehills, intentionally pressing the wrong buttons, ones guaranteed to spark an argument or cause emotional withdrawal.

I was not going to abandon my marriage. I loved her. We would make it. For better or for worse; till death do us part.

Brooke

So far, I'd kept my promise to Destiny. Come hell or high water, we'd talked every single day since that day at the gym. I had, however, faltered on my workout regimen. Patrick found one reason or another to nitpick about something I was not doing, or not doing right, around our home. When I was not working, I was trying to keep him content. I'd started fucking him whenever he wanted, and I would suck him dry on demand. I even tried anal again and endured the pain to please him.

I washed clothes, dishes, and even his ass when he would beckon me into the shower for hot sex amid the steam. I thought that we were making progress. Then his mother showed up at our door.

When the bell rang, I assumed it was the doorman delivering a package that a messenger had dropped off. Instead, I found the queen of all bitches.

"Good morning, dear," she said, brushing past me in a bunch of silk scarves and almost knocking me down with her $2,000 handbag.

"Patrick is in court." I walked behind her, hoping that she would turn right around and leave. "He won't be in until tonight."

"Good." She made a show out of sitting down elegantly on the sofa as if she were royalty. "That gives us an opportunity to get to know one another."

"Excuse me?"

"You heard me." She patted the spot beside her. "Sit down, Brooke. We need to have a one-on-one discussion about what it means to be a woman."

I stood by the sofa and crossed my arms in defiance. "I have a wonderful mother who has already taught me what it means to be a woman."

She smirked. "Oh, yeah, the schoolteacher."

I sat down on the armchair opposite her, realizing any hopes of her immediate exit had vanished. "Teaching school is an admirable profession. Even the socially elite get an education, right?"

"We're provided the best education that money can buy."

"But you're taught by teachers."

She cleared her throat. "I feel a bit parched."

I motioned my head to the left. "There are two faucets in the kitchen; full of plenty of water."

Her head flew back in alarm. "Tap water? Are you insane?"

I laughed. "Mrs. Sterling, you and I have zilch in common, so it's useless for us to even attempt to engage in a discussion. I did ask Patrick to speak with you about being civil toward me, but, believe me, I wasn't seeking any form of attention or affection from you."

"You're wide off the mark, Brooke. We have something very important in common. My son."

She had a valid point. "That's true enough, and I'm doing my part to keep him satisfied. By being nice to me, you can make his life a whole lot easier."

"Or you can make everyone jump for joy and depart the premises, and Patrick's life."

I stood up. "This conversation is over. I'm going to politely ask you to leave . . . now."

"This is my son's place. I'm not going anywhere."

"This is *our* place and you *are* going. How did you even get up here?"

"The doorman let me up, of course. I'm his mother."

"You keep flinging your motherhood around like it's a recent development. We all recognize that you're Patrick's mother, but I'm the woman who shares his bed every night and—"

"One of his beds, dear. *One* of his beds."

"What the fuck do you mean by that?"

She got up from the sofa and started gathering her things. "I didn't come here for you to curse me. This is so below my level." She eyed me up and down. "And so are you."

"Everyone's below your level!" I yelled at her as she headed for the door.

"No, not everyone." She turned to face me and stopped in her tracks. "I have plenty of friends who meet my standards, and they have stunningly beautiful daughters who are better suited for Patrick's needs."

"I fulfill his needs," I stated defensively. "If Patrick didn't love me, he wouldn't be with me. *Only me.*"

Mrs. Sterling laughed. "You're completely delusional. Look at you, all fat and nasty. I'm mortified that my son has resorted to dealing with scrap waste."

"You're scrap waste, with your cosmetic surgery, tummy tucks, and Botox injections."

"The best Botox that money can buy." She touched my stomach

and I pushed her hand away. "That's it. Isn't your birthday coming up? Why don't you let me give you gastric-bypass surgery for a present? George Washington Hospital has this great doctor who—"

"First off, fuck you and your offer. Second, I wouldn't put it past you to attempt to pay some doctor to kill me on the operating table."

Mrs. Sterling laughed. "I'd never take things *that* far. Things will work themselves out perfectly. They always do."

"Now what does that shit mean?"

"I don't know why I'm so surprised at your rank mouth, based on your upbringing, but it still upsets me."

"So fuckin' what?"

She flung her bag up on her shoulder. "Before I *depart*, I have one last thing to say to you. Feel free to take it any way you wish."

I put my hands on my hips. "Take your last dig at me and bounce."

"If you think for one second that my pussy hound of a son is being faithful to you, you're an idiot. He'll never be faithful to one woman; especially one who has let herself go. Don't be surprised when all of this blows up in your face. After you're long gone and nothing but a distant memory, I will *still* be his mother."

She walked out and started pressing the button for the private penthouse elevator.

"No, you will still be a bitch!" I yelled, and slammed the door.

When I arrived home from the diner around eleven thirty that night, Patrick was lying in wait for me at the door.

I decided to preempt his verbal abuse. "Yes, I did call your mother a bitch and I don't feel one iota of regret for it. She is a bitch."

"You always ruin things," Patrick said, dropping his arms to the side and leering at me. "I'm not standing here to start an argument."

"Oh, come on." I kicked my shoes off in the foyer, as always. I hated to trek the odors of the food from the diner throughout the penthouse. It was bad enough that they were in my hair and on my clothing. "I'm sure your mother couldn't wait to call you to tell you what transpired."

"Actually, she didn't call. She was in my office when I got out of court."

I closed the closet door, after putting my shoes inside, and leaned on it. "Great! I'm sure it was very theatrical. She showed up here and started in on me; not the other way around. I told you before that I was sick of her treating me like shit. She had the audacity to call me a piece of 'scrap waste.'"

"I understand," he said, shocking the hell out of me. "She was totally out of line and I told her so. I asked her to never come over here and bother you again. If you don't want to deal with Mom, you don't have to. That's a bunch of unneeded pressure and stress on our relationship, and we have an adequate amount of issues already."

"You can say that again. I'm beginning to feel like we can't resolve them either."

"Yes, we can. Things have been going good between us the last couple of weeks. Haven't they?"

"I've tried, but I didn't need your mother showing up here. What was her point? Did you know she was coming?"

"Brooke, I wouldn't be crazy enough to stroll out of here and leave you to face my mother alone. If I'd known, I would've cut her off at the pass or even missed court if I had to. She insists that she was trying to make amends with you and things went awry."

"Your mother came here to belittle and demean me, *period*. She came here to plant a seed in my head that you're cheating with other women, too."

Patrick stood there like he was stunned. "Cheating!"

"Cheating, as in sticking your dick inside other women. You know, doing the nasty; knocking boots; fucking."

"I know what the hell *cheating* means. I don't have a clue what Mom was thinking. I haven't so much as looked at another woman since we've been together."

I rolled my eyes and sighed. He was lying and we both knew it. All men look at other women and contemplate the possibilities, whether they take action or not.

Patrick took my hand into his. "I want you to recognize the strength of the love that I have for you. I asked you to marry me, but you refused and—"

"I didn't refuse. We're not in that place yet; that's all. Nothing would make me happier than to eventually become your wife, but . . . we have some things we need to work out."

"Okay, well, I am ready, willing, and able. First, I want you to see your surprise."

"Surprise?"

"Yes, that's the reason I was standing in the doorway. After hearing about what happened between you and Mom, I wanted to try to ease your stress, so I planned a special evening for us."

"But it's almost midnight, and I smell like grease and a bunch of other crap."

"That's why you need a nice, relaxing bath."

Patrick pulled me into the living room, and a wide grin spread across my face. Roses of all different colors were all over the place— red, white, yellow, and pink. "Wow, did you procure the entire florist shop or what?"

He chuckled. "I left a few for the next man who wants to make an impression on his woman."

"I'm definitely impressed . . . and grateful. I don't want you to think that I don't appreciate you, Patrick. I realize that you do so much for me; that's part of what bothers me. I should be able to do more to make this relationship equal."

"It is equal."

"No, it's not. I'm a waitress and you're a lawyer, for goodness' sake. Then, to top it off, you come from old money and I come from no money."

"Your parents are great!"

"Yes, they are, but any way you size it up, we come from diverse worlds."

"I met you waiting tables. Did that stop me?"

"No, but—"

"But nothing. You're the woman for me, the only woman I need. If it takes me forever and a day to prove it to you, then so be it. I'm never giving up on us. Never."

Patrick had a luxurious bath waiting for me, complete with more roses surrounding our step-down tub and petals scattered across the top of the water. We drank champagne and gazed into each other's eyes for more than an hour.

The water began to turn cold, despite our letting some out and replacing it with hot water every ten minutes or so.

"You're getting goose bumps," Patrick said as I sat between his legs with my back snuggled up against his chest. "Ready to get out?"

"No, it's so peaceful here. Besides, I got a buzz and I might bust my ass trying to get out of this tub right now."

Patrick laughed and rubbed my shoulders before planting a kiss on the left one. "You know that I'll always protect you."

"I didn't mean to yell at you earlier." I took soap and a washcloth and starting washing his legs. "I jumped to conclusions when I saw you standing in the doorway."

"You thought something was about to get set off, huh?"

We both laughed.

"Something like that," I replied. "I must admit that I'm shocked."

"About what?"

"Do you realize that this is the first time that you've ever actually defended me with your mother?"

"No, it's not. I've spoken to Mom plenty of times, but she's set in her ways."

"Well, her ways could use a lot of improvement."

I could hear Patrick suck in air, trying to hold back a comment.

"I realize that you don't like someone talking about your mother, baby. Nobody does, but I only come out swinging when she attacks me."

"Brooke, my mother is used to me dating more—"

I turned to face him. "More what?"

"Never mind."

"No, fuck that. More what?"

He shrugged. "You're the first woman that I've been with who doesn't have a graduate degree or a real profession."

I started to get up, covered with suds.

"I thought you wanted to chill in here for a while," he said.

"Never mind!"

By the time Patrick came out of the bathroom, I was under the covers with thermal pajamas on, even though it was midsummer. I didn't want him to get any funny ideas. The pajamas didn't deter him for a second. As soon as he climbed in behind me naked, I could smell his minty-fresh toothpaste breath as he whispered in my ear, "You want some of this dick, don't you?"

"No, I'll pass."

He started groping at my top and rubbing my breasts. "Oh, come on, Brooke. Don't be that way."

"Patrick, if you think that I'm so beneath you, why bother? I'll pack my shit and be out of here tomorrow morning."

"You're not going anywhere," he blared, and started to yank my top up, exposing my chest. He rolled me toward him and started devouring my right nipple.

"Stop!" I tried to push him off, but he kept on sucking.

Patrick knew how to pacify me. When he sucked on my breasts, it was my weakness. Soon, I'd calmed down and was content to allow him to have his way. He pulled the top completely off me, then yanked the bottoms off.

He buried his face in my pussy and started licking and moaning, and I let it go and enjoyed the ten minutes or so that he satisfied his hunger.

I was hoping it would last longer because I knew what came next. As soon as he came up for air, he was pulling his body up toward the headboard. His dick slapped me in the forehead. At first, I turned my head to the left.

"Brooke, you know I need my medicine. Come on. Don't be such a bitch!"

I glared up at him. "What did you call me?"

He sighed. "It's a figure of speech." He tried to use his hand to guide his dick in my mouth. "Suck it for a few minutes. It'll make us both feel better."

"Fine, let's get it over with." I engulfed as much of his dick in my mouth as I could manage.

"That's right, baby," he whispered, grabbing on to the headboard so he could maneuver the way he fed me his dick. "Take all of Magnum in. Aw, you excite me so much, baby, even though you've gained a lot of weight."

I rolled my eyes, despite the fact that he had his closed and was lost in his own little world. I always felt humiliated when he insisted that I suck his dick on demand. It was different when I actually wanted to give head—which was rarely—but it was exhilarating because it was something I yearned to do, as opposed to being pressured into. That weight comment didn't sit right with me either. Why did he always have to bring it up?

Patrick came in my mouth and I swallowed quickly, hoping he would get off me so I could go brush my teeth and gargle. Instead, he lowered himself down, placed his flaccid dick between my legs, and started grinding against my wetness to get another erection.

He started kissing me on my neck, then had the audacity to try to kiss me on the mouth.

"Are you crazy?" I asked. "I have your semen in my mouth."

"So, it's my semen," he said, making another attempt. I turned my head. "Don't be so frigid."

"It has nothing to do with being frigid. It has to do with being nasty." I tried to get up, to no avail. "Let me go gargle and then we can kiss."

Patrick flew into a rage. "Brooke, I'm so sick of your shit!"

"Then get off me."

He spread my legs open wider and held them open, starting to grind harder. Damn if his dick was not hard in a few seconds. All the blood must have *warped* into his scrotum.

"I'm going to give you this dick. I know you want it!" he nearly yelled.

"I want to go to sleep," I said, realizing that he was going to fuck me senseless regardless.

"After I'm done," Patrick said, and started handling his business.

Damon

August 4, 2007
Hot Springs, Virginia

DECIDED to surprise Carleigh with a weekend getaway to the Homestead resort in Hot Springs, Virginia. It had long been on our list of places to visit during our marriage; yet we had never managed to get there. She was feeling depressed. Two more house sales had fallen through; neither couple could qualify for a loan. Carleigh lost nearly $40,000 in commissions that she had been counting on. She was devastated and contemplating a change of profession.

Realtors and mortgage companies in the area—and nationwide, for that matter—were shutting down daily, vacating their luxury offices in upscale office complexes. People who had paid 900K for their homes a year or two before were sick to their stomachs when signs in their communities advertised the same homes for 600K and up. Even I was getting heated because the median home price in my neighborhood had taken a nosedive. I dreaded finding myself in the midst of people who couldn't sell their house for what they'd paid for it—or even for what they still owed on it.

The Homestead offered an "Enchanted Romance Package"

from May through October. It included a suite upgrade, breakfast and dinner daily, champagne, flowers and chocolates upon arrival, a carriage ride, and a fifty-minute Swedish massage for each of us. We had arrived the night before and made love from nine until midnight. It was incredible. Now it was Saturday and we were ready to explore the resort. They had three championship golf courses. I'd brought my clubs along, just in case. Carleigh didn't golf, but if she wanted to split up and indulge in some additional spa services, I would certainly play a round. However, only if she suggested it; I wasn't going to leave her side otherwise. I wanted to re-kindle our relationship; things were going well thus far. The Friday-night sex was the best we'd had in quite some time, with no feelings of animosity.

Carleigh was stunning in a black shorts set and flat sandals. She always kept her toes pedicured, and her skin was as smooth and flawless as ever. Her hair was swept up into a bun and held with a gold hairpin. Even in a simple outfit, my wife was still a looker. Yet, as we walked through the resort, all eyes seemed to be more on me. I had on a white golf shirt, khaki, knee-length shorts, and sneakers. Women were trying to get my attention, and some were brazen in their efforts, not caring whether Carleigh was aware of the mockery they were making of themselves or not. As usual, she seemed to take pleasure in it. At one point, during breakfast, she whispered, "Do you realize that half the women in this dining room want to fuck the living daylights out of you?"

I laughed uneasily. "Only half?"

"Okay, so maybe three-fourths."

She took another bite of her scrambled eggs and clamped her mouth shut to chew. When she was done, she added, "I wonder if I walked up to one of them and made a proposal, if they'd be willing to give up some cash."

"Carleigh, you can't be serious!" I gawked, then pointed to her plate. "You're trippin'. Finish your food so we can go for a walk."

Carleigh rolled her eyes. "Yes, master. I was joking. I love that dick; the way it fits perfectly inside of me. Ain't no other woman getting that; now or ever."

"Is that all I am to you? A piece of meat?"

"Oh, Damon, stop being overdramatic."

I was determined not to allow the weekend to be ruined. I reached over and took her free hand while she put another forkful of food in her mouth.

"Honey, I'm glad we were able to escape. It means so much to me; you and I, alone." I gazed lovingly into her eyes. "Even though we live by ourselves and don't have kids *yet,* it's still difficult to carve out moments like this . . . like last night . . . when we're so busy dealing with the daily grind."

Carleigh took a sip of her orange juice. "Damon, you're the best husband any woman could ever ask for. Sometimes it might seem like I don't recognize that, but I do. I'm trying to work through all the emotional baggage that I'm boggled down with. I really am."

"I'm not any of the dudes from your past. I married you. Doesn't that prove anything?"

"It proves everything!" Carleigh lifted my hand to her mouth and kissed my knuckles. "Lately, things have been crazy, with the mortgage crisis, and you trying to get that website going."

I cringed a little when she said "that website." Carleigh must have felt it because she grasped my hand tighter. "I don't mean anything negative by that, but, it does seem like you're trying to reinvent the wheel. Those other sites have millions of members. There's no way you can possibly catch up."

"I'm not trying to catch up. I'm only trying to get my piece of the American pie. From childhood, I've always wanted to run my own business. I didn't know in what kind of industry for sure, but I was never cut out to take orders."

"I know that, baby. I'm the same way. That's why I went into real estate. Picture me trying to pull a nine-to-five in some stuffy office."

I could see the regret on her face by the time the last word escaped her lips. I was working a nine-to-five.

"So why is it okay for you to be free from the shackles of corporate America, but for me to be trapped there?"

Carleigh let my hand drop out of hers. After an uncomfortable few seconds, she giggled. "Look at us. I may have a lack of restrictions, but, shit, real estate is flushing down the toilet. You're making over a hundred grand a year, but you're not happy."

I chuckled. "It seems like we need to reassess some things, make some changes, so we can be happy . . . again."

The insinuation hung in the air like fog. Carleigh was no dummy. "Are you saying that you're not happy with me? I was talking about your job!"

"I'm saying that happiness is defined by many things. I feel like outside influences are affecting what we have together. You feel me?"

She bit her bottom lip seductively. "Well, didn't you enjoy last night?"

"Every second of it," I responded without hesitation, "but sex is only a temporary fix and not a cure."

I felt Carleigh's bare foot—she must have slipped it out of her sandal—rubbing up against my crotch underneath the table. I glanced around to see if anyone was looking.

"Don't worry," she said. "They can't see anything through the tablecloth."

I felt myself getting hard. Carleigh always had that effect on me.

"I wouldn't mind a temporary fix right now," she said suggestively, digging her toes into my balls and moving them clockwise.

"Let's head back to the room." I used my hand and pushed her foot off me. "I don't want to have to walk out of here with a hard-on."

"Too late for that." Carleigh laughed. "There are only two things that will tame that snake, now that it's awake. My mouth or my pussy; or a little of both."

"Both sound good. Let me carry your tote bag."

"You? The ultimate alpha male, carrying a tote bag?"

I grinned. "Oh, so now you've got jokes."

"Okay, you can carry the bag, but only on one condition."

"What's that?"

"We don't go back to the room."

"Then where do we go?" I wondered.

Carleigh got up, handed me her bag, then started walking toward the door. I had no idea what she was up to, but I hoped it was something rocking-chair memories were made of.

We ended up by a waterfall. The view was spectacular, both of the mountains and of Carleigh. The way the sun shone down on her hair and skin was like a prize-winning photograph.

I sat down on some rocks near the bottom of the falls as Carleigh slipped off her sandals and kicked around in the water like a little girl. She giggled and hopped as she stepped on rough rocks and pounced around, her breasts jiggling in her top.

She stopped and asked me out of the blue, "What?"

"Huh?"

"What are you thinking about over there?"

I grinned. "The good times, all the ones we've had and all the ones yet to come."

"You want a baby, don't you?"

"Wow! Where did that come from?"

I stood up, took off my shoes, and walked toward her.

"Where did it come from?" I asked again once I reached her.

She placed her hands on my chest and leaned into me. "You keep hinting that you're not happy."

"No, I don't." I wrapped my arms around her. "We're both dealing with some things, but that's what marriage is about . . . dealing with things together."

"I figured that a baby might bring some joy into our lives."

"Carleigh, when it's time for us to be blessed with a child, God will handle that. It's not like we've been using protection. What's for us will happen. Until then, it's me and you."

Carleigh started trembling, even though it was in the nineties. It was bad nerves. I knew the symptom well.

I gently pushed her back a little and looked down into her eyes. "What is it?"

Carleigh seemed like she was fighting back tears. "I wanted us to have some time together before we started a family."

"And we've had four wonderful years. I'm in no rush, baby. It'll happen."

"What if I told you that I've kind of *prevented* it from happening?"

"Prevented it how?"

She bit her bottom lip and moved away from me.

"Prevented it how?!" I yelled, as all sorts of things rushed through my head.

"I'm on the pill," she whispered.

I shook my head. "I must be hearing things. It sounded like you said that you're on the pill."

"I've always been on the pill."

"You've been taking birth control pills all this time and you never thought to discuss it with me?"

"I . . ."

"You what?!"

"I was going to tell you. When the time was right."

"So now is the right time?" I headed back to the rocks where I'd been sitting before, to get my shoes.

"Where are you going?" Carleigh called behind me.

"Away from you!"

Before I knew it, she was behind me, pulling on my shirt. "Please, Damon, let's talk about this."

I turned and glared at her. "What's there to talk about? Our marriage has been based on a lie, and not a little one. Children, Carleigh. You decided on your own to control when we could have children. My mother has been asking me when we were going to give her a grandchild. My friends have been asking."

"I know that," she said, lowering her head. "I made a mistake."

"A mistake is when you forget to turn off the faucet and the tub overflows. A mistake is when you take machine-washable clothes to the dry cleaner's. A mistake is when you spill grape juice on the carpet. Playing with my emotions is not a mistake."

A flood of tears was streaming down Carleigh's cheeks by that time. "Please forgive me, Damon. I love you. You know that I love you. We can work this out."

Most men would have walked away and left her standing there. Most men would have cursed her and banished her to burn in hell for eternity. But I was not most men. I was one of the last good ones.

"Carleigh, for the life of me, I don't understand why you'd do this. I've never given you any reason to feel like you have to keep secrets from me. If you didn't want to have children yet, you should've told me."

"You're right, and it's been balled up inside me like a knot all this time. I've been trying to find a way."

"Why didn't you stop taking the pills?"

She fell silent. We both realized that it was a logical question.

"If you had stopped," I said, "there would be no reason to tell me now."

"I'm going to stop . . . right now . . . today. I hadn't planned to tell you, but I had to. I do need to know if you really want a child though. Do you?"

"Of course I want kids."

"But the real estate market is shitty and you're trying to get that site up and running. Don't you think we should be more financially stable first?"

"We're not destitute, Carleigh." I waved my hands around at the picturesque surroundings. "Look at where we are—at a resort. If we can afford a weekend here, we can afford a child. I make a decent living."

"But you're not happy."

"You keep saying that I'm not happy. How can you determine how I feel?"

"It's written all over your face, Damon!"

As I analyzed her words, I wondered if she could be right. Was it possible for a man to have so much and still not be content?

Carleigh fell down on her knees in the water and placed her hands over her face, trying to hide her shame. She was like a broken doll, and I had to put her back together, which meant keeping my own emotions in check.

I knelt down and picked her up, carrying her to the grass. I laid her down and she took me off guard by pulling me on top of her and burying her tongue in my mouth. Her kiss was intense, needy. I had to meet her needs. She was my wife . . . for life.

We made love in the grass, beside the waterfall, that day in the mountains. It was the closest we had been in years. We tossed around naked in the grass, covered by pollen and insects. Nothing mattered.

Then we walked hand in hand into the waterfall and made love again, standing up against the rocks as the water cascaded down our bodies.

Brooke

So how are things going?" Destiny asked as we shared the huge chocolate-chip-brownie dessert at Red Lobster in New Carrollton, Maryland. "You and Patrick still involved in your passive-aggressive kind of love?"

"Very funny. I've been giving you daily updates," I replied, shoving another spoonful of fudge and vanilla ice cream from the top into my mouth while Destiny tackled the brownie itself.

"Exactly! Every day when you call, it's something new." She paused. "By the way, thanks for keeping your promise to me thus far."

"It hasn't been easy, but I'm trying."

"I'm glad you didn't kill Mrs. Sterling that day she showed up at your crib. That was some soap-opera-meets-*Jerry-Springer*-type shit right there."

"Hey, don't knock my Jerry. He deserves an Emmy." We both laughed. "Patrick's mother is fortunate that I'm not a violent person."

Destiny gave me a serious stare. "Have you ever thought about hurting Patrick? Honestly."

"What woman hasn't contemplated killing her man at one point or another? I'm normal."

"I have to admit that I've lain in bed next to Harold quite a few nights, wondering what he would look like with a bloody stub in place of his dick. I've even thought about using his balls as tea bags. Wonder what that shit would taste like."

"You are sick!" I shook my head at her, then giggled. "Okay, here's my honest answer. Yes, I've thought about it, but not since early July. Before then, I was having constant flights of the imagination involving him and various harmful devices. I hated having sex with him because of the way he would talk down to me about my weight."

Destiny looked at the dessert. "I confess that I'm not trying to lose, but are you?"

"I am, but sweets and fats make me feel better. I've only been to the gym once or twice since I met you there. I guess my diet is starting tomorrow, too."

She giggled. "I'm happy being me, and if Harold doesn't like it, he can move the fuck on."

"Harold doesn't harp on your weight. Not like Patrick does with me."

"Harold wants me to break his ass off with great sex. As long as I'm doing that, he doesn't care if I'm as big as his whole damn house."

"So that's why you don't care about your size?"

"Oh, I care, but not because of what he thinks. I care because of health reasons."

"That's my main thing, too. I have a coworker who was recently diagnosed with all kinds of ailments, and she's not even thirty-five yet."

"I'll bet she's had a rough life."

"Yes, she has."

"Thank goodness we both come from decent families."

"Not according to Mrs. Sterling."

Destiny and I had been raised together in Northwest, D.C. Her father was an electrician and my father a plumber, which meant that neither family had to pay for those types of bills. Our parents were the best of friends—extremely close. Her parents still lived in the same home, but mine moved into an apartment after Daddy fell on hard times for a year or two and they couldn't keep up with the mortgage payments.

Mama was heartbroken when we had to move. My brother, Jacob, who was three years older than me, enlisted in the navy because he didn't want to encumber them with additional bills for college tuition. He occasionally wired money to help out but pretty much lived in his own world. His one serious relationship ended short of marriage. Now he was playing the field, for all we could tell. Every time he called either my parents or me, he was vague and avoided discussing women altogether.

"Mrs. Sterling needs to ride back out on the broomstick she flew in on," Destiny said.

I laughed. "From your mouth to God's ears."

"How are your parents?"

"They're great. I'm going by there for dinner."

"After this big-ass lunch?"

"I know, shame on me," I said. "I'll bet Mama is going to cook up a storm, too. It's Friday."

"If she makes any of those collard greens, potato salad, or bread pudding, let me know. I'm coming through."

"After this big-ass lunch?" I said jokingly, repeating her words.

Destiny smacked her lips and waved our waitress over to get the check. "I can't believe they gave you a day off from that diner."

"If they legally didn't have to, they wouldn't."

"Why don't you work for Patrick in some capacity? I'm sure he can hook you up with an administrative position at his firm. He's a partner and—"

"I *will not* do that. I won't be that dependent on him. Even though I live with him and, technically, he supports me, I pay my basic outside bills. I'm going to start searching for another job. I'm not dumb."

"I never said you were, Brooke. You're the smartest chick I know."

"I fucked up in college and I don't have anyone to blame but myself. I had a full academic scholarship and blew it on partying and trying to please a man who meant me no damn good."

"Geesh, let's not conjure him up. I want to be able to keep my food down," Destiny said.

"I agree. Let's leave that past in the past . . . for good."

After dinner with my parents, I decided to drive past Patrick's firm. He told me that he would be working late and that's why he couldn't come with me. Mama was disappointed. She hadn't cooked the collard greens, potato salad, and bread pudding Destiny had craved, but she had put her foot into what she did fix. We had pot roast with vegetables and gravy, egg noodles, and chopped salad. She made a homemade apple pie for dessert. I was determined to hit the gym the next day.

When I was less than a block from the front of the firm, I spotted Patrick's Bentley pulling out of the underground garage. I started to blow my horn, but decided it was pointless. We were both on our way home so I would see him there. I needed gas and planned to stop at the Exxon closer to home. Trailing behind him about a quarter of a mile, I debated whether to call him on his cell to tell him to stop so he could pump the gas for me. It was nighttime and I was always apprehensive about doing it after dark. My finger was on the talk button to speed-dial him when he turned right onto Sixteenth Street, headed toward Maryland. He should have kept going and made a left onto South Capitol Street.

I had this instant pain in my stomach, alerting me that something was off-kilter. *Where the fuck is he going?* I asked myself.

Ten minutes later, Patrick turned off onto one of the streets in an upscale area of Washington known as the Gold Coast. I cut my lights and continued to follow him down the narrow, dark street. He pulled into the driveway of a majestic home at the end of the street, right next to the DEAD END sign. The word *dead* jumped out at me because if he was going to see some other bitch, he was going to be one dead motherfucker.

I sat there, about five houses away, with my lights and engine off, as Patrick got out of the car, locked it, and headed to the side door of the house. Instead of knocking, he took a set of keys out of his suit pocket and unlocked the door. I was weak. This shit was not happening.

Mrs. Sterling's words flooded through my head. She had made an outlandish comment when I said that I shared Patrick's bed with him every night. She had said, "One of his beds, dear. *One* of his beds."

"I know this bastard does not have another house!" I screamed into the steering wheel of my Toyota Corolla. "What the fuck?!"

I reached for my cell phone and started to call him to curse him out, but I stopped. I dialed Destiny, but she didn't pick up; it went right to voice mail. I was hyperventilating as I said, "This is Brooke. We saw each other earlier today so I don't owe you a daily

phone call, but I need to talk. Call me when you get this message."
I paused, sucked in a deep breath, then added, "Oh, if something
should happen to me . . . any something . . . I want you to know
that you've been a wonderful friend to me and I love you."

I sat there for the next fifteen or twenty minutes, watching lights
flick on and off inside the stone house that was obviously worth a
couple of million based on the neighborhood alone. I spotted a sil-
houette here and there but couldn't make out more than one at a
time, so I had no idea if he was in there alone or not. All kinds of
crazy thoughts ran through me at the speed of light.

*What if he bought the home for us? Yes, that's it! He purchased the
home for us and plans to surprise me with it.*

No, that doesn't make any fucking sense and you know it.

*Maybe it's one of his parents' numerous homes that I've simply never
been to.*

No, that doesn't make any fucking sense either.

*Maybe he's feeding the dog, cat, or fish for one of his law firm partners
who's out of town.*

No, they wouldn't ask Patrick to do some shit like that.

Maybe he's visiting a client.

At this time of night, with his own damn key?

*Maybe it's exactly what you think it is! He's in there fucking his other
woman, in his other house.*

"One of his beds, dear. *One* of his beds."

I couldn't take it another second. I started my car, left the lights
off, and drove down to the end of the street, parking on the opposite side near the neighbor's driveway. I exited the vehicle as quietly
as I could and walked over to the house that Patrick had entered.
No lights were on in the front; even the porch lantern had been
turned off. Shit, was he planning on spending the night? In the time

that we had lived together, Patrick had never spent the night away except— *Oh, hell no!* I thought as it hit me. Patrick took a ton of business trips. I never called the hotels because everyone uses their cell phones these days and Patrick had two of them, one for business calls and one for private, but I was one of the few people who had both numbers. What if half of those trips were right across town to be with another woman? But that meant the other woman would have to be cool with his coming home to me nine out of ten times. It was all ludicrous and totally implausible. I'd learned a lot in my twenty-eight years on earth. The most ludicrous and implausible things often turned out to be nothing but the truth.

"One of his beds, dear. *One* of his beds."

An adrenaline rush attacked me as I walked to the rear of the house, desperate to catch a glimpse of anything that would answer my questions. A bay window overlooked the stone patio and in-ground pool. I stood there and watched in disbelief as Patrick took another woman—a petite woman with long, brown hair, and a body most woman would slaughter for—into his arms. They were surrounded by candlelight and I could hear faint music playing—soft, romantic music. He kissed her with passion, like he kissed me, and it made me sick. Not sick enough to stop watching. I wanted to watch. I wanted to take it all in, so I could commit his betrayal to memory. Sure, I could have stopped it, but what for? This was not their first, second, or even third time together. He was comfortable with her as they engaged in their sexual ballet. They kissed for a while longer, then she dropped to her knees, on a pillow, and started maneuvering to get his dick out of his pants like her life depended on it.

She engulfed him with her jaws and seemed genuinely happy to be pleasuring him in such a fashion, something that I'd never been too keen about. She was unrelenting with him as, disoriented, he threw his head back and started shaking. She took him deep, for long periods, then would come up for air long enough to work magic with her tongue ring, which I could see even from that distance. Eventually, Patrick collapsed back on the sofa, which caused her only to adjust her position slightly to accommodate him. He grabbed the back of her head and guided it up and down, as she tugged on his balls and kept up a steady pace. Then he exploded and the tears began to stream down my face.

Even after he came, she kept right on sucking, her ass bobbing up and down along with her head, in a pair of tight blue jeans. Patrick's dick sprang right back up to attention. He pulled her up to him on the sofa and started kissing her again, which was plain old nasty to me. That was about the time when I would have been brushing my teeth and gargling. I couldn't comprehend his kissing her with the remnants of his own semen in her mouth . . . then he planned to come home to me and act as if it had never fucking happened. My knees almost gave out on me completely, but I leaned on the windowsill and continued to watch as they removed each other's clothing and started twisting and turning on the sofa like one large, nude mass.

She climbed on top of Patrick, shoved his dick inside her pussy, and started riding him as he sucked on her nipples one at a time, then pushed her breasts together so he could go at them both . . . like he always did with mine.

Every woman wants to imagine that the sex she gives her man is the best that he has ever had. Every woman wants to believe that he could never want another. I felt that same exact way until I saw Patrick deriving so much pleasure from being with this woman. Sure, I'd been with men who cheated, but they didn't mean as much to me. I didn't live with them and they hadn't asked for my hand in marriage. Patrick had, even though he was doing this shit behind my back.

They really started going at it. The sex was animalistic. Sweat poured from both their bodies. She began to scream out his name: "Patrick!" I wanted to scream it out as well, but for totally different reasons. Then my cell phone started belting out "U Can't Touch This" by MC Hammer, and I could have killed myself for not thinking to turn the damn thing off before I went on a surveillance mission, and for picking such a loud, attention-getting song for my ringtone. The point was for me not to miss a call, but no one else could miss it either.

Both of them looked toward the window, and Patrick pushed the woman off him.

"Brooke!" I heard him scream.

I don't think he actually saw me but what were the odds of another woman with the same distinctive ringtone as mine watching him fuck.

I ran back to my car and hopped in, starting it and backing into the neighbor's driveway so I could turn around and head back up the street. The front door of the house flew open, and Patrick was rushing out, trying to pull his pants up and button his shirt at the same time.

"Brooke!" he yelled out again. "Wait!"

I could see the woman in the background of the doorway. *Bitch!*

I rolled down the passenger window with the automatic button.

"I hate you!" I yelled back at him. "I hate you and she can have your ass!"

As I turned onto Sixteenth Street, I called Destiny back because she was my missed call.

"What's going on?" she asked before I could even say hello.

"I'm on my way over there. Be there in twenty minutes."

I hung up on her as she threw out more questions. I would answer them all soon enough because there was no way that I was going back to that penthouse—never that.

Damon

IT was a Sunday when all hell broke loose. Carleigh and I returned from church to find Jordan's fire-red BMW in the driveway.

"Oh, great! What is she doing here?" I asked in disgust, before I even killed the engine.

"I don't know," Carleigh said. "I wasn't expecting her."

Jordan climbed out of the driver's seat as we exited my car. She had on a dress that seemed more suitable for the bedroom than the street. It was thin, lacy, and all her goodies were popping out at the seams. She had on a pair of fuck-me pumps and enough makeup for three women. There was no shame in her game.

Carleigh rushed up to her, in her powder-blue church dress, and they hugged. "Hey, sis, what's up?" Carleigh asked.

She's no sister of yours, I wanted to yell out, but walked toward the front door, loosening my tie instead.

As I unlocked the door, I could hear Jordan say, "Do I have some shit to tell you!"

Our house was not a mansion, by any stretch of the imagination, but I wanted to rush in, change into some shorts and a T-shirt, and try to find at least one spot where that pigeon's voice wouldn't carry and irritate the hell out of me.

By the time I came back out of the bedroom in fresh clothes, the two of them were in the kitchen sipping iced tea and talking trash . . . about my website.

Something told me to leave it alone, to walk right past the kitchen doorway and go bury myself in my office. But I stood there, at the corner where they couldn't see me, and listened.

"Carleigh, I'm telling you. That website is nothing but a big joke. Have you logged on to it lately?" I knew where Jordan was headed.

"No, I haven't been on there in months," Carleigh replied. "I figure the less that I know about it, the better. Damon is constantly accusing me of making disparaging comments—"

That's because you do!

"—I try to keep my knowledge limited so I won't have anything to say at all."

"Well, maybe I shouldn't say anything."

I could hear Carleigh sigh when Jordan said that. She wanted to hear the dirt and we all knew it.

After a dramatic pause, Jordan continued, "Last good men, my ass. That site has turned more into pitbull-in-my-bed-dot-com."

Carleigh gasped. "What do you mean?"

"Damon claims to have that damn screening process. Bullshit! Those pits gnawed right through the damn screen and have been leaving bite marks all over the country." Jordan paused. "After they tear up some ass, doggie-style, that is."

"Jordan, speak English."

Jordan laughed. "Over the past month or so, the feedback comments from women have been *fugly*."

"English!"

"Women are coming on there talking about how the men they hooked up with on there are a bunch of users, abusers, losers, and back-door infusers."

"Back-door infusers?"

"Yeah, you know, as in they like to take it up the ass. They prefer to be on the receiving end of the dick action."

"You mean they're gay!"

"Not all of them, but quite a few. They claim that bisexual non-sense, but the hell with that. If you have sex with another man, you're gay." Jordan paused, and I could hear ice cubes swirling around in a glass and her gulping the tea down. Then she burped. *Nasty-ass whore!* "Most of them are straight-up whack. One young woman said she flew from Seattle to Philly to see some man, and it turned out that he was married, broke, and high on coke."

"Damn!" Carleigh exclaimed, undoubtedly taking it all in so she could throw it in my face later. "I'm going to have to go on there and check it out."

Just wonderful, I thought.

Things had taken a turn for the worse on the site, but I viewed it as growing pains. I still stood by my contention that a little bit of screening—even if some of the men perpetrated a fraud to get past it—was better than no screening at all.

"Yeah, girl, you have to see the madness for yourself! The chick that flew to Philly . . . she said she was a virgin and this piece of shit had convinced her to let him bust her cherry."

"Wow! She must be devastated."

"She is, but she asked for it."

"Jordan!"

"She did. I'm sick of these chicks out here, especially the young ones, thinking that throwing pussy at a man is going to get them anything but the motherfucking blues."

I had to literally clamp both of my hands over my mouth to keep my comment in. No, that hooker was not in there putting other women down for the same shit she did daily.

"How do you know so much?" Carleigh asked. "Were you on there trying to find a man?"

"Please, the day that I have to resort to internet dick is the day I'm slitting my own fucking throat! The girls at the office are always on there, desperate sluts, trying to see what they can see. I kept hearing about the comments and decided to log on to get some good laughs. I'm telling you, it's better than watching *Jerry Springer.*"

"Well, there's only one thing to be done," Carleigh blurted out. "Damon is going to take that site down, no questions asked."

"That shit should have been down like yesterday," Jordan said, cosigning on the idea. "But he's not going to do it."

"Oh, yes, the hell he is," Carleigh stated with authority. "I run this house!"

They both started laughing, and I entered the kitchen with fire in my eyes.

"What did you say?" I asked Carleigh.

Jordan cackled and said, "Uh-oh." She looked at Carleigh. "Tell him what you said, Carleigh. Repeat it. If you do, you're one bad bitch, and I will bow down to you."

"Yeah, Carleigh, repeat it. I dare you," I said, crossing my arms in defiance.

Carleigh sat there for a moment, drinking some more of her iced tea, then shocked everyone—probably even herself—when she threw the glass at the wall.

She stood up and put her hands on her hips. "Who the fuck do you think you are, talking to me like that in front of my friend?"

"Friend!" I shot a dagger at Jordan. "She's no friend; she's in line to be your replacement."

Jordan got up. "Maybe I should go."

I grabbed her wrist. "No, Jordan, why don't you stay awhile? Let's tell Carleigh about the countless times you've offered to suck the skin off of my dick. The times you've showed up here, when you knew good and damn well she was showing a house, and tried to take me for the ride of my life. Let's tell her."

"Carleigh, he's lying," Jordan said uncomfortably, yanking her wrist free. "He must've overheard our entire conversation and now he's being the typical man. Trying to start a bunch of shit and cause a sisterly divide."

Sisterly divide! Was this chick for real?!

"Jordan, have you been trying to fuck my man?" Carleigh asked.

"Who, me?" Jordan slapped her hand over her chest like she was appalled. "I would never!"

I stared at Carleigh. "You know how all your friends are constantly talking about my looks, how good I must be in bed, how they wanna watch, be a backup, have a threesome? The list goes on and on. You've always thought that shit was cute, but they were serious . . . *all* of them." I pointed at Jordan. "Especially this one. She even followed me into the house on the Fourth of July and tried to fuck me in my office while I was putting my camera away."

Carleigh was so mad that she started trembling. She turned around and faced the sink. The kitchen was so quiet that you could have heard a mouse pissing on a cotton ball. Then she shocked everyone again—*definitely even herself*—when she suddenly swung back around with a big-ass butcher knife in her hand.

I assumed she was going to go after Jordan, and so did Jordan because she flew out of the kitchen without her purse but grabbed her keys. Carleigh came at me with the knife and tried to stab me. I managed to get a grip on her arm and redirect it.

"Carleigh, what are you doing!?" I yelled.

"You fucked my friend!" she screamed.

"I didn't fuck anybody!"

"But you just said—"

"—I said that she *tried* to fuck me! That all of them tried but I never did anything, Carleigh!"

Carleigh collapsed in the kitchen chair as the knife fell to the floor and tires were squealing on the driveway. She broke out in tears.

"How could you?"

How could I? She was still not receiving the data.

I got down on my knees and tried to put my arms around her, but she pushed me away.

"Don't touch me! Don't you ever touch me!"

"Carleigh, with God as my witness, I have not been with another woman, in any manner, since we've been together."

"You're a typical man. Mama was right."

"Your mother doesn't know anything about me!" I lashed out. "But you know me! You know that I would never betray you!" I shook her shoulders. "Tell me you know that!"

Carleigh wouldn't answer. Nor would she look at me. Her eyes took on this glassy look and she hid herself away in a private place in her mind. I sat there for a good ten minutes, hoping that she would acknowledge my presence, but fearful of saying anything more. I'd done the one thing that I swore to myself I would never do. I'd hurt my wife . . . intentionally. I knew that by telling on her friends, it would damage her. But when I heard her comment about running the house, something snapped. Something snapped in both of us that Sunday.

I got up from the floor, went outside, and sat in my car with the engine running. There was no place that I wanted to go, no place that I needed to be other than with my wife. I sat there for more than four hours, suffering through crying spell after crying spell, listening to first gospel music and then the jazz that followed on the same station.

I didn't even realize that Carleigh had come outside until she opened the driver's-side door.

"Come inside, Damon," she whispered, staring at me with bloodshot eyes.

"For what? So we can fight some more? So you can actually stab me this time?"

Carleigh reached in and cut off the engine, removing the keys. "I'm not going to hurt you. I love you. I was just . . . just upset."

I looked up at her. "I would die for you, Carleigh. Don't you realize that? I would take a bullet for you!"

"And I you. I'm in this for the long haul . . . no matter what . . . unconditionally."

Carleigh helped me get out of the car, a broken-down man, and we walked into the house—our home—hand in hand.

Brooke

Men amaze me. They can do the most low-down, dirty shit to women, then expect us to simply overlook it. I often wonder if men back in the wild, wild West and other times treated their women the same way—like they were interchangeable pieces of chattel. Most profess to want love—to give it and to receive it—but few believe in doing what is necessary to nurture and sustain that love. Granted, no relationship is ever perfect, but Patrick had taken betrayal to an entirely new level.

I had Destiny go over to the penthouse the morning after I'd caught him and that woman together. He tried to insist that I come to get my own things—to face him—but she informed him that the situation was not going down like that. Destiny and Harold had been dating for a while but were not officially shacking. She started dividing her time between his place and her own, so she could keep a watchful eye over me. I assured her that I was fine.

The truly fucked-up thing was my job. Because I was a waitress in a public establishment, Patrick showed up almost every day, begging and pleading for me to listen to him. Instead of my boss being understanding and taking my side, he threatened to fire me if I didn't get the situation under control. I thought about taking out a temporary restraining order but decided against it. Patrick was a prominent attorney, and having that on his file wouldn't have been a good look. I realized that Patrick and I could never have any real closure without talking it through. I'd seen enough, but part of me still wanted to hear his explanation. In the end, none of it would ultimately matter, but I wanted to understand why he would do such a thing and who this woman was to him.

"What am I lacking as a woman? Is it because I gained so much weight?" I asked him as we walked along the waterfront in George-town as the sun set one evening. Numerous couples were down there, walking lovingly hand in hand, some with their kids in tow, enjoying a family outing. Patrick made a futile attempt to touch my shoulder and I pulled away. "Please, don't touch me."

"You aren't lacking anything, Brooke. I love you," the dirty liar had the nerve to say to me. "And you know it's not about your weight. I'm with you because I want to be with you. I've asked you to marry me since you gained, so don't even go there."

"Define love." I stopped and stared at him. "Define what it means when you say that you love me."

"You know what love means."

"I know what I believe love means, but I want to hear your defi-nition of it. It's obvious that we don't have the same one."

"Love is a feeling that you get when you look at someone, when you hold them in your arms and gaze into their eyes. It's when your heart starts to race when you think about them throughout the day and you can't wait to see them again, or hear their voice, or feel their touch. Those are all the things I feel about you," he said. "You're always on my mind."

"Was I on your mind when that woman was sucking and riding your dick?" I blurted out at him. "Was I on your mind when you were driving over there instead of driving home to me? Who is she? Is that your home?"

He sighed. "You remember when I told you about my ex, Mandy?"

My mind rewound itself to our earlier conversations when we first started dating. "The Mandy who dropped you like a hot potato to marry another man? The one who said that you didn't measure up to her new man because he was already established in his career while you were still in law school? That Mandy?"

"One and the same. She moved back to the D.C. area a few months ago. That is not my house. It's hers. Her ex-husband owned it before they got married and moved to Atlanta, but it was awarded to her in the divorce anyway."

"So let me get this straight. She moves back and you start fucking her so much on the regular that she gave you a key?"

"It just happened."

My right hand had slapped the living daylights out of him before I even realized it was in motion. He held on to his cheek but didn't strike me back.

" 'It just happened' is the most ridiculous and overused excuse in the world. Men kill me with that. 'It just happened.' I saw you, and that didn't just happen. It was orchestrated. You told me that you couldn't go to my parents' with me; that you had to work late."

"I did work late, but—"

"But you decided to make a booty call on your way home. How many times did you fuck her and then come home and do the same thing to me? How many times did I kiss you while her pussy was still on your tongue? How many times, you disgusting bastard?!"

I could see the wheels moving inside Patrick's brain as he tried to come up with something—*anything*—that would afford him a segue into possible forgiveness. That was not to happen.

"You know what?" I said. "This is pointless. I was foolish enough to believe that meeting you here would bring about some type of closure, but all I feel toward you is hatred."

"Don't say that, Brooke. You don't mean that."

"Don't tell me what I mean." I realized that we were being loud and started walking farther away from a half dozen people who were within earshot. Patrick followed me as I added, "I should have known that this could never work. Your parents despise the fact that their precious little boy lowered his standards to be with me. Your friends act like our relationship is some sort of joke. Hell, you don't even respect what we had together."

"I haven't seen Mandy anymore since that night. I told her that all bets were off." He crossed his hands and then spread them apart like an umpire. "She knows that I love you, and I do . . . love you. I made a stupid mistake, a really stupid mistake, but if you give me another chance, I promise that I'll make it up to you."

"How could you possibly make it up to me?" I leaned against the railing near the water. "I can't get the image of the two of you to-gether out of my head. That was not something you did with her in the past. That was something you did with her during our present, while we were making plans for our future."

Patrick fell silent and looked down at the ground.

"Men feel like it's cool to do whatever and expect us to brush it off and get back in the saddle, but not me . . . not this time . . . not in this place. From this moment on, I don't give a damn whom you fuck, because it won't be me."

I walked off, paused, and turned around. He was standing there, staring at me. "Oh, and tell your mother, Miss High-and-Mighty, that I should have listened to her. In her own sick, perverted way, she was the only one who at least tried to warn me. Now she can hook you up with all her friends' daughters . . . who are worthy of you."

Patrick didn't call me anymore after that day. I was relieved and disappointed at the same time. It had to end, that was without question, but he had seemingly given up and that made me feel dejected. Life had changed for me within the span of such a short time. Little did I know that the worst—and the best—was yet to come.

PART TWO

LUNAR ECLIPSE

Lunar eclipse—the obscuration of the
light of the moon by the interposition of
Earth between it and the sun

Damon

September 1, 2007, Labor Day Weekend

CARLEIGH was having a fit to go to the D.C. Blues Festival, not because she was into that type of music but because she wanted to show me off to her friends and business associates, who all planned to attend. The more I thought about it, the more I understood how women who were simply showpieces to their men felt. I'd heard about rich men who intentionally planned on shifting wives every five years or so in order to keep a "fresh piece" on their arm. As long as I kept in shape, Carleigh was bound to get attention from other women who wanted what she had.

Things had been much improved between us since she'd actually let me enlighten her about what had transpired between her friends and me, in particular Jordan. She confronted them all, then forgave them, after they put their bullshit spins on it. Only one of them tried to blame me for actually coming on to her— Raquel—and Carleigh did stop speaking to her, but only for a little over a week.

Women are funny. There must be some secret code of ethics because if a man finds out that his buddies have been trying to fuck his woman, nine times out of ten, those friendships are dead and buried. That is a critical lack of respect when it comes to manhood. Lions even piss on their territory to let the other male lions know where to draw the line.

Despite all of that, Sharon and Jordan had actually ridden with us that day like we were some blissful family. They were singing to the latest Mariah Carey CD the entire way there. The mixture of their perfumes made me queasy. When we arrived at the Carter Barron, an amphitheater in Rock Creek Park, parking was at a premium. We ended up having to park on a residential side street and hike it.

Being a history buff, I made it my mission to know the background of most of the architectural sites in the area. Most people have never given a second thought to who Carter Barron really was. They had simply enjoyed coming out to the events. When I was a child, my parents used to take me to see Stevie Wonder, B. B. King, Smokey Robinson, the O'Jays, and the Four Tops at the forty-two-hundred-seat complex named after the vice chairman for the Sesquicentennial Commission, who died from cancer at the young age of forty-five, a mere three months after it opened. In fact, it was originally called the Sesquicentennial Amphitheater when it opened in 1950, but President Truman renamed it the Carter Barron in 1951 as a legacy to Barron's dedication to being a link between the performing arts and the government. I hoped to one day do something so significant in life that, upon my death, a street or a place would be named after me. I have yet to figure out what that would be.

Carleigh was off the pill and we were trying to conceive. We had a ceremonial flushing of the remaining pills down our toilet—popping them one at a time out of the foil packet before tossing them in. Our sex life had intensified, surely because Carleigh was trying to make up for her betrayal. We had a lot to overcome, but no one ever proclaimed that marriage would be easy. Despite our ups and downs, I was confident that we could make it work.

The 19th Annual D.C. Blues Festival had a great lineup: Zac Harmon & the Mid-South Blues Revue; Delta-blues guitarist and vocalist Lil' Dave Thompson; the Charles "Big Daddy" Stallings Band; ACME Blues Company; the Country Bunker Funky Blues Band; and more. I was excited to attend the free concert, scheduled to run from twelve-thirty to seven. With everything gratis, everyone and his mama was in the house. It was a great cheap date. Free parking; free music. The only thing that the single brothers trying to get some play had to splurge on was food. You could tell that many men were thinking that, too, because couples were hugged up all over the place as we went inside to track down some decent seats. We managed to find four about twenty rows up and got settled in.

I recognized quite a few people. Some from work, but others that I'd crossed paths with in various places, like the gym. I spotted a young, attractive woman that I'd seen a couple of times when I was working out. She had never come back, to my knowledge. The first time I'd seen her, she had been with a friend who was choking down a Snickers bar. I remember chuckling about it. In fact, she was with the same friend that day at the Carter Barron. They had on matching colors; she had on a red sundress, and her friend had on a red halter top and red shorts.

For some reason, I found myself drawn to her, but not because I wanted to date her. I was married and content, but she had a sadness about her, even though she was gorgeous. I'd sensed her insecurities at the gym. Both times she had had on loose clothing, attempting to mask her body. She was slightly overweight, but not a beach whale by any means. I could appreciate women with a little meat on their bones.

Carleigh noticed that I was distracted and looked in the same direction. With the sea of people there, she couldn't tell whom I was concentrating on.

"See something that interests you?" she asked sarcastically as she started rubbing my thigh.

I glanced at her, then put my sunglasses on. "It's ironic that you'd be concerned about me surveying a crowd but be carefree about your piranha friends sitting beside you." I nodded in the direction of Sharon and Jordan, sitting on the opposite side of her.

"They've apologized," Carleigh said. "Besides, nothing happened."

"Not because they backed down. The only reason nothing happened is because I am one of *the last good men.*"

Carleigh smirked at the reference to my website. Registration had slowed down, and it was gradually becoming one of those sites with a bunch of registered members but with the majority of them inactive.

Saved by the music, I thought as the first act took the stage. I didn't want to chat about any of it. I saw the woman from the gym and her friend sit down on a blanket on the grass and immediately start swatting away insects.

Brooke

I T was hot as hell out at the Carter Barron that day. The body heat emanating from all those people didn't help. Destiny had somehow convinced me to go to the D.C. Blues Festival with her. I didn't know anything about the blues, other than suffering through my personal blues. Destiny wanted to get my mind off the obvious. I still felt like such a fool for ever believing that Patrick would take me seriously in a relationship. We had been doomed from day one because of our diverse backgrounds.

As the last act was finishing up, I started voicing my thoughts out loud. "I still can't believe I was such an idiot!"

Destiny brushed her shoulder against mine on the blanket. "You need to let that shit go."

"But how could I have not seen it coming?"

"Oh, please. No woman could have seen that coming. Sure, you and Patrick had issues, but another woman never crossed your mind and you know it."

"He made me think he cared."

"That's because he does care."

I glared at her. "You really think so?"

"Brooke, it isn't like he was making booty calls over at your crib like he was doing with Mandawhore."

I couldn't help but giggle at the nickname Destiny had given to Mandy.

"He moved you in," she continued. "He took you around his friends, his coworkers, his snooty parents."

"You have a point." I slammed my palm down on a gnat that was attacking my leg. "It took a lot of nerve for Patrick to present me to his parents." I paused as a guitarist started ripping up a tune onstage. After a moment of thought, I asked, "So why would he cheat on me?"

Destiny smacked her lips. "Because he's a man, Brooke. You used to criticize me for accepting Harold's creeping, but that is what men do. I would rather have a man who steps out every now and again to experience some variety in life than not have a man at all."

"Are you suggesting that I take Patrick back?"

She shrugged. "I'm simply saying, if not Patrick, then who? Look around. Nothing but a bunch of no-good men who think they're the salt of the earth because of the male–female ratio in this town. Most men today act like they're doing you a favor by even paying you attention. That's why I'm keeping Harold for as long as he'll have me. Ain't shit else out here. Either way, odds are, we will all be sharing dick."

Destiny's dismal outlook on love and relationships was actually beginning to make sense to me. I thought Patrick loved me down to my dirty drawers, despite the disrespectful things he'd said from time to time. Lord knows that I hated the B-word. But he did look out for me and take care of me. Now I found myself crashing with Destiny, still working in that dump, and the few men who had tried to talk to me, I wouldn't have fucked for bone marrow.

"Patrick's giving you a chance to cool off," Destiny said. "It hasn't been that long, but trust me when I say that he'll be calling soon or showing up at your job again; hoping that you have come to your senses. You need to figure out what you plan to do when he does show up."

"He's not going to bother me anymore. He knows it's over."

"I doubt that, because men never truly believe that we will leave them. In their convoluted minds, they are supposed to walk away from us. Especially men like Patrick—rich, successful, named as a great catch in magazines. Brooke, that man thinks that you're coming back and . . ."

"And what?" I waited for her to respond, but she didn't. "And you think I'm going back, too? Right?"

"I honestly believe that you need to weigh your options. Peep out all these skinny chicks running around here half-naked. Competition is thick. If you have a man willing to make any kind of commitment to your ass, even if it isn't a total commitment, you need to consider yourself lucky as shit. Harold may not be a super-hero, but he is damn sure my superman. He might dilly and dally with some whores, but he knows who keeps the home fires burning."

"You sound foolish!" I damn near yelled at her. "Do your parents know you feel like this?" I asked, trying to make her feel even an ounce of shame.

"My parents don't love me, not with the kind of love a man brings to the party."

"Let's drop it," I said, totally disgusted. Not with Destiny—with myself. Part of me was wondering if I should at least hear Patrick out at some point.

The amphitheater was full of beautiful women . . . most of them with other women. The young ladies had it rough. They had to dress sexily to compete; they had to lower their standards to get a man; and a lot of times they even had to support a man to have one in their bed. Shit, Patrick was looking better by the second.

Damon

AFTER the concert ended around eight, an hour later than expected, people started flooding out of the seats like there was free money out in the parking lot. Sharon and Jordan had made a mockery out of themselves the entire time, throwing themselves at men who walked past our seats and shaking their asses in the faces of the women seated behind them trying to see the stage. Blues is not booty-shaking music; it is slow-grinding, finger-snapping music, but they were acting like 50 Cent and Kanye West were performing.

We had quite a way to walk back to our car, and I was ready to get the hell away from Carleigh's friends. I couldn't wait to get back to the house so they could hop in Sharon's car and roll out. They had been talking about hitting two or three clubs later that night. Good for them; that meant I could have some quality time with Carleigh. Things were still tense since I'd found out about the birth control pills. Even though we were back on track and planning to have kids as soon as possible, I was still struggling with that betrayal. What upset me most was her taking the choice away from me when I might actually have agreed with her decision. It should have been *our* decision and not hers alone.

"Honey, Sharon and Jordan want to know if we can stop by Jin for a drink before we head home."

I gawked at Carleigh in disbelief. The three of them were standing there on the grass near the parking area waiting for my reply.

I took Carleigh's left hand into my right. "Baby, I thought we were going to spend tonight alone. We hung out with your friends. Now it's our time."

"Just one drink." She pouted. "I'm not ready to go home yet."

Jordan suppressed a laugh and I rolled my eyes at her.

"It's Labor Day weekend," Carleigh added. "Let's hang out and have some fun."

"Why can't your friends have fun on their own? Or with their men?" I paused, then went in for the kill. "Oh, that's right. They don't have any men, except the ones who drop by to fuck them and then bounce."

"You know what?" Jordan said, stepping closer to me with much attitude.

"I know your breath reeks," I answered. "Other than that, I don't know anything about you, nor do I care to know."

"Fuck you, Damon," Jordan hissed.

"No, you can't fuck me and that's the problem. You wish."

Sharon jumped in then. "Can you two stop acting all childish? This shit ain't that damn serious." She turned to Carleigh, who had let go of my hand and now had her arms crossed defiantly across her chest. "Carleigh, let's head back to your place and then Jordan and I can come back down to Jin."

"It makes zero sense to go all the way out to Wheaton and then have to come back down to Fourteenth and U when we're right off Sixteenth. Damon is being difficult," Carleigh said.

"I'm being difficult?" I shook my head. "You asked me to come out here with them and I agreed. I even offered to drive so we wouldn't have to bring two cars. Now, because I was being *nice,* you want me to continue to cater to them. Damn, no good deed goes unpunished."

Carleigh started trying to gratify her friends' emotions instead of mine by telling them I would change my mind by the time we got to the car. That she would talk to me about it. She was whispering like I couldn't hear every word; like I wasn't even standing there. It was totally disrespectful, and I wasn't about to change my mind either. We were headed out to Wheaton, which was less than fifteen minutes away, and not two or three hours like she'd tried to make it sound.

I spotted her again. The woman in red. The one from the gym. She and her friend were headed straight in our direction. Our eyes met, then she looked away. She must not have remembered me. It wasn't like we had ever spoken. They were less than ten yards away from us when she glanced back at me and smiled. Beautiful smile. Beautiful eyes. It wasn't a flirtatious smile; merely a "How are you doing today?" smile. I smiled back, still wondering why I was so drawn to her.

"Sharon and Jordan are going to the bathroom," Carleigh said, as they walked off toward the outside restroom facilities. "While they're gone, we need to hash this out."

"There's nothing to hash out." I watched the woman in red as she said something to her friend. Then her friend in the halter top and shorts walked off toward the bathroom as well, and the woman in red came even closer to us. She was probably planning to stand in the same general area to wait for her friend to come back. She was less than five feet away from us when someone screamed.

It all happened so quickly. The screams . . . the headlights . . . the expression of terror on Carleigh's face . . . the reflex to save her life . . . the impact . . . the pain . . . darkness.

Brooke

September 3, 2007
Providence Hospital, Washington, D.C.

My head was killing me; *literally*. Not the kind of tolerable pain that some Motrin or Tylenol can knock out, but the kind of pain that made you yearn for certain death. Then it hit me. Where the hell was I?

I fought to open my eyes, and a bright light flooded down from the ceiling, causing me to wince before struggling to steady them. I could hear beeps and suction noises coming from the machines surrounding me. I realized that my leg was elevated in a cast, and all kinds of tubes with liquid were running in and out of different parts of my body.

The hospital, I thought, trying to remember what had happened before everything went black. *The concert . . . Destiny went to the ladies' room . . . a big-ass SUV . . .*

I darted my eyes and found the call button for the nurses' station. I tried to maneuver to reach it, to no avail. A sharp pain shot through my leg and all the way up to the top of my cranium, which was already killing me, *literally*.

Right then, a male nurse came into my room. "Ms. Alexander, don't try to move."

I tried to speak but only a gurgle came out of my mouth.

He looked down at me and compassion was in his eyes. "Wait one second. I'll go get the doctor and a pitcher of water. Don't try to speak yet. Your mouth is bone-dry."

I lay there as told, waiting for him to return. It took less than five minutes before he came back with a female doctor in tow. "I'm Dr. Hackett. Glad to see you're back with us. A lot of people were worried."

The nurse adjusted my bed so my head was elevated enough to sip some water through a straw. I watched Dr. Hackett take my pulse and check on some levels on the various machines. When I felt like something other than garbage might come out of my mouth, I asked, "What happened to me?"

She stopped what she was doing and gazed into my eyes. "You were in an automobile accident . . . at the Carter Barron Amphitheatre. Do you remember anything?"

"I remember going to the blues festival . . . with my friend Destiny." I suddenly jerked in the bed. "Is Destiny okay?"

"She's fine. She's been keeping a vigil by your bedside with your parents for the past two days. Wonderful young lady and a very caring friend."

I was trying to wrap my mind around her having said "two days." "I've been unconscious for two days? No wonder my head is hurting."

"We'll get you some pain medication for that. It's to be expected. You suffered a concussion that caused you to lapse into a temporary coma. We've done several brain scans and everything appears to be fine."

I glanced at my leg. "It's painfully obvious that my leg is not fine."

"It was fractured in two places, but it seems to be healing nicely. All in all, you are a very fortunate woman. If that young man hadn't pushed you out of the way, chances are it could have been fatal."

"Young man?" I sat up farther, despite the pain. "What are you talking about?"

"He saved your life."

Destiny entered my room less than an hour later. Both the doctor and the nurse were gone, having left me so the pain medication could kick in.

"Aw, look at you," Destiny said giddily. "Wide-awake and looking like sunshine."

I gave her the finger. "Kiss my monkey!"

"Please, I ain't your man. I don't kiss snatch." She leaned over and kissed my cheek. "A peck on the cheek is all you get from me."

After she sat down, I asked, "Can you believe this shit?"

"I don't have to believe it. I was there." She sighed. "It scared the hell out of me. One second I'm taking a leak in the bathroom, and the next second I'm watching you flying up in the air and landing damn near at my feet."

"But . . . but . . . what the hell happened?"

"This crackhead lost control of her vehicle and started using the crowd as bowling pins. It's been all over the news. Nineteen damn years old. I'm telling you. The entire world is headed to hell in a handbasket."

"Is she locked up?" I asked, getting angrier with each word that left Destiny's mouth. "She needs to be up underneath the jail."

"She might still be in the hospital. Some of the people decided to open a can of whup-ass on her before the police got to her."

I could see the guilt written all over Destiny's face. "You wouldn't happen to have been *some of the people,* would you?"

She glanced away from me at the window. "Maybe, maybe not. I may have gotten a good kick or two in."

"Destiny!"

"Brooke, you would've done the same thing if the shoe was on the other foot. Besides, there were officers on the scene because of the concert. It was only a minute or two, and some other people beat her way worse than me. I had to damn near fight them to get in on the action."

My anger began to subside, and something about me felt sorry for the girl; even though she was the cause of it all.

"How many people did she hit? Did anyone get killed?"

"About twenty-five people got injured, but no fatalities, thank heaven. A lot of broken bones and shit. And then there's Damon."

"The Damon who pushed me out of the way? The doctor and nurse mentioned him but didn't give me many details."

Destiny grew really quiet.

"What happened to him? Is he dead?"

She shook her head. "No, he's not dead, but . . ."

"But?"

"They had to amputate his arm."

We sat there in silence for a minute.

"They said he saved my life. Are you telling me that the only reason he got hurt was trying to shield me?" I finally asked.

"He pushed you and his wife out of the way. He saved her, too."

I stared at the ceiling. "I'm so sorry."

"You have nothing to feel sorry for." Destiny pulled her chair closer and caressed my hand. "See, this is why I wish you never had to find out. I know how you are. You're going to feel responsible and somehow put a 'this is all my fault' spin on an incident that was out of your control."

"He lost his arm . . . because of me." A tear cascaded down my right cheek. "How can I live with something like that?"

"Brooke, you were merely a side reflex to what the man would've done anyway. A man will instinctively attempt to save his woman; at least a real man will. This proves that chivalry is not altogether dead, like it seems these days."

"So, did his wife get injured?"

"No, he took the brunt of the impact. What happened to you was that when he pushed you out the way, and the SUV hit him, he was thrown into you and you flipped up in the air and then landed on your leg . . . and your head."

"Oh no!"

"I heard your leg actually snap into pieces. It's a miracle that you didn't lose it, like he lost his arm."

"Are he and the others here, in this hospital? I want to thank him."

"The girl who ran your asses over was here, but I believe they moved her to the infirmary at the jail. Who gives a damn?! I believe Damon was flown to George Washington. He's not here. I know that for sure."

"So how do you know so much about him?"

"I only know what they've said on the news and in the papers. I've never met him . . . but I have seen him before. So have you."

I stared at her. "What do you mean I've seen him before?"

"Before that day." She released my hand, stood up, walked over to the window, and opened the curtains. "Let's bring some of the outdoors indoors. This place is depressing." She turned and looked at me. "Remember that day when I met you at the gym? The one and *only* time I met you at the gym?"

"Yeah, I remember."

"He was Mr. Fine, the one in the white wifebeater we were checking out."

My mind raced. The man who was smiling at me right before everything went crazy. The one that I smiled at first because he seemed familiar. The attractive man from the gym. *Oh my goodness!*

Damon

September 15, 2007
The George Washington University Medical Center,
Washington, D.C.

"THEY said you can go home on Monday." Carleigh was sitting beside my bed, a mere shell of the woman that she used to be before the accident.

"Great!" I feigned a smile. "Did you let the office know that I need a couple of months before I return to work?"

"I don't know why you insist on going back to work *period*, rather less so soon."

"I don't get your meaning."

Carleigh glared at my shoulder and then at me. "Damon, you lost a fuckin' arm. You're disabled."

"You use that term like it's a dirty word, Carleigh. My arm is gone, not my mind. I'm still the same man."

Carleigh started crying again—a daily occurrence. I couldn't stand to see her in so much agony, but I was dealing with my own issues. As much as I wanted to pretend otherwise, I was devastated that a part of me was lost because of someone else's stupidity.

Lisa Grant, the young woman who had abused crack to the

point of making an SUV a weapon, was facing numerous charges, and her life was pretty much ruined. At least she still had all of her limbs. She had been banged up pretty good in the crash and the crowd had attacked her, but she had fully recuperated. Unlike the other two dozen or so people who were all dealing with the aftermath, Lisa Grant made a choice that none of the rest of us had.

"Baby, why don't you go home and get some rest?" I told Carleigh. "I'll be fine, and Bobby and Steve said they were coming through later."

"Are you sure?" I could tell that the thought of getting the hell out of my hospital room excited her. "I can stay until visiting hours are over, if you need me to."

"I'm okay. All of you don't need to baby me. My parents are in here constantly and so are my friends. I appreciate all the attention, but—"

"You don't sound like you appreciate it!" Carleigh snapped at me. "You blame me, don't you?"

"Blame you for what?"

She pointed at the bandage. "For that! I didn't cut off your arm, Damon."

"Don't be ridiculous. None of this is your fault. A drug addict did this to me, and everyone else. How could you possibly believe it's your fault?"

Carleigh swiped at her tears with the sleeve of her jacket. "Somehow, some way, I know that you'll eventually blame me for this."

I tried to put myself in her place. How would I have felt if she had lost a limb trying to protect me? I quickly decided that I would have blamed myself for her getting hurt.

"Carleigh, look at me, baby." When she planted her eyes on mine, I said, "I understand how you must be feeling right now, but you have to believe, we *both* have to believe, that everything happens for a reason. I cannot begin to explain the purpose behind what happened, but there is one."

"That's ridiculous, Damon. There was no purpose to this." She stood up and started gathering her things. "There's no justification for that little girl's actions. She was strung the fuck out on drugs and had no business being behind the wheel of that truck."

"No, she didn't, but you and I are spiritually mature adults. We attend church every Sunday because we know that there is only one powerful being in the universe. We were all brought together, in that park, for this to occur, because He wanted it that way."

"So how does that help us now? How does that help us cope with this?"

"People suffer loss every day, different kinds of loss. I'm alive and I'm grateful for that. Can't you be grateful for that, too?"

"I'm grateful that you didn't die, Damon. If you had died, they would've had to bury me right along with you. I wouldn't have been able to deal with that. Your death, and because of me? No way."

"Well, you don't have to deal with that. I'm not going anyplace." I tried to sit up higher in the hospital bed, but cringed in pain.

"Damon, don't try to overdo it like you're Superman. The doctors already made it clear that you have a long road to recovery."

"I realize that. They gave me a pamphlet from the National Limb Loss Center. It's in the drawer."

Carleigh couldn't hold back any longer. The floodgates opened and she broke out into a full-fledged wail. Then she collapsed back into the visitor's chair.

"Baby, I'm still your husband, minus one arm. That's it. Nothing's going to change."

"Everything's going to change. You loved to work out at the gym every day. You were so vibrant and full of life."

"And I can still work out at the gym and I *am* full of life. None of my aspirations have been altered. I still have my career. I still have my website."

Carleigh let out an audible gasp.

"What?"

"Nothing."

"What, Carleigh?"

"I can't believe that you're lying there worried about that stupid website. That should be the least of your concerns. It's a joke."

"What makes it a joke? You might find all of my hard work humorous, but I don't. I will make thelastgoodmen.com profitable. Very profitable. If you don't want to support my efforts, cool."

Carleigh wiped away the last of her tears. Now she was getting irate. "Look at us. Sitting here arguing about something irrelevant." She reached over from the chair and took my remaining hand. "You're going to have to learn to write all over again. You were right-handed."

I forced a grin. "I had to learn to write the first time, so we both know I can do it."

Finally, a smile out of her. "We also both know that your handwriting looked like gibberish, so hopefully you'll do better this time."

I laughed. "Go get you some rest."

"You sure you don't want me to stay?"

"I want you to get some sleep. To get out of this dismal place for a while. To live life."

About an hour and a half after Carleigh had left the hospital, the phone rang in my room. I was surprised because even in the hospital everyone that I knew had been calling on my cell number. I as-

sumed that it was something pertaining to hospital business and
started not to answer. Yet, something compelled me to pick it up.

"Hello."

"Hello." The voice on the other end of the line was soft and female. "May I please speak to Damon Johnson?"

"This is Damon."

I braced the phone on my shoulder so I could free up my hand
to turn down the volume on the television. I was watching an episode of *Judge Mathis*. I'd always been a fan of his, but after reading his memoir, *Inner City Miracle,* I realized how cool the brother
truly was.

The woman had yet to say another word so I repeated, "This is
Damon. Who's this?"

"My name is Brooke. Brooke Alexander. I wanted to thank
you."

The lady in red!

"There's no need to thank me. I did what anyone would've
done."

"That's not necessarily true. There are a lot of heartless people
on this planet, and even though I realize that your main purpose
was in saving your wife, a lot of men would've stood by and done
nothing."

"Not *this* man."

"That's apparent."

I sat there, listening to her breathe, possibly trying to figure out
what to say next.

"I appreciate you calling. That means a lot."

"But it's not enough. How can I ever repay you?" She sighed.
"That's a stupid question, isn't it? I could never repay you. Not in
the true sense of the word. If I could, I would give you my arm to
replace the one you lost."

The sincerity in her voice was overwhelming. Somehow, I knew that she actually meant it. A lot of people might have thanked me, but most wouldn't have felt so obligated. She was really hurt about my amputation.

"You really want to do something for me, Brooke?"

"I'll do anything—anything at all."

"Be happy from this day on. Appreciate life as much as it appreciates you. Wake up every morning and embrace each day as a gift. Don't waste any time. Don't let anyone hurt you. That's what you can do for me."

"That's really deep, Damon. I'm going to try my best to honor your request. I wish that we were in the same hospital. I would come see you and thank you in person."

"Your phone call has touched me. I wasn't expecting it."

"Then that means you are truly a giver. You give and don't feel entitled to anything in return. That's rare. Very rare."

"You take care of yourself. You're a beautiful woman, Brooke."

It is strange, but I swear that I could feel her smile through the phone.

"You think that I'm beautiful?"

"I know that you're beautiful. This might sound crazy, but the other day isn't the first time that I've seen you."

"You remember me from the gym?"

I am not sure who was more stunned. Her or me.

"Yes, I remember you, and you obviously remember me," I said, blushing.

"You're a hard man to forget."

We both grew quiet.

"I'd better go," Brooke said. "Would it be all right if I call you again?"

"Sure, but let me give you my cell number. I don't know how long I'll be here; in this room or in the hospital."

After I gave Brooke my phone number, we hung up, but I didn't want to end the conversation. She sent me a text message with her number and I found myself looking forward to using it. That was not a good thought for a married man and I knew it. *What the hell was going on?*

Brooke

EVERYONE thought that I was plum foolish; including me. Foolish for even considering Patrick's offer to stay with him after I left the hospital. For the past week, he had shown up at the hospital daily, expressing his undying love and concern. He would take a pencil and scratch the itches inside the cast on my leg. Give me sponge baths with my favorite shower gel because I couldn't stand what the nurses used. Patrick would rub me down with lotion, every inch of me except for the part of my leg covered by the cast; so gently, so lovingly.

Of course, I was still pissed off about Mandawhore. But I also remembered what Destiny had said to me that day at the Carter Barron. How all women have to share dick at some point if they want a man in their life. Now I was not about to sit there and allow Patrick to parade other pussy in front of me and have some kind of open relationship. I guess that I was prepared to accept the circumstances and understand that the possibility of his straying again existed. For all I knew, he might still have been tied up with Mandawhore, only denying it.

Nevertheless, he insisted on my "staying with" him as I refused to make it official and move back in—lock, stock, and barrel.

The first day went well. Roses everywhere; a $1,500 bottle of Dom. Romane Conti 1997; the latest Will Downing CD blaring through the speakers. Patrick had surprised me by purchasing an Esse, a luxury chaise lounge made expressly for fucking the daylights out of somebody. He claimed it was for my benefit, but I am sure that he wanted to make sure he could get some unrestricted pussy, even with my leg in a cast.

The Esse did make life a lot easier. My head, neck, and back were cradled in the soft, black material while the rest of me was perfectly positioned for him to try to knock my insides out. Patrick's dick felt different, better. I am not sure if it was because I had had a close call with death. Or maybe something had shifted in my pussy during the accident. It sounds ridiculous, but our organs do tend to shift in our bodies over time. That is why so many women started wearing that body shaper, to put everything back into place. Maybe my pussy had fallen out of place and now Patrick could hit it at a different angle.

I made the mistake of mentioning my theory to Patrick, and once he stopped laughing uncontrollably, he told me his own theory.

"Maybe you just finally realize that I have some good-ass dick!" We were in the kitchen eating vegetarian omelets that Patrick had prepared after a long, drawn-out night of fucking. "I've been trying to tell you that all along."

I snickered. "Whatever, baby. I'm telling you though, there's something different about my pussy. You didn't notice anything?"

"I noticed that I missed it, that I missed you." Patrick reached over the table and took my hand. "If I had lost you, I wouldn't have been able to survive, Brooke. I mean that."

I hesitated, then pulled my hand back away from him. "Funny how you never appreciated me until I almost got killed."

"That's not true."

"It is true, Patrick. Sure, you had your good days and your bad days, but for the most part, you never truly respected me as a person." I sighed. "I only hope you mean what you say and that you've changed."

"I have changed. I'm going to be the man you need, from this moment on. I promise."

I gazed into his eyes. "Please don't make promises you can't keep."

"I'm not."

We finished eating the rest of our breakfast in silence, then Patrick left for his law office.

I sat down on the sofa and flicked through the channels. I hated being on crutches, hated having a cast, and hated the world for my problems. Everyone but Damon Johnson; he had saved my life.

The Tyra Banks Show was on and I watched about thirty minutes of it. My mind kept drifting off to Damon though, wondering if he was still in the hospital and how much pain he was going through . . . because of me.

I decided to call him, telling myself that it was simply to check on him, but something else about the mysterious stranger drew me to him. No one had ever given me a gift like the one he had bestowed upon me.

"Hello, this is Damon," he answered on the second ring, sounding cheerful and shocking the hell out of me. "Hello?"

"Hey, Damon. It's Brooke. Brooke Alexander."

"Nice to hear from you, Brooke." He paused. "I knew it was you. I plugged your number into my phone."

But you haven't called me! Why am I bothering this man!

"Oh, did I catch you at a bad time? I was just calling to see how you're doing. Are you still in the hospital? How's your arm?" *Stupid-ass Brooke! His arm is gone!* "I mean, um . . ."

He must have deciphered my apprehension. "I still have part of it, at the top. It hurts, but, all things considered, I'd rather lose my arm than my life."

"Well, I for one, am glad that you didn't lose your life. I'm sure your wife is delighted to still have you around. You're a great man."

I could hear him suck in a breath on the other end of the line; I was not quite sure what to make out of it.

"I don't know about great. I did what anyone would do."

"No, some people wouldn't have done a thing. In fact, there were a bunch of other people there and no one else reacted but you."

"I'm sure there were others that day who prevented somebody else from being hurt, but I drew the shortest straw."

He had a valid point. Lisa Grant had had herself a field day using people in the crowd as human bowling pins. Someone else was probably pushed out of the way and slammed to the ground just in time to avoid being hit.

"Possibly," I said. "But you're the one who intervened on my behalf, and for that I will be eternally grateful."

"Aw, you're so sweet."

There was a long silence as I struggled for something to add. I could hear someone in his hospital room—a nurse asking if he needed any more water—which answered my question about whether he had been released. I waited patiently until he finished their conversation.

"So, I see you're still in the hospital."

"Yes, but I'll be out in a few days. I can't wait either. I'm not used to being waited on hand and foot."

"I hope you're not one of those *alpha men* who's going to rush your recuperation and act a fool."

"You sound like my wife. She's already fussing about me going back to work months from now."

"What do you do?"

"I'm a human resources director. You?"

"Nothing worth mentioning."

"Why do you say that?"

"You have a career. I make ends meet. It's not the same thing."

I was really ashamed of being a common waitress. I hated to admit it, but Mrs. Sterling was right. I was not doing enough with my life. Even though I hadn't been afforded the same opportunities as Patrick, that was no excuse for not pursuing a dream. Too many people spend the majority of their lives hoping for a change but do nothing to evolve. Their biggest fear is taking the risk to be alive. I needed to begin my evolution and become a risk-taker.

"Brooke, tell me, what you do? You have a job, right?"

"Yes, I have a job."

"Then that puts you in front of legions of other people. Come on; tell me."

"Why's it so important?"

"It's not. At least, it wasn't until you seemed like you don't care to discuss it."

How dare him! "I'm not a hooker or a stripper or anything like that, if that's what you're thinking," I lashed out at him.

He laughed and I frowned.

"What's so funny?"

"Even if you were a hooker or a stripper, it's no big deal. People are just people, and they do what they have to do to, like you said, to make ends meet."

"So, if I told you that I lay on my back and went through four sets of kneepads a month, you wouldn't judge me?"

"No, I'd probably find it fascinating."

Fascinating!

"Brooke? What do you do for a living?"

"I'm a waitress," I blurted out. "At a diner."

Damon chuckled. I wondered if he was making fun of me.

"That's a great profession, and it *is* a career. It takes a lot of skill to wait tables without dropping dishes, dropping trays on someone's head, and keeping up the pace . . . especially in a diner. Everyone's always in a hurry."

"You know what? What you said makes a lot of sense. I guess that I never thought about it like that. It's just . . ."

"Just what?"

"I used to work at more *upscale* places and my tips were a lot bigger. I feel like I got a demotion."

"Have you applied other places, Brooke?"

"No, not really." *Not at all!* "My schedule's so crazy that I really don't have the time."

"Didn't you injure your leg?"

"Yes, it's in a cast."

"While you're laid up, apply for some other jobs. You don't have to confine your search to waitressing either. You have internet access?"

"I'm not that destitute!" I exclaimed. "I didn't mean to come off like that. I can get on the internet."

"Then there are a lot of websites where you can search for a new job, and they're open twenty-four/seven."

"You're really trying to make me feel bad." I sighed. "I get what you're saying."

"I didn't mean to make you feel bad. I'm sorry. It's that human-resources part of me that kicked in. But seriously, it's a lot easier to find a new job when you already have one. A lot of people don't realize that."

"True. True."

"As the primary decision-maker at our corporation, when someone comes in with a huge gap in his employment history, sometimes even a small gap, it sends up a red flag. Unless, of course, a woman's been taking care of kids, or a sick parent."

"What if a man's been taking care of kids, or a sick parent?" I found myself asking, getting caught up in the conversation to my own surprise.

"Then he's not a real man."

"There are plenty of house husbands these days. Women are capable of bringing in the money. Not me, but *some* women." I snickered at my own comment. "I could never cover all the bills in a household."

"That must mean you don't live alone. Are you married?"

"I'm not married. Never been married." I tried to think of what to say next. "My situation is *complicated*. I'm kind of between households right now."

"You're not homeless!"

"No, not that. I was living with this guy but we're not officially together anymore. I'm staying with my best friend, Destiny, but sometimes I'm back and forth. Is this making any sense whatsoever?"

"It makes total sense. I only hope you do whatever makes you happy."

There was an uncomfortable silence on the phone for a few seconds. Then I said, "Well, Damon, I don't want to keep you. Thank you for your advice about looking for a new job."

"Are you going to do it?"

Probably not! "Yes, definitely," I lied.

"Will you call me again sometime?"

"Sure, or you can call me." *After all, you have my number!*

"I'll do that. Maybe we can have lunch one day soon, after I get released from lockup."

We both laughed.

"That sounds like a winner. You take care."

"You, too, Brooke."

And that was that. We hung up without saying another word.

Damon had definitely given me some food for thought, but the odds of my stepping outside of my comfort zone and leaving the diner were slim. Hell, Patrick had over and over offered to help me get a better job. Fear was definitely keeping me from doing things. I had to somehow overcome my apprehension. Damon was a nice man, and I hoped that he would call me to have lunch.

I turned the television back on and *Maury* was playing. For the life of me, I couldn't figure out why men would allow themselves to be trapped making moves on other women in the greenroom. Some of the men would ask for numbers and talk about fucking, but some went as far as to be slobbering the female decoys down. Then there were the paternity shows that Maury did regularly. How could a woman have to test a dozen men for the same child and still not figure out the father? I swear, some of that stuff had to be staged. Either way, it was entertaining, so I turned up the volume, grabbed my Pepsi, and got lost in the madness.

Damon

September 22, 2007

Y OU'RE making too much of a fuss over me," I said in protest
to Carleigh as she led me through the door to our home. "I
can walk."

She was holding on to my elbow like I'd lost a leg instead of an
arm. It had been bad enough to be escorted out of the hospital in a
wheelchair, but it was their policy. I could deal with that. What I
didn't want—and couldn't stand—was Carleigh babying me.

"Damon, let me be the wife and chill out," she said as we entered the dark house.

"Why are all the lights out? Did you pay the bill? Carleigh, please
tell me you paid the bill!"

I always took care of all the household expenses. Carleigh was a
good real estate agent, but when it came to paying bills on time, she
was the worst.

"You haven't even been in the hospital an entire billing cycle.
The electricity's not off, Damon."

"Then why is it so damn dark in here?"

"Watch your mouth!" I heard my mother yell out from someplace. Then the lights flickered on.

Everyone stared at my mother as she clasped her hand over her mouth on the living room sofa, then looked at Carleigh and me and yelled, "Surprise!"

One by one, friends and family members approached me to give me a kiss on the cheek or a hug. Most of them seemed totally uncomfortable as they looked at my arm, or what was left of it, covered by a shirt with a pinned-up sleeve.

Carleigh's four-year-old niece, Natalie, came up to me and hugged my leg. She looked up at me and asked, "Uncle Damon, are you contagionic?"

"No, I'm not *contagious*."

"Good, because my mommy said I have to stay away from kids at day care who are contagionic."

Natalie was so proud of the big word that I decided to play along. "Well, don't worry. I'm not contagionic. I'm still the same old Uncle Damon."

As I watched Natalie rush off to join her parents, Carleigh's brother and sister-in-law who lived in Richmond, I couldn't help but wonder what our children would look like. Natalie was a doll, and I would've given my other arm to have a daughter like her.

It was finally Mom's turn. She threw her arms around my neck, while my father shook my hand.

"Welcome home, Son," he said in a strained voice.

Even though they had been to see me in the hospital almost daily, Dad was still struggling with what had happened.

"I can't believe I spoiled your surprise," Mom whispered into my ear. As she let me go, she added, "I'm such an idiot."

"You're a lot of things, Mom, but an idiot isn't one of them."

She smiled and pinched my cheek. "I love you, Damon."

"I love you, too." I glanced at my father. "Both of you. Thanks for being here for me, throughout this ordeal."

"There's no other place for us to be," Dad replied. "You're ours."

"Are you hungry, sweetheart?" Mom asked. "We've got all of your favorites prepared."

"Actually, I'm so happy to see everyone, I really want to sit and talk." I glanced around the house as I walked farther into the foyer. "I can't believe so many people traveled here."

A lot of my aunts, uncles, cousins, as well as many of Carleigh's family members, were there. I still never figured out where everyone had hidden their cars in order to surprise me. They must have damn near hiked to the house. The one person who was obviously missing was Carleigh's mother. My mother-in-law hadn't visited me even once in the hospital. I guess hunting down dick action was her full-time gig. Fine by me. She could have crawled back in her cave for the remainder of her life, for all I cared. Whenever she was around, she seemed determined to cause turmoil in my marriage, and I loved my wife too much to sit back and willingly put up with it.

I was elated to be around all of the people who were concerned about me. Her being there would have put a damper on the entire evening. Made everything else seem fake.

Speaking of fake, Jordan walked up to me next.

"Hey, Damon." She wrapped her arms around my neck, and I wanted to push her ass down on the floor. She let go and looked into my eyes—phony heifer. "I'm so glad you're feeling better. Sorry I couldn't make it past the hospital, but you know how that goes."

Good! I didn't want your ass at the hospital!

"Wow, that was so scary. I saw the entire thing." She started staring at my pinned shirt. "Sorry about the arm, but such is life." She shrugged like it was no big deal. "Carleigh will get used to it, I'm sure."

"I'm sure she will. Right around the same time *I get used to it.*"

Jordan laughed uneasily. "Of course. You have to get used to it, too. You know what I meant."

"I know what you *implied,* Jordan." I started to walk away from her. "Where are Bobby and Steve?"

Bobby and Steve were the last ones to arrive, hours later. Carleigh had gone into the bedroom to give us some privacy.

"So, what are you going to do now?" Bobby asked as he guzzled down his third or fourth beer of the evening.

"The same thing I've always done," I replied sarcastically. "I'll be back at work in a couple of months and I'm still going to run my website."

Steve picked up a pretzel out of the bowl on the kitchen table, where we were seated, and snapped it in half. "Don't you think you should slow down a little bit?"

"Would you . . . slow down?"

He shrugged. "I can't answer that but—"

"But nothing." I stood and walked over to the sink to put my plate in there to be washed. "Both of you need to chill the hell out." I sat back down and looked back and forth between them. "My life has been forever changed, but I still have a life. My arm is gone. No big deal. I can still see. I can still hear. I can still think. There's no way that I'm going to sit around and act like some kind of invalid. This isn't a damn dress rehearsal. I've got things to do."

Bobby looked at Steve, who had lowered his eyes to the table. "Hey, no one's saying that, Damon. Steve didn't mean any harm. We're all still dealing with what happened. I wish that I could've been there for you, man. That I could've done something. *Anything.*"

"Bobby, don't get overdramatic on me. It's okay." I reached over and grasped his hand. He put his other hand on top of mine and grabbed it. "I'm a grown-ass man and I'll deal with this. People come back from the military all the time fucked-up; even some of our friends."

"Yeah, but you didn't volunteer for this shit!" Bobby exclaimed, letting go of me.

He stood and started pacing the floor as Steve and I watched him go through whatever he was going through. Until that moment, I never realized how much Bobby really loved me. Sure, we had been kicking it together since forever, but it is true that your darkest hour is when you determine who your true friends are. Bobby and Steve were my true friends. My blood brothers, even though different blood flowed through our veins.

Steve cleared his throat. "Bobby, we should go. It's late and Damon needs to get some sleep."

It was late; very late. "You two can crash here, in the guest bedrooms."

"That's not a bad . . ." Bobby was saying until Steve glared at him. "Oh, no, I need to get home."

"Why don't you want to stay, Steve?" I asked.

"This is your first night back. Everyone's imposed enough." He nodded toward the hallway. "You need to go in there and spend some quality time with your wife, if you know what I mean."

We all chuckled. They knew the deal. I had one hell of a buildup in my balls. Shit, all that time in the hospital without sex; not even being able to masturbate because someone might have walked into the room. I was about to go insane.

After I saw them out, I turned off all of the lights and headed to the bedroom. Carleigh was fast asleep. I bent over and kissed her on the

forehead. She was freshly bathed and smelled like lavender and vanilla. As much as I needed some pussy, I yearned for a shower even
more. They had given me sponge baths the entire time that I was in
the hospital, but I needed to feel the power of high-pressured water
on my body. They had given me a bag to place over my bandages
when I showered or bathed, but told me to be careful. A home nurse
would be coming by daily to check on me and to change the bandages for at least the next month, so I was willing to take my
chances.

I got into the shower and finally let it all go. I had the water so
hot that the mirrors instantly got foggy, and the soap was invigorating. I cried for nearly an hour, right there in the confines of the
shower, coming to terms with how my life would change. As much
as I hated putting on pretenses, I now had to do that very thing. I
couldn't let my parents or Carleigh or my friends know how deeply
I was affected by the loss of my arm. Those emotions and the disappointment that I felt would have to forever be my secret.

Once I climbed under the covers with Carleigh and placed my
remaining arm around her waist, I immediately felt her tense up.

"Do you feel better?" she whispered, shifting her weight so she
could look at me. "You were in the shower a long time."

"It's been weeks since I've been able to bathe the way I like. You
know how I am."

She sighed and fingered my chest, then stared at my bandages.
"Does it still hurt?"

"Yes, but I'll get through this. I have a very high tolerance for
pain." I winced as I tried to move and a pain shot through me. "At
least, I think I do," I added, then chuckled.

"I keep telling you that you have to take it easy and try not to
overdo it, Damon."

"And I keep telling *you* that I'm not going to allow this to be some kind of crutch to prevent me from doing what I need to do, as a man, and as your husband."

"Your job said you can stay off for up to a year; I called Samantha Howard and asked her." She ran her fingers over my cheek. "But you knew that already, being that you're the head of human resources."

"Yes, I did know that already, but I'm not staying off work for a year. I'd go bananas. A couple of more months and I'll be fine. It's not like my job is strenuous."

Carleigh kissed me and it felt great to know that she even still wanted to kiss me. I hungrily explored her mouth, remembering what it was that I was prepared to fight for—my life. I started pulling her nightgown over her head. She broke the kiss and hurriedly took it off. She was nude underneath and I had come to bed that way. I entered her with a grunt and lay there for a moment, gathering my bearings. Women could never understand what pussy really feels like to a man; never.

I fucked Carleigh without mercy for the next thirty minutes or so, until her head, shoulders, and arms were hanging backward off the bed. I kept on thrusting deep into her, even though I was sure the blood was rushing to her head. She seemed to love it though and moaned and yelled out like it was our first time together, all over again.

After I climaxed the first time, Carleigh started sucking my dick, and it was a welcomed kind of pain; the best kind of ache. Once I was hard again, she got on top of me and started swiveling her hips like she was twirling a hula hoop. I grabbed her waist with the one arm that I had, then started slapping her on the ass.

"Ride this dick, baby," I told her. "Ride it faster."

Carleigh placed her hands on my chest and pounded my dick

even harder with her pussy, like she was trying to draw out my soul with her pelvic muscles.

"I want you to fuck me from behind," she announced before climbing off me and quickly getting into the doggie-style position. "Hit my G-spot. Work my shit."

I was gasping for breath, but I was not about to give up. If my doctor had been there, he would have been ready to put me back in the hospital. I was acting a fool; we both were.

Carleigh was on all fours as I pounded into her, using my curved dick to hit the right spot. I had figured out when I was a teenager that something about my dick was special, besides it being long and thick. It being curved drove women insane. When I fucked them from the back and rubbed it against their G-spot, they experienced incredible orgasms, like the one my wife had about fifteen minutes later.

Totally spent, we both collapsed back onto the bed. Carleigh pulled the covers over us and laid her head on my chest.

"The sun's almost up," she said. "What time is your therapy tomorrow?"

"You mean today." I kissed the top of her head and ran my fingers through her hair. "The therapist is due here around noon, but, shit, I've already had all the therapy I need for the day."

We both laughed, then shared one last kiss before falling off to sleep in each other's arms.

Brooke

October 10, 2007

I CAN'T believe your ass is up in here!" Destiny was all loud as she sat at the counter at the diner. "You can't wait table on crutches!"

"Then how come I'm doing it?" I said, and used one crutch to make my way over to the serving window to pick up a customer's plate of corned beef hash, if you wanted to call it that. "I may be moving a little slower, but I'm still faster than most of the people in here."

"She needs to be at home in bed," Tony chimed in. "And Hank ought to be ashamed of himself. This has got to be against *some-body's* labor rules."

Hank had made a run to a distributor to get some more ketchup. How the hell could he run out of ketchup, of all things? With the way the food tasted, most people had to drown it in some kind of sauce to make it edible. It was amazing how many regulars Hank had. Some of them had been coming there for decades. I guess if you eat enough bad food, it eventually starts to taste good. They must have built up immunity to his poison.

"Well, complain when he gets back," I dared Tony, knowing he wouldn't say jack shit about it. "I need to work. You know as well as

I do that Hank doesn't have benefits in this dump. Luckily, I had a private health-insurance plan. Thank goodness I didn't fall behind on my premiums. I would've been screwed."

"Why don't you let Patrick cover your car payments and bills while you're laid up?" Destiny suggested. "You don't have to worry about paying me rent. Sheesh!"

"I'm not about to lay up in your apartment and not pay rent, Destiny, no more than you'd ever do that shit to me." She got quiet and stirred some more sugar in her iced tea. "And you're going to get diabetes if you keep putting twenty damn sugars in one glass of tea."

"I used fourteen packets, thank you very much," she stated sarcastically. "You don't need to pay me any rent. You're over Patrick's most of the time anyway."

"But I live with you," I insisted.

Destiny rolled her eyes. "I still say this is ridiculous, you working like this. I was telling your mother that—"

"My mother? Don't tell me that you called my mother on me! You might as well have called the po-po."

"Somebody needs to talk some sense into your ass."

I sensed Tony motioning behind me and swung around in time to see him swirling his finger around his temple region, implying that I was crazy.

"Takes one to know one," I said, and tapped his foot with the bottom tip of my crutch.

Tony screamed like I'd shot him, and everyone in the diner stared at us.

"Stop being such a baby," I told him. "I barely touched you."

He snapped his fingers. "I only like tender touches, chile. I'm not into that S-and-M shit, living behind the veil and all of that."

Destiny almost choked on her tea. "I don't even want to think about you in leather thongs."

"And I don't want to think about you in them either," Tony snarled at her. "Not unless you're hiding a dick under that dress."

Joe, the cook on duty, yelled from the back, "You all need to shut it up before you both get fired. Hank will be back any minute, and you know he has his spies." Joe peeked over the serving window and looked to see which regulars were there.

"Fuck a spy," Tony said to Joe. "Hank needs me, and he needs Brooke. If I get fired, I already have my plan B and plan C laid out. Plan B is to become a stripper at the Mill over by the Navy Yard, and plan C is joining the damn navy."

"Navy!" Destiny, Joe, and I all exclaimed at the same time.

"The navy's not ready for you," I informed Tony. "They'd have to put you in a private barracks. You'd be trying to get down with every man there."

"What's even wilder is that all of them would be trying to get down with me."

I ignored that comment. Tony was constantly swearing that every man was a creeper, a booty bandit.

Destiny got up from the counter. "I'm going back to the office. Back to my daily grind." She looked at me. "You need to take your ass home."

"I love you, too, boo-boo," I said teasingly, then blew her a kiss as she left out.

My next order was up, so I limped over to get it and took it to table 12.

When I got to Patrick's penthouse later that evening, my parents were inside, lying in wait with him. They were determined to convince me to "stay off my feet" a little longer.

"We can help you out some," my mother said, sitting beside me on the sofa while my leg was propped up on the coffee table. "You're still our daughter and we have a little extra money."

Daddy was seated in an armchair and was eyeing Patrick, who was standing by the window, with disdain. Patrick had his back to us, probably because he was angry with me for making him look like a total cad.

He definitely felt that way because when Mama said that, he turned to face us and then looked right into Daddy's eyes. "I'd be more than willing to provide Brooke with everything she needs. She's stubborn."

My father sighed and nodded in agreement. "She's always been stubborn. She gets it from her mother."

Mama and I glanced at each other and fell out laughing. We knew that we were stubborn, but I preferred the term *determined*.

"Daddy, I want to work," I said. "I don't want to sit around here all day, watching television. That's boring. If there's nothing else you know about me, it's that I hate idle time."

"You always say that idle hands are the devil's workshop, dear," my mother said to my father.

"How much longer is that cast going to be on?" Daddy asked me.

Patrick jumped in like he was the authority. "The doctors said she has a few more weeks."

I can speak for my damn self, I thought.

"Daddy, it's not like I'm racing cars or herding cattle. I take a cab to work because I can't drive yet, but I'm telling you, I'm fine." I took my leg off the coffee table, got up from the sofa, and stood up. I beckoned Patrick to me with my finger. "Come here."

Patrick grinned and walked over to me.

"Dance with me," I said.

We started doing the tango, and my parents both laughed. When Patrick dipped me and my leg stood straight up in the air, Mama said, "Be careful, Brooke. We don't want you to break something else."

Daddy stood and folded his arms in front of him. "We better go. It's getting late and I don't want to miss *48 Hours Mystery*."

"You still watch that show, Daddy?"

"He never misses an episode," Mama replied. "It is a pretty good show, but he turns the volume up so loud, sometimes it drives me wild."

"Maybe I like driving you wild," Daddy said with a little too much seduction in his tone for me.

"Oh, boy, please don't flirt in front of me!" I exclaimed, letting go of Patrick and shielding my eyes. "Next thing we know, you'll be swapping spit."

Mama laughed. "We swapped a whole lot more than that to get you and your brother here."

Her last statement made even Patrick uncomfortable. "Let me get your coats," he said, heading for the closet in the entryway.

Daddy followed behind him and I heard them talking in hushed tones while I helped Mama gather her belongings. I am sure they were conspiring on how to keep me from going to work, but that was not happening.

"Brooke, promise me that you won't overdo it."

"I promise. I'm almost thirty. You and Daddy have got to cut the umbilical cord."

She rubbed her belly. "Never."

We both laughed as I walked her out.

• • •

Patrick and I were in the kitchen an hour later. I was sautéing some tomato-garlic chicken and fettuccine. Patrick was finishing up the spring-mix salad with balsamic dressing.

"I hope you're hungry," I said. "You've got me slaving over a hot stove."

"I told you that I would cook."

"I'm kidding, Patrick." I limped over to the fridge to get the Parmesan cheese off the door. "I like cooking."

"Then I like eating . . . *everything* you're serving up."

"Umm, that sounds very enticing. We might have to hit the Esse again tonight."

"Even though you're feeling better, I think we should be more careful with the sex."

I looked at him. "I know those words didn't just leave your mouth. Not Mr. Freak-of-the-Week."

"Your parents are really concerned that you might get hurt, and I feel bad enough, allowing you to go back to work in that diner."

"You didn't *allow* me to do anything, Patrick. I'm my own woman. You can't keep me from working."

He stared at me and I could tell he was angry, but he held it back. "Like I said, stubborn."

I walked toward him and kissed him. "Sometimes being stubborn can be a good thing." I grabbed his dick through his pants. "Like if I decided that I wanted some dick right now, I wouldn't stop until I got it."

"Far be it from me to stand in your way."

I continued to caress his dick. "But you'd try to stand in my way from earning a living?" I pushed his back against the counter. "If you're going to admire my traits some of the time, then you have to admire them all the time."

I lifted up my dress and told him, "Tear my panties off."

Patrick eyed me seductively. "I'll do better than that. I'll tear them off with my teeth."

I giggled as Patrick swung me around and put me up on the counter. Then he bent down and started gnawing at the right side of my bikini underwear. The slice of material was wafer thin and he had no problem biting through it. Then he started working on the other side. This savage act turned me on beyond compare.

I pulled his cashmere sweater off him, then anxiously worked at his belt and zipper. His pants dropped down around his ankles, and he was inside me in mere seconds.

"Hold up; let me show you some of my moves," I told him.

I lifted my well leg up over his shoulder, then used my hand to lift my leg with the cast over his other shoulder. I was on the counter with my legs spread into a *V*. Patrick pounded into me, and I swear, there was something *different* about my pussy. Patrick was hitting spots that he had never hit before. I came all over the kitchen counter as my chicken started burning in the skillet on the stove.

"Move the pan," I told Patrick. "Before the smoke detector goes off and the doorman and half the complex end up in here."

When the fire alarm goes off in a building, that is bad enough, but when it goes off in the penthouse of a building, everyone panics. Even with the water tanks on the roof and the sprinkler system, people don't like the idea of a fire starting at the top of a building, or in the basement. That always means that it could spread up, or down, like a matchstick.

Patrick tried to grab the pan without taking his dick out of me. I started scooting my ass, legs still spread in a *V*, to the right so we could get closer. He was able to grasp the pan and pull it off the flames, just as the detector gave off a little beep.

"Just in the nick of time," he said, and we both laughed.

Then he went right back to rubbing the hell out of my walls. We forgot all about eating and took it to the bedroom, where we went another *four* rounds, breaking our relationship record. Patrick was in rare form; very rare form.

Damon

November 1, 2007

My therapy was going great. I was learning to control my new prosthetic arm. It was not easy at first, but between the home visits and my workout sessions at the hospital, things were moving along.

I had called Brooke the evening before, feeling bad that I hadn't reached out to her before then. Part of me had expected her to call me again, to take me up on my lunch offer. She said that she was at the diner when I called, working the late shift, and could only speak for a moment. It worked out perfectly that she was working nights that particular week because that afforded her the opportunity to meet me for lunch.

I asked if she wanted to meet at America in Union Station. It seemed like a neutral point for us, and I figured that being in such a crowded place would make her feel more at ease. I didn't want to ask her to go someplace quaint—or romantic. She might have got the impression that I expected something "warm and juicy" in return for saving her life. I really wanted to see her and was anxious as I sat at a window table, awaiting her arrival.

She came in, limping a little, and I recognized her right away.

She was stunning. She spotted me as well and came over to the table, with a wide grin on her face.

"Damon!" she squealed out.

I stood up and gave her a hug. Our embrace lingered for a bit longer than a casual moment, and then she sat down. I took my seat again and smiled at her for a few silent seconds.

"I'm glad you could join me," I said. "You're looking well."

"Thanks, so are you." She picked up her menu. "I got my cast off last week."

"Cool. I've had my arm for a few weeks."

She suddenly seemed uneasy. "I'm so sorry about your arm."

"I hope that you don't keep saying that every time we talk."

"I'm sorry." She laughed after she realized she had done it again. "Oops! I'll try not to say it again."

"It's okay, Brooke." I pointed to the menu. "See anything you like?"

"I think that I'll go with the fish and chips, unless you have a better suggestion. Have you eaten here before?"

"No, never."

"So, you picked this place out of a hat?"

I chuckled. "No, I'm in Union Station quite often. I catch the train back and forth to New York several times a year. Our corporation is headquartered there."

"Oh, that's right. You actually have an exciting career; unlike me."

"I can see that you're the queen of putting yourself down."

"No, I'm not," she said defensively as the waitress came over to take our order. After we both ordered the fish and chips and lemonade, she continued, "What makes you think that I put myself down?"

I raised an eyebrow. "The words you say. What happened to you looking for a better profession? Something that you can be passionate about."

"It's been so long since I've had an actual dream that I don't know what to be passionate about."

"Come on. There has to be at least one thing you're interested in."

Brooke bit her bottom lip and got lost in deep thought for a moment.

"Well?" I prodded her.

"It's funny, but since the accident, I've been going to the pharmacy so much that it's started to seem interesting to me."

"So you want to be a pharmacist? That's great!"

"No way. It would take me years to become a pharmacist." She paused. "But the people who work in the front, the technicians, seem like they have a lot of fun."

"That should be easy to achieve. I can help you figure out how to do it."

"I'm sure you have plenty of things to occupy your time already." Brooke smiled at me and started snickering.

"What's wrong?" I asked, wiping my face with the cloth napkin. "Do I have something on my face?"

"No, silly. You haven't eaten anything yet."

Right on cue, the waitress returned with our food.

"This looks delicious," Brooke said. "Wise choice."

"I picked the place; you picked the food." I picked up a fry and dipped it in ketchup. "Dig in."

"The reason that I was laughing earlier is because I did some research on you on the internet and—"

"Instead of going to the employment sites that I told you about?"

Brooke smirked. "Yeah, instead of that."

"And what did you discover about me, Miss Brooke?"

"I found out that you have a dating website."

"I do. I own the Last Good Men. We've been around for a bit." I sighed. "Let me guess. You think it's foolish for me to have a dating site."

"No, I think it's sweet. You're like a modern day cupid. What made you want to start it?"

I shrugged. "It's a long story."

"My shift doesn't start until four. I'm all ears."

"Are you telling me that you're genuinely interested in it?"

"For sure. Why'd you start it?"

"Because I felt that there were a ton of sites out there, but none that had an actual screening process. Most of them are mere online meat markets. I wanted a site that focused on men—and women— who are searching for something real; something that will last."

"Are you a good man?" she asked me before taking a sip of her lemonade. She was picking at her food and I got the feeling that she was self-conscious about her weight.

"I like to think so. My wife's opinion fluctuates from day to day though."

Brooke gasped. "How is your wife? I never thought to ask if she was injured during that collision."

"No, she's fine; at least physically. She's struggling with the loss of my arm though. Before that day, she sported me as a trophy husband. Now I'm the blemished version."

"An arm doesn't make a man. His heart does, and you have an extremely big heart, Damon Johnson. Extremely big."

I found myself blushing. It was not every day that I had a woman like Brooke compliment me. I take that back. Women had complimented me before the accident, but most of them were trying to get into my pants, especially Carleigh's friends. Now I would walk past the kitchen or family room and hear them whispering about my "injury" like it was the end of the world as they knew it.

Carleigh would listen to them making disparaging comments about me, and I didn't like it. I had yet to confront her though. It had to be hard on her, going from having what she conceived as the perfect husband to a having a man with a physical flaw. But she had married me with the expectation that one day—if we lived long enough—both of us would end up sick, elderly, and looking totally different than we did when we met. Isn't that the way love, commitment, and lifetime commitment are supposed to go?

I looked at Brooke and she was still picking at her food.

"Since I have such a big heart, let me help you become a pharmacy technician. I can make a few phone calls and see what it would take, even help you get a jump start on a position after you complete your training."

Brooke looked at me, then shook her head. "I can't."

"Why? Because it's out of your comfort zone?"

"No, because I don't have the time."

"You can make the time." I gazed into her beautiful eyes. "We make time for what's important."

"I guess I see your point."

"You wanted to be here today, right?"

"Yes, I did." Now she was blushing.

"And you made the time."

"But school is something different."

"Isn't your boyfriend a prominent attorney?"

She was stunned. "How did you know that?"

I shrugged. "I heard someone mention it someplace." It had been all over the news; how Brooke was the girlfriend of one of the District's most prominent men. "Can't he help out?"

"Patrick would like nothing more than for me to be in the

kitchen, barefoot and pregnant with a huge diamond on my finger."

"What's so wrong with that?"

"He and I have a lot of issues."

He's a damn fool if he cheated on you, I thought. "I see. Well, if you decide that you want to do it, the pharmacy thing, let me know."

"Okay, I will."

Brooke and I finished up lunch, then walked around Union Station for a while, window-shopping. She saw this elegant, pricey dress at one store and stared at it for a long time.

"You like that dress?" I asked.

"It's awesome . . . but I can't afford it." She paused. "And I wouldn't look right in it, even if they had it in my size. This store caters to skinny women, looks like."

"Well, I prefer women with meat on their bones."

She looked up at me. "Really?"

"Yes, really." She looked back at the dress in the window. "You're a beautiful woman, Brooke. Your boyfriend's very lucky."

She giggled. "And you're very charming. Your wife's lucky, too."

Brooke was blushing and I'm sure that I was as well.

A little while later we parted with another big hug and a smile. As I watched her walk away with a slight limp, I marveled at what a wonderful woman she was and hoped that our lunch would be the beginning of a wonderful friendship.

Brooke

November 21, 2007

Over the next few weeks, Damon and I had lunch about twice a week. We always went to America, or one of the other restaurants in Union Station, and it was always perfectly innocent. We become good friends, and it seemed like we had known each other our entire lives. I'd always heard people talk about feeling that way about someone—like they had known each other in a previous life. I'd never experienced it until Damon.

I took the plunge. I let him talk me into registering for an online course to be a pharmacy technician. It would be a struggle, but at least I could do the classwork on my own time. I was required to go to campus to take tests, and I don't blame them for that. Imagine if someone else fronted and did the course and then you ended up working in a pharmacy, messing up everything. I had to show photo identification when I took the exams. Like most women, I hated my license picture. It was my own fault. I should have made sure my hair was freshly done and my makeup tight before I stood in the long-ass line at the Department of Motor Vehicles. All the other women in there had looked worn-out the day that I renewed my license. After all, that is not exactly the kind of place you get dressed up to go to. You grab a good novel, a bottle of spring water, your cell phone, and sit on those hard-ass benches for your number to be called.

Patrick wasn't happy about my decision to pursue school—probably because he had nothing to do with the decision-making process. I told him after the fact, when I already had my textbooks. I was still living with Destiny, but spent most of my time at his penthouse. He had ordered a bunch of other sex furniture from the Liberator website, even though my cast was a distant memory. The guest bedroom was beginning to look more like a sex club or porno-film set than anything else. We would go in there and fuck each other's brains out to try to keep our minds off our problems.

I still didn't trust him and didn't think that I ever could again. I had no ready-made alternatives, so I hung in there. There were good days and bad days. One of the good days was when Patrick took me up on the roof and made love to me on a blanket underneath the stars. One of the bad days was the day he talked shit about my weight and tried to get me to do a bunch of perverted sex acts.

"I'm not doing that," I told Patrick as he tried to shove a glass dildo up my ass.

"Come on, Brooke, you'll like it. It's not that big."

He had placed it in the freezer earlier that day and it was ice-cold. I was tempted to grab it out of his hand and clock him upside the head with it.

"You are not sticking that Popsicle up my ass, Patrick. Now leave me alone and let me go to sleep."

I turned over on my side and pulled the comforter tight around my body, to make sure that he didn't try to pull a fast one and ram it up me. I could have kicked myself for coming to bed nude. I was prepared to give him some pussy, but that was it. Not have my insides feel like the north fuckin' pole.

"Just let me stick it in your pussy," he whispered in my ear.

"You're not following me." I looked over my shoulder at him. "What would you get out of it anyway? That's for a woman who wants it; for her enjoyment."

"You will enjoy it, if you just try."

"No, I won't. I damn sure won't enjoy that."

Then he went and did it. He spewed the words: "Fat bitch!"

I sat up. "What did you say to me?"

"There's nothing wrong with your ears and I didn't stutter."

I sprang from the bed and headed for the walk-in closet.

"Where the hell do you think you're going, Brooke? It's the middle of the night."

"I don't give a shit what time it is!" I yelled from the closet. "I'm out of here!"

Patrick came and blocked the doorway of the closet. "You need to bring your ass back to bed and give me pussy."

"You need to get a grip on reality. The days of you talking trash about me and then forcing me to spread my legs are over."

"I've never forced you to do a damn thing."

I sighed as I pulled a sweatshirt over my bare breasts. "Okay, I'll give you that, but the days of me giving in to your nonsense are over." I pulled on a pair of jeans and brushed past him. "Sometimes I fuckin' hate you, Patrick."

"You love me, Brooke. Always have, and you'll never find another man like me."

I paused and stared at him. "I pray that I don't."

"Let me guess. You're going to run back to Destiny's. You're probably fucking that ho."

"She could probably do a better job than you."

Patrick's face became contorted as his anger rose. "You know you love this big dick."

"If I didn't have another dick to compare it to, it might be a big dick. Magnum, my ass."

I was bent over putting on my shoes when Patrick grabbed my hair and flung me back on the bed.

"Who have you been fucking? Whose dick have you been comparing mine to?"

I smirked, even though it felt like he was ripping my hair clean off my scalp. "That's too much for you, isn't it? The thought of me giving up my pussy out of both sides of my drawers to another man. You can't handle it, but you expect me to handle everything you dish out."

Patrick let go of my hair and sat up. "I'm sorry if I hurt you."

"No, you're just plain sorry." I slid on some shoes and left the bedroom, slamming the door behind me. "A fuckin' sorry-ass bastard!" I yelled as I headed down the hallway to the front door.

As I drove out of the garage in my car, the tears started to flow.

What are you doing, Brooke? What the hell are you doing?

I waited for someone to answer, but no answer came.

Damon

CARLEIGH dropped by my office to see how I was readjusting to being back at work. She was a welcome surprise . . . at first. Then things quickly turned ugly, when I shared with her what I *thought* was good news.

"I registered a new domain name today!" I told her once she was seated across from me at my desk. She didn't comment, just looked down at her hands, so I asked, "Want to know the name?"

Carleigh sighed. "Can you tell me over lunch? I'm starved."

"Sure. We can go downstairs to the cafeteria."

We had a great cafeteria in our building. It put most of the restaurants in the vicinity of the office to shame. That was not good enough for Carleigh though.

"You know how I despise cafeteria food. Can you have your secretary make us a reservation at La Ferme?"

"That's all the way out in Bethesda."

"And?"

"And it'll take a good forty-five minutes to get there in traffic."

"And?" Her voice was dripping with heavy sarcasm.

"And you just said you were starved." I sighed and tapped my fingers on my desk. "How about B. Smith's? You love the food there."

Carleigh rolled her eyes at me. *Say what!* "I'm in the mood for some French food."

"Then I'll have her call Brasserie Beck. They've got great duck."

"I want to go to La Ferme."

"Then I can't go," I said vehemently. "I'm not driving all the way out there for lunch; not today. We didn't even have plans."

"I wasn't aware that I need to make *plans* with my husband."

"You do when I'm in the middle of a workday." I got up from my desk and paced the floor for a moment, intentionally keeping my back to Carleigh. Then I turned and faced her. "Listen, I'm going to grab a sandwich at the cafeteria and then eat at my desk. I don't feel like playing this game with you today."

"What game, Damon?"

"You have an attitude and I'm not going to be your willing victim. You pretended to come here out of concern, but obviously your panties are in a bunch because of something." I thought of the date in my head. "It's not time for your period."

Carleigh rolled her eyes again. "Why do men always try to put a woman's emotions off on her period? As if we only have emotions for part of the month."

"At least that would be an excuse, but it looks like you don't have one," I stated. "I wanted to share some good news with you since you popped up, but forget it."

I sat down on the leather sofa in my office. Carleigh got up from where she was seated, came over, and plopped down beside me.

"Crandall and Dee want to go biking across California again in the spring."

Crandall and I had attended college together. He and his wife,

Dee, short for Demetria, lived in Los Angeles. Carleigh and I had gone on motorcycle excursions with them for the past three years in a row. We would fly out and then ride motorcycles up and down the coast. Harleys. The best of the best. Crandall collected them.

"Sounds great!" I said.

"Great?" Carleigh looked like I had slapped her. "What are you talking about, Damon?"

"Tell them we'll go; just like we do every year."

"They didn't know about . . ." Carleigh stared at my arm. "About the accident."

I slapped my thigh. "Things have been so crazy that I haven't had a chance to even shoot Crandall an email. I'll call him."

"Call him and say what?"

"That we'll narrow down some dates in a month or so."

"You can't ride a motorcycle," Carleigh said. "And I'm not getting on the back of one."

I glared at her. "Why not? Because you think I can't ride with one arm? Rarely do I ever hold both handlebars anyway."

"I'm *quite* sure that if you ran this past your doctor, he'd think you were a fool, too. Driving a car is one thing, Damon. Riding a fucking motorcycle is something else."

"Don't curse at me," I said, getting loud. "Don't curse at me and don't talk down to me." I shook my head in dismay, then changed to a nod. "This proves that I'm on the right track."

"On what right track?"

"My *news* is that I'm starting a new website called Able Minded Dating, for people with disabilities."

Carleigh gasped. "Tell me you're joking."

"I'm not joking. I'm dead serious, Carleigh. I'm going to continue running the Last Good Men site, but I'm also going to do this one."

"So now you're going to set up poor women in wheelchairs to be run over by four-legged creatures!"

"Your low opinion of men is astounding."

"I don't know why you'd find it astounding when most men are pieces of shit. Besides, most people with disabilities don't even have sex."

"That's not true, and how can you make such a blanket statement about other people's lives? I'm technically disabled, even though I disagree, and we have sex."

"But you're not confined to a wheelchair and you don't have a spinal-cord injury." She sighed. "Are you talking about people who are cuckoo, too?"

"What the hell do you mean by *cuckoo*?"

"You know what I mean, and now you're cursing at me, so watch it." Carleigh was really testing my patience. "I *mean,* people who can't even think straight."

"Do you ever listen to a word that comes out of my mouth? I said it is called *Able Minded Dating.* Obviously I am not suggesting that someone take advantage of a person who has dementia or Alzheimer's. You're trippin'."

"No, you're trippin' if you think that nonsense is going to work for five seconds. How long have you been doing that Last Good Men crap? I went on there the other day and the women on there are pissed off."

"We've had half a dozen couples get married after meeting on my site. I know that for a fact. Why don't you read the testimonials we post, instead of feeding into all the negativity? You're the most negative person that I know."

"Then why are you married to me?"

"Why are you married to me?" I asked back. I immediately reached out and took her hand. "I'm sorry. I didn't mean that. I love you, Carleigh."

She yanked her hand away. "I'm going to go to La Ferme for lunch *by myself.*" She stood up. "Jordan and I are hanging out tonight. It's her birthday."

I didn't realize witches had birthdays, I wanted to say. "That's nice," I blurted out instead. The mere mention of Jordan's name still stirred me the wrong way. "What time will you be in?"

"When we're done celebrating! I came over here to spend some quality time with you this afternoon so you wouldn't feel neglected tonight, but we both see how that turned out."

I stood up. "If you really want to go to La Ferme, I'll go. Let me clear a couple of things off my schedule for this afternoon."

"No!" Carleigh walked toward the door. "Do your thing. I'll tell your secretary to go get you a turkey club sandwich on my way out. You do still eat those, don't you?"

"Yes, of course I do."

"Just checking. You've changed a lot lately."

Carleigh left without saying another word.

"No, you've changed a lot lately," I said, after she had closed the door behind her.

That evening, I was sitting in my study, going over the initial concepts for Able Minded Dating. My mind wandered to Brooke and I wondered what she was doing. It was late, close to midnight, but I decided to take a chance and give her a call, hoping that I wouldn't interrupt quality time with her man. She answered on the third ring.

"Hello, Damon. Is something wrong?"

"No, nothing's wrong. Sorry to call you so late."

"Oh, it's no problem. I'm awake." I could hear her trying to mask a yawn on the other end of the line. She was so sweet, telling fibs to accommodate me. "What's up?"

"I decided to start a new website today."

"That's great! What's it called?"

Wow, she actually cares! "It's called Able Minded Dating, for—"

"That's wonderful! For people with disabilities?"

"Yes, exactly."

"That's so wonderful, Damon. You're such a compassionate person. Is there anything I can do to help?"

I found myself grinning from ear to ear. Someone once told me in a seminar that the world is full of dream stealers and reality stealers. The man giving the lecture stated that if you tell ten people close to you about a new business venture or life aspiration, eight out of the ten will say something negative. The other two will be happy for you and ask if they can do anything to help. Brooke was refreshing, and I was not surprised that she was in the positive 20 percent. Carleigh was in the negative 80 and had always been.

"Sure, I would love your help," I told Brooke. "Maybe we can meet for lunch tomorrow."

"Oh, I have to work tomorrow, but I work the late shift on Thursday. Can we meet up then?"

"That'll work. I'll give you a call to confirm on Wednesday."

"I'll be waiting. Meanwhile, I'll do some brainstorming and try to come up with some ideas."

"I appreciate that."

"I appreciate you, Damon. More than you realize." Brooke paused before adding a sweet "Good night."

"Good night, Brooke."

After she had hung up, I tried to focus back on the outline of the site, but I couldn't. Brooke Alexander was invading my thoughts. So much so that it got to the point where I tried to turn in, but couldn't get to sleep. I finally took a pain pill that I had left over and knocked myself out, but then she consumed my dreams.

Brooke

February 12, 2008

Over the following months, Damon and I spent a lot of time together planning out Able Minded Dating. My admiration of him grew tenfold, and I couldn't help but wonder what the hell was wrong with his wife, Carleigh. She must have been half-blind in one eye and unable to see jack shit out of the other. Damon was an incredible man, but whenever I brought her up, his entire demeanor changed.

Is that bitch being mean to you? I often found myself wanting to ask.

I decided to be there for him whenever he needed a friend. As much as he tried to pretend that losing a limb was no big deal, I would catch him staring at his prosthetic arm with a sad expression. A person with self-esteem issues finds it easy to recognize them in someone else. He was a beautiful man—*handsome* didn't do him justice. Even though they say you should never call a man beautiful, that is exactly what he was to me. Not just on the outside, but on the inside as well.

I had taken him over to my parents' place for dinner one night. They didn't know what to think of the situation. Of course, they knew that Damon was the man who had pushed me out of the way of Lisa Grant's SUV, but it may have come off as more of a date. Once during dinner I spotted Mama's eyes glued to his wedding ring. She sensed that I was staring at her, and her eyes met mine. That's when I brought up Carleigh and explained that they were trying to conceive their first child.

His having children was one of the main staples of our conversations. Damon told me about Carleigh's taking birth control behind his back for the first four years of their marriage. I wanted to strangle her. But she was supposedly all happy-and-go-lucky about getting pregnant at present. I prayed for them to conceive, sometimes even with Damon out loud. We would pray about a lot of things together, but I didn't attend church on the regular. That didn't mean that I didn't believe in God. The devil was a liar and I knew that God existed. He carried me day to day, and even though I may not have been front and center in a pew every Sunday, I loved Him and I was sure that He loved me.

Damon and Carleigh did attend church together religiously, no pun intended. They had attended a couples' retreat for a weekend up in the mountains. I asked Damon how things went, and he seemed reluctant to respond. Finally, he admitted that while he and Carleigh had both put on pretenses for the other couples in attendance, and the minister, the tension in their marriage was still as thick as wool.

I felt like a schoolgirl with a kindergarten crush. Damon was everything that I'd ever wanted in a man, but he could never be mine. I understood and accepted that, which is why I was still seeing Patrick. Despite the disrespect and Dr. Jekyll/Mr. Hyde personality that Patrick had going on, it was still a relationship. Not a great one, or even a particularly good one, but it was safe. He was there when I needed to be held and gave me the distance that I needed when I asked him for it.

Lisa Grant finally went on trial in January, and, of course, she was easily convicted. There were thousands of witnesses, including police officers, numerous victims, and their families. And high levels of drugs were detected in her system. It was what they call "a wrap" in Hollywood. Her public defender might as well have been a public-school teacher. No argument was going to shed a positive light on what she had done. She was sentenced to eight years, plus time served, in a high-security prison. I didn't necessarily agree with the "high-security" thing. Even though she was a drug addict, her actions didn't lead me to believe that she would commit an all-out violent act. Part of me felt bad for her. She would enter prison as a confused young lady and come out a hardened woman, more than likely continuously abused and molested by the other inmates.

The trial lasted for nearly three weeks, but I only attended one day, the day that I testified. Hank would have had five thousand heart attacks if I'd tried to take off to witness the entire trial. Patrick attended court with me, to make sure that I was not mistreated by the defense attorney. I told him that it would be senseless for the man to try to make me look bad. I was standing outside the Carter Barron, waiting for Destiny, when the shit went down. Still, Patrick was babying me and it was awkward when I introduced him to Damon. They spoke briefly, in hushed tones, in the hallway. I didn't hear what they said because I was distracted by the prosecutor trying to prepare me. I am willing to bet that Patrick made it clear that I was his woman though.

Damon was there every day. His buddy Steve went with him. Damon testified on a different day from me, but he told me all about it. We traded horror stories of having to relive that moment. Honestly, I didn't remember much, just the aftermath. Damon was apparently able to describe seeing the SUV careening through the crowd, headed straight for Carleigh and me. I was shocked when he told me that Carleigh had missed his testimony—the entire trial in fact—because she was trying to sell some houses.

None of my business, I kept telling myself, but that was a difficult pill to swallow.

Some of the other victims decided to file civil lawsuits against Lisa Grant. That was pointless, in my opinion. The woman was more penniless than me and was about to do eight years. Even if they were awarded a judgment, where was the money going to come from? Out of her ass? Damon didn't sue her either. Both of us wanted to move on with our lives and put it all behind us. What neither of us understood was the roller-coaster ride we were about to go on together—the one called *life*.

PART THREE

TOTAL ECLIPSE

Total eclipse—an eclipse in which
the surface of the eclipsed body
is completely obscured

amon

May 3, 2008

My big day had finally arrived; everyone was so excited. Everyone except Carleigh. She mysteriously had "other plans" and couldn't attend the launch party for Able Minded Dating. She claimed that a new client insisted on viewing a few homes on that same Saturday and that rescheduling was out of the question. She stressed how much she needed to earn some commissions; I must admit that she had a valid point. However, my launch was only going to last a few hours, and her client should not have come before her husband. Then again, that was only my opinion; obviously, not one that she shared.

This was a once-in-a-lifetime event. When I started the Last Good Men website, there was no launch party or fanfare. Let's face it, dating websites were everywhere, but not sites like Able Minded Dating. The few other websites for people with disabilities had not gotten much exposure; I was determined that mine would be different. When I thought of the concept of the Last Good Men, I was trying to capitalize on the huge internet dating trend. With Able Minded Dating, my motivation was completely different.

Having met so many people—during therapy and in my support groups at the hospital—who had faced many issues when it came to meeting new love prospects, I felt emotional about my new site. On the existing, bigger dating sites, I noticed that few people on them were in wheelchairs or missing limbs or deaf, etc. I did a test myself and joined a few—not looking for love but performing an experiment. Even with an attractive face and physically fit body, no women sent me a message or even flirted once I mentioned that I was missing an arm. Nothing.

I'd met one young lady, Summer, who had lost both of her legs during a suicide-bomber attack in Iraq. She was over there in the military and believed that she was doing the right thing. I will never forget her expression when she described her feelings one day in the hospital weight room.

"Damon, do you think that I'm pretty?" she asked me out of the blue.

"No," I said. Once she frowned and looked away, I added, "You're not pretty; you're gorgeous! Little girls and teenagers are pretty. Women are gorgeous."

A smile spread across her face. "You really think so?"

I stopped walking on the treadmill, grabbed a towel, and went to sit beside her. She had been lifting hand weights from her wheelchair.

"Summer, I realize that this is hard on you. Losing your legs, in such a horrible way at that, must have been terrible."

"You lost your arm."

"Yes, I did, but it's okay." I moved my prosthetic arm back and forth. "I'm as good as new."

"How did it happen?"

I shrugged. "I got hurt trying to do the right thing, just like you. I wasn't fighting a war, not in the literal sense, but we're all victims of certain types of wars every single day."

"What do you mean?"

"I was at an outdoor music festival with my wife and some of her friends, and this young lady, a drug addict, careened through the crowd in her vehicle." I laughed slightly. "I ended up with the short end of the stick."

Summer giggled, then reached out and touched my real hand. The warmth of her skin was invigorating. "So, you're saying that we all are in a drug war?"

"In a sense. We all have to feel the effects, one way or another, of the rampant drug abuse in this country. It's not going anywhere. As long as there is a demand, there will be a supply. People will die. Some guilty, some innocent. All in the same boat together."

"A lot of the soldiers started using when I was over there, in Iraq. It was a way to escape reality."

"And people here in the States also use drugs to escape reality. With the economy the way it is today, the problem will only get worse. People are losing their sources of income, their homes, and even if they are willing to bust their asses to make ends meet, they have no way to make it happen."

"That's true." Summer glanced down to where her legs used to be. "I guess that I better count myself lucky that the government has to take care of me." She pulled her hand away and swiped at a tear that had escaped her right eye. "I'd rather take care of myself though."

"Don't cry, Summer. Every day is a new day. We both have to deal with some things, but we're still here."

"Yes, we're still here, but . . ."

"But what?" I prodded.

"You have someone . . . a wife. I'm only twenty-three years old and now I'll never know what true love feels like."

I sighed and fought back the sharp pain that exploded through my heart for the young woman.

"True love is unconditional," I told her. "What matters is the inside of a person and not the outside."

"What man would want a woman without legs when he can have millions of women with them? I can't compete with all of these model types—even regular-looking women. Who would want to love me?"

"Lots of men . . . good men. There's nothing wrong with you, Summer. A real man would appreciate the fact that you went overseas to fight for this country. A real man would understand that we are all victims of circumstance. A real man would embrace your beauty instead of reject it."

I will never forget the words that left her mouth next: "Where are these real men?"

When I left the hospital that day, I'd made up my mind to start ablemindeddating.com. I went back to my office, realized that I was blessed when the domain name was available, registered it, and started making my plans. Now, several months later, I was at the Carolina Kitchen in Hyattsville, Maryland, about to make a dream come true . . . for both myself and Summer.

Summer was there in her new wheelchair. She was still getting used to it, but she was a real trouper; she had to be to survive that ordeal in the war. Lance London, the proprietor of the soul-food establishment, was busying about making sure that everyone who entered was properly greeted and guided to the buffet, which featured everything from spicy Thai wings and catfish nuggets to collard greens and sweet potatoes. The food was incredible. Steve and Bobby were there to support my latest effort. My parents were out of town attending my cousin's wedding, but that was okay. They were there in spirit, and that is all that mattered.

A lot of the county and state politicians were there; I invited them and figured that they wouldn't miss out on an opportunity to shine in a positive light. With all the layoffs of police officers and firemen and furloughs of government employees, they needed to look good, if even for a day. A lot of press people were also in attendance. The local Fox affiliate had sent a camera crew and reporter, and the *Washington Post,* the *Washington Times,* and the local *Gazette* were all there as well.

I'd taken my place at the podium and was about to begin when I noticed Brooke come in the front door. She tried to ease her way in without being noticed; she was crazy for thinking that could happen. She was stunning in an orange sundress that accentuated her smooth complexion. I was glad that she was there, to support me . . . unlike my wife.

"Good afternoon, everyone," I said, then cleared my throat. "I want to thank you very much for coming. This won't take long; I'm not much of an orator."

Everyone laughed; I wondered what I'd said that was so amusing.

"I'm a bit nervous, but I'm extremely proud. Able Minded Dating means a lot to me . . . the world to me. It is a dating concept that I feel is long overdue. People with disabilities are often overlooked when it comes to so many things, and that includes love. They are . . ."

I hesitated and thought about how I had been about to segment myself away from the group.

"We are as capable of loving and having fruitful, fulfilling relationships as anyone—probably even more capable. Why? Because people with disabilities, whether born with them or acquiring them later in life, have a greater appreciation of what the world has to offer. In my case, having had a close call with death has revitalized my will to live."

I meant those words with all sincerity. I recalled reading a recent article on the internet about a man who had died on the operating table six times after suffering a widow-maker, a heart attack so severe that it was believed to be impossible to survive. Somehow he did though. They had had less than five minutes to get him to a hospital before sudden death, and he got there in three minutes and twenty seconds. He had none of the factors that generally caused a heart attack and was quite active. Yet, it happened out of the blue. He spoke about how he viewed every day differently from that point on. So did I.

"I hope that all of you will be inspired by what is happening here today," I added. "So many times we complain about little, practically insignificant things . . . until something major happens and we realize that things could be a lot worse."

Everyone started clapping; I waited a few seconds for them to stop. Many cameras were flashing in my face and I was blinded for a moment. I was thinking, *Wow, this is really happening!*

"I would like to thank all of the county and state executives who have taken time out of their busy schedules to be here today. I realize that a few of you want to make remarks, so I am going to keep this short. Able Minded Dating is for people, like me, who may not have arms, legs, hearing, or even sight, but we all have a heart."

By that time, Brooke had inched her way up closer to where I was, and I could see her waving at me and grinning. I couldn't help but blush.

"I want to acknowledge a few people. Mr. Lance London, I appreciate you opening up your establishment for us today and providing everyone with such delicious food and a warm atmosphere."

Lance waved from over near the bar, then came over and shook my hand. He stood by me as I continued, "I would like to thank my two closest buddies, Steve and Bobby, for being there for me in the past, being here for me in the present, and undoubtedly being there for me in the future. Nothing will ever come between us, and I love you guys."

Steve rested his elbow on Bobby's shoulder and appeared on the brink of tears, while Bobby clapped so hard that I thought his hands might fall off—bad thought.

"I would also like to thank the young lady who gave me the inspiration to start this website." I could see Brooke bite her bottom lip and start trembling, like she was nervous. She was off the mark. "Summer Kendrick, thank you for that talk in the hospital gym that day. You will never know how much that touched my heart."

I could see Summer's mouth fall open from across the room. Then she placed her hand over her chest and mouthed the words *Thank you.*

I looked directly at Brooke then and said, "But most of all, I would like to thank Brooke Alexander, who has become one of my dearest friends in the face of my darkest tragedy. Without you, I am not sure that I would have made it through the past several months. We share a bond that no one else will ever understand, and you will forever have a place in my heart."

Brooke stood there for a few seconds, then turned away from me and started pushing her way through the crowd toward the other side of the restaurant. I noticed Bobby and Steve both staring between her and me; it was obvious what they thought.

"Thanks again, everyone, for coming out to share this experience with me," I said, finishing up. "Who would like to say a few words next?"

Lance said, "I want to say a few words before the politicians start coming up here. We all know how long-winded they are."

Everyone laughed while Lance continued speaking and as I made my way toward Brooke. I had to find her. People were trying to shake my hand and talk to me, and even Summer tried to get my attention, but I had to find Brooke. I told Summer, along with the photographers who wanted to take pictures, that I would be back in a few minutes.

Brooke was standing in the back room, looking at Lance's collection of model automobiles enclosed in glass cases. Her back was to me.

"Brooke, are you okay?"

She turned and I noticed that she was holding a stack of napkins—tear-soaked napkins.

"I'm fine." She sat at one of the tables.

I went and sat across from her. I reached out and took her hand. "What's wrong?"

"Nothing." She still clutched the napkins in her other hand and wiped away more tears. "What you said really touched me; that's all."

"I meant it."

"I know; that's why it touched me."

We both chuckled.

"I guess you were thrown for a loop when I mentioned Summer," I said, hoping that a jealous streak would come out, but realizing at the same time the implications of my wanting Brooke to be envious.

"Kind of. I didn't know you had grown close to another woman . . . I mean, other than your wife."

"Summer and I aren't that close. Not like you and me. She and I were working out in the hospital gym one day, and she expressed to me how she felt about trying to find love without legs."

It didn't escape me that I had found myself explaining my connection with Summer to Brooke like she was my woman and she deserved an explanation. This was not a good look.

Brooke glanced toward the direction of where everyone else was. "I saw her in there; I noticed she was in a wheelchair."

"She's still getting used to her condition. It's extremely hard on her."

"What happened to her?" I could tell that Brooke's concern was genuine.

"Suicide bomber in Iraq."

Brooke shook her head. "Poor woman. It's a damn shame, the war. Pointless."

"She's really lonely. She doesn't have much family, but she stays alone with her father. He's a borderline alcoholic, and a lot of the friends that she had before she was deployed don't want to be bothered with her now."

"Are you serious?" Brooke asked in disgust.

"Yes, that what she says. They don't think she's able to hang out with them like she used to. Stupid people."

Bobby and Steve had stood by me and treated me no differently. I was blessed. Sure, they stared at my prosthetic arm from time to time, but our conversations rarely changed. Then again, it was not like we had ever played golf or basketball together—not in many, many years. We always chilled out and we could still do that.

Brooke grinned at me and tightened her grip on my hand, bringing me back from my thoughts. "So you took it upon yourself to help her find a man?"

"Well, having done thelastgoodmen.com already, I had a degree of experience." I paused, then chuckled. "Yeah, I'm going to find Summer a man. In fact, Summer is my first featured member, so everyone who logs on will automatically view her profile."

"That's great. I noticed that you don't have your other site mentioned on any of the handouts, and it wasn't on your invitation for the launch party either. How come?"

I shrugged. "My other website is a moneymaker, a cash-cow business. Able Minded Dating serves a much deeper purpose for me. I didn't want to taint that, in any way."

"You're sure a good man, Damon. Your wife doesn't realize how lucky she is."

"No, she doesn't."

Brooke suddenly pulled her hand away. "We shouldn't be sitting back here holding hands like this. What if Carleigh sees us?"

"Only if she has supersonic vision. Did you not notice that her name never escaped my mouth while I was making my speech?"

Brooke gasped. "I came in late so I didn't have a chance to look around for her." She sat up in her seat. "Are you telling me that she didn't come today?"

"Carleigh had to show some houses to a new client."

To be honest, I suspected that Carleigh was too embarrassed to come with me. She didn't want to be affiliated with anything that had to do with "less than perfect" people, and lately it had seemed like that included me.

"But this is such a special day for you," Brooke said. "I mean, I took off to come, and Hank, my asshole of a boss, gave me a hard time, but I set him straight."

"How'd you handle ol' Hank?"

"I told him to kiss my monkey."

I laughed. "Kiss your monkey? You mean your ass?"

"No, my monkey." Brooke dropped her eyes. "My monkey."

I was completely lost. "What's a monkey?"

"Damon, I'm talking about my pussy," Brooke whispered. "A monkey is a pussy."

The mere mention of Brooke's pussy made me feel uncomfortable. I got up from the table.

"I'd better get back. They're probably looking for me."

"Of course they are." Brooke got up as well. "You're the man of the hour." She put her arms around my neck and hugged me, then gave me a kiss on the cheek. "I'm so proud of you, Damon." She gazed into my eyes. "You will forever have a place in my heart as well."

It took every ounce of restraint in my body not to bury my tongue in her mouth. I wanted to so badly, but I couldn't do that to Carleigh, or to Brooke. She deserved better, and while I didn't believe for one second that her current man, Patrick, was worth her time, I couldn't be that man.

She let go of me and we went back into the other section of the restaurant. Perfect timing; the last politician was finishing up his remarks. I went back up to the podium to pose for photos and talk to the press, while Brooke lagged behind. I was going to make sure that she was in at least some of the pictures before the event ended—both her and Summer.

Brooke actually went over to Summer and started talking to her. Not only was Brooke not jealous—something that I had mixed feelings about—but she seemed to be embracing Summer and befriending her. I saw her take out a piece of paper and write something down and hand it to Summer—probably her number. That meant the world to me. Brooke has the kind of heart that all people on this earth should have.

Brooke

May 3, 2008

CAME by the diner this afternoon," Patrick said before I could even get into the door good. "I also called to see if you had a doctor's appointment. Where were you?"

I glared at Patrick like he was crazy. "Patrick, it's late. My class ran long tonight and I really need to take a bath and hit the sack. I have to be at work early. I promised Hank that I would work a double shift to make up for today."

Patrick grabbed my upper arm. "Stop all that yakking and rambling and answer my damn question. Why weren't you at work today?"

"Let go of me, Patrick," I warned him. "I'm not a rag doll; I'm a human being."

Patrick released me reluctantly. I was waiting on him to revert back to his old ways and call me a bitch. I would have been out the door so fast that it would have made his head spin.

"You keep saying that you've changed," I said to him. "And you've been doing better lately, I will give you that, but don't mistake my being here as submission. Most of my shit is still over at

Destiny's, so if you want to come out your mouth at me any kind of way, I can give a brand-new meaning to the term *gone in sixty seconds.*"

I walked into the living room and put down my backpack.

"So how was class?" he asked, trying to change up his game and be nice.

"It was fine. Everything's coming along."

"You don't have to take those night classes, Brooke. You don't even have to work. Why won't you let me take care of you?"

"Two reasons, Patrick. I want to have a purpose to my life." I used the word *purpose* because Damon had used it earlier that day. His purpose was Able Minded Dating, and I had to have a purpose as well.

"Okay, so you want to have a purpose. What's the other reason?"

"If I ever allowed you to take care of me completely, that would only signify control to you. I may not have your economic stature and I probably never will, but I do have pride and I won't be controlled. Not anymore."

"Are you trying to say that I've controlled you in the past?"

I sat down on the sofa and he took a seat beside me, glaring at me; I could tell that he was trying to hold back his anger at my implication.

"Yes, Patrick, in many ways, I allowed you to control my mind and my actions in the past. Catching you with Mandawhore changed all of that for me. It made me realize that your love for me can be easily penetrated. It made me—"

"I have not talked to Mandy. Not Mandy or anyone else."

"I want to believe you . . . I really do. Once trust is lost, it does not come back on autopilot. It has to be regenerated, and all I can say is that I'm trying. I'm making a serious attempt to have faith that I'm woman enough for you." I paused. "No, I take that back. I *am* woman enough for you; I am woman enough for anybody, but I am not *for* everybody. Now I have to determine if I am for you."

"You're not making any sense, Brooke." He shook his head in dismay. "We've been a couple for a long time. I take you around my friends, my family. We live together. I want to marry you. I adore—"

"We don't live together. I'm staying here temporarily."

"Whatever, Brooke!" Patrick got up and walked over to the wet bar to fix himself a snifter of brandy. "You're here every night and have been for months. If it makes you feel better to perpetrate by keeping some items at Destiny's, so be it. As long as you're here, that's all that matters."

"Your friends and family think that I'm beneath you. You take me around them, but I don't want to be there. I tolerate it, for you."

"Maybe if you were friendlier toward them, they would open up to you, but you don't even make any effort. You run around telling everyone to kiss your monkey and roll your eyes at them."

I suppressed a laugh, thinking about how I had had to explain the term *monkey* to Damon earlier. When I mentioned my pussy, he seemed uneasy. I wondered what kind of lover Damon was—surely nothing like Patrick. I was willing to bet that he didn't attempt to fuck his wife's skull and call her a bitch. He was probably tender, slow, and took his time with a woman's body, making sure that every fiber of her being was catered to.

"Did you hear what I said, Brooke?"

I pulled myself out of my wet dream. Damon was at home with Carleigh, and I was at Patrick's home—not mine—with him.

"I heard what you said and I never started any of the drama with your people. They prejudged me before I could ever open my mouth. But we made a decision to be together, and you knew, from jump, that it was going to be an issue. Maybe you should have left me where you met me."

"This is silly." Patrick started walking off to the bedroom. "I'll go run you a bath."

After my bath, I lay there in Patrick's arms, feeling his chest rise and fall against my back as he slept. He was making a sincere effort to work things out with me; that point couldn't be denied. But could a man really change overnight? Could his train of thought, his tendency to troll for pussy, his need for complete control, all evaporate into thin air in the name of love?

My mind wandered to Damon. I wondered what he was doing at that very moment. I imagined him sitting at a computer—maybe in a home office—logged on to the administrative back-end office of ablemindeddating.com, watching the membership numbers increase by droves. I prayed that he was not in bed with his wife, making sweet, passionate love to her. Then again, how was that any of my business?

I sighed and stared up at Patrick's face. He seemed so peaceful having me there. I realized that his behavior was not all his fault. Hell, all of us are simply culminations of everything we have ever been taught, experienced, or observed. His parents had money, true enough, but money damn sure couldn't buy happiness. They were living proof of that. So were Patrick and I. People don't realize that they can live in the biggest palace in the world and have all the riches, but sooner or later, after entering big iron gates and driving up a winding driveway hundreds of times, complacency sets in and it's no longer a big deal.

I really wanted to work things out with Patrick. For so long, he had meant the world to me, and I had put a lot of time, sweat, and emotion into our union. There was another problem. My feelings for Damon. What on earth was I going to do?

Brooke

May 4, 2008

WOKE up the next morning with Patrick's dick trying to part my lips.

I turned my head slightly, so that I could speak. "I don't feel like it."

"Come on, Brooke. I need my medicine."

I decided to get the ordeal over with, positioned my head in place, and started sucking him off. After he came in my mouth, I tried to make a beeline for the bathroom to brush my teeth and gargle with mouthwash; he wouldn't let me.

"Give me a kiss."

"I don't want to," I protested.

"Baby, you agreed that you'd be more experimental when it comes to sex. That's the only reason that I . . ."

"That you what? Fucked Mandy?"

He didn't respond. Instead, he started lifting up my nightgown, then moved my panties to the side so he could ram two fingers up my pussy.

"Patrick, you don't have to remind me of how Mandy broke your ass off. I witnessed it, remember?" I pulled his hand out my monkey. "If you're implying that you might cheat on me again since I won't kiss you with your sperm in my mouth, then commence to cheating. I am not doing that shit—today, tomorrow, or ever!" I jumped off the bed. "What kind of freak are you, anyway? Why would you want to taste your own semen?"

He followed me into the bathroom, where I brushed my teeth like I had six months of plaque buildup.

"Actually, I was thinking, maybe we could try some new things."

I paused and stared at his reflection in the mirror over the sink. "Like?"

"I was talking to this friend of mine, another attorney, and he told me that he eats his woman's pussy and lets her cum in his mouth."

I shrugged. "And? You eat my pussy all the time and I cum."

"Yeah, but once she cums, he doesn't swallow it. He holds it in his mouth and then kisses her and feeds it to her."

I stood straight up, with toothpaste hanging out of my mouth and drizzling on my chin. "That is the most disgusting shit I've ever heard!"

He folded his arms across his chest in defiance. "See, that's exactly what I mean. You refuse to experiment."

I rinsed my mouth out and gargled twice before I responded. Then I turned to face him. "That's not an experiment, Patrick. That's a travesty to mankind. News flash: the human race has evolved since the days of barbarians."

I brushed past him on my way into the bedroom to get dressed. I put on some deodorant, body spray, and lotion, all the while listening to him rant.

"This is the twenty-first century, baby. You need to get with the program. People today are different."

"What's so damn wrong with regular, old-fashioned lovemaking? Why does it have to be dipped in perversion and kinkiness? I don't mind different positions, Patrick. Hell, I'm the one that bought that book about sex positions, and the one about erotic massage. I'll do the *Kama Sutra;* I'll do a bunch of shit." I finished getting dressed and grabbed my purse and keys. Then I glared at him. "But we won't be swapping spit-and-cum mixtures in this lifetime, and if you don't like it, you can kiss my monkey and my entire ass!"

Patrick glared at me. "I'm going to pretend like you didn't say that. I'm going to head over to the firm. I have court this afternoon and need to prepare some documents."

I chuckled. I was the one dressed and about to haul ass. Yet he tried to make it seem like I was suddenly holding up his day.

"Well, I'm going to head on over to the diner and serve breakfast and lunch, and then I'm going to spend the night at home."

"Cool. I should be back around six."

He didn't get it. "Have fun then. Destiny and I are going to watch some classics on AMC."

"This is your home, Brooke. No matter how much you deny it. Home is where the heart is. Remember that."

Patrick walked off into the kitchen to make his morning pot of coffee. I stood there for a moment, then headed out. I was so confused. One minute I wanted him—truly wanted him—and the next I wanted to get as far away from him as possible.

Destiny came to the diner for lunch. I waited on her at the counter after she took the last stool near the restrooms. She grimaced as a man exited the men's room and a stench came out behind him.

"For the life of me, I don't know why restaurants put *any* seats so close to the damn bathroom."

"Destiny, please, look at the size of this place. The only other place they could put them would be outside, and how nasty is that?"

Destiny swatted at her nose with her freshly manicured fingernails.

She had a valid point; the bathrooms at the diner gave a new meaning to *stanky*. I would often wait until after my shift to even take a piss. That was not healthy though. I heard about one woman who refused to use public bathrooms and ended up with a bad appendix. Our bathrooms were disgusting, but I was not about to make a comment to Hank. He would have tried to make bathroom cleaning one of my duties, and that shit was not happening.

"Can you take a break now?" Destiny asked, scanning the menu she had seen a hundred times. The selections hadn't been updated in years.

"Not officially, but I can talk. What's up?" I poured her a glass of sweetened iced tea from a metal pitcher.

"How did it go yesterday? At Damon's event? Sorry I couldn't make it. You know how I love soul food."

I rolled my eyes at her. "So all you were worried about was the food?" Destiny shrugged, and I leaned on the counter with my elbows and grinned, ignoring her selfishness. "Yesterday was great! Damon's really doing something powerful with that site. It's funny how you never recognize the needs of others unless you can directly relate to them."

"True. I guess having a disability himself gave him a reality check. This man who works with me is going to join. He's in a wheelchair."

"What happened to him?"

"Car accident, last year. His wife left him and is already remarried. That's fucked-up."

I sighed. "Love is supposed to be unconditional, but it rarely seems like it."

Destiny pouted. "Tell me about it." She closed the menu and stuck it back into the metal holding bracket. "He was with her for almost fifteen years and they have three kids. That tramp still rolled out on him in her car, leaving him to roll around in his wheelchair alone."

"What do you want for lunch?" I asked, deciding that the topic was depressing me.

"I'm going to be good today. Give me the chicken-strip salad with low-fat ranch dressing."

"Grilled or fried chicken strips?"

"Fried."

"Then you're not being *too* damn good," I said, chastising her.

She laughed. "Whatever, hooker. Harold and I are going out to eat tonight so I don't want to overdo it."

"Speaking of tonight, I lied and told Patrick we were having movie night at your place. You mind if I crash there?"

"Of course not." She took a sip of her tea. "Sick of his ass again, huh?"

"Something like that."

I walked away for a second to stick the order sheet on the revolving clips so they could start preparing Destiny's salad. After catering to a few others seated at the counter—with fresh coffee and one slice of key lime pie—I came back over to her.

She continued like we hadn't missed a beat. "Something like that, huh? What happened this time, Brooke?"

I was getting irritated, even though I realized Destiny meant well. "No one is perfect. Not Patrick and not Harold."

"Okay, forget it. I don't want to play tit-for-tat relationship drama with you. I'll stay with Harold tonight so you can meditate on some things. Cool?"

"Thanks, Destiny."

"You're welcome." She nodded toward the heat counter where her salad was waiting. The cook must have thought we were playing that *Diner Dash* video game because he broke a record making it. "Now go get my shit so I can eat and get back to work on time."

We both laughed.

After Destiny was gone and the lunch crowd had slowed down, I made a mug of hot tea, leaned onto the counter, and observed people. One couple in particular caught my eye. They had been in the diner for a good two hours and were seated in Tony's section. Normally, they would have been asked to give up their booth by now, but since they didn't seem homeless or like they were using the seats as a waiting room, no one had bothered them.

They were obviously having a deep, heated conversation. Drama recognizes drama, and I'd had enough arguments with Patrick to recognize one. I wondered which of them had fucked up the relationship first. Was it intentional or a mistake? Had one cheated on the other? Or were they both caught up in a toxic situation because they were trying to hang on to each other?

"What are you staring at?" Tony asked, walking up behind me at the counter.

"Your customers over there." I nodded and cut my eyes toward him. "They've been here for a minute."

"I wish they would get the hell on," he said in his high-pitched voice. Tony was openly homosexual and I could appreciate his not playing games. "I've refilled their damn water glasses a hundred times."

"Stop exaggerating." I slapped him playfully on the arm. "They're into something heavy over there."

"Don't I know it!" Tony smirked. I looked at him and he raised a brow. "What? So I may have overheard a word or two."

"Okay, spill it."

Tony sighed. "Well, Miss Thing wants to take their relationship to the next level and move in together, but Mr. Player is not even having it. He wants to be free to roam and eat a variety of cookies."

"Is that so?" I asked, prodding Tony to continue.

"She thinks he's cheating on her, and that's a safe bet. Shit, he's even been checking me out."

"Be for real!"

"I'm serious, Brooke. You'd be surprised how many men who look like him really want some of my ill na na." Tony started gyrating his ass cheeks while he had a coffee urn in his hand. "I might slip him my number when he pays the check and see what's up."

I took a long look at the man in the booth and couldn't believe that he'd have sex with another man. Then again, what the fuck did I know? I didn't think Patrick would have sex with another woman and cheat on me.

"This world has truly gone to shit," I said to Tony.

"True, but I'm going to enjoy my time here. And if that brother over there wants some of my goodies, I'm willing to give them to him all . . . night . . . long."

Suddenly, the man got up from the booth and walked toward the bathroom. Tony smiled at him, and I will be damned if the man didn't blush. As he passed us, Tony sniffed the air to inhale his cologne—which did smell good—and then whispered to him, "Don't you wish your girlfriend was hot like me?"

The man blushed even harder and continued on to the bathroom.

Tony put the coffee urn down and straightened up the folded apron around his waist. "Forget about waiting to slip him my number on the check. I'm about to make my move."

As he walked around the counter, I was stunned. "Tony, what are you doing?"

Tony glanced at me and winked. "Just keep an eye on my section for a few, especially that floozy." He looked toward the booth where the man's girlfriend was seated. "Keep a lookout for a brother."

I couldn't believe what was happening. Not in the diner! Not in the nasty-ass bathroom! Yuck!

Sure enough, Tony and that man didn't reappear for a good fifteen minutes. I kept an eye on Tony's section and even poured the poor woman another cup of coffee while she waited for her man. Hank was busy in the kitchen yelling at the cook and the dishwasher, who probably didn't understand a word he was saying. They understood limited English, but not all of that bullshit Hank was spewing.

Finally, the man emerged from the bathroom first, zipping up his jeans, with a big old grin on his damn face. I watched him walk over to his girlfriend, but he didn't sit back down. He threw a twenty on the table and told her, "Come on, let's jet. I have a meeting."

She said, "What took you so long in there? Are you feeling okay?"

He chuckled. "I'm feeling great. Just needed some relief, that's all."

Relief, my ass, I thought.

No sooner had they walked out of the diner and pulled off in a white Lexus than Tony was coming out of the bathroom, wiping his bottom lip and then licking it like it had honey on it. Yuck!

Once he was back behind the counter beside me, I said, "Please tell me that you didn't do what I think you just did."

Tony giggled. "I got me a little sample. It was good, too. Tasted like sweet cream." I shook my head in dismay as he added, "Byron's going to call me later. I wrote my number on his dick so he wouldn't lose it."

I whispered, "You wrote your number on his dick?"

"Yes, and I wrote it *big*. All over his ten inches."

"Ten inches! Damn, what a waste!"

"Ain't a damn thing going to waste around me. Bank on that."

As I watched Tony switch off toward the kitchen, I shook my head again. Out to lunch with his woman and that man went into the bathroom to get a blow job from another man. The world had *truly* gone to shit.

When I got off work that evening, I was headed toward my car on the side of the diner when I noticed a black stretch limousine parked next to it.

"This is not happening," I said aloud to myself. "I don't need this shit today."

I was expecting Mrs. Sterling to get out of the car as the driver rushed around to open the back passenger door. Instead, Mr. Sterling climbed out. I forced a smile as I approached him.

"Brooke, how are you, dear?" He hugged me and I gave him a one-handed hug back. "We were waiting for you to get off. We didn't want to disturb you in there."

"We?" I asked, getting a bad feeling.

"Yes, the missus and I." He pointed toward the open door of the car. "Can we have a word?"

"I really need to get going. I have plans tonight." I was lying, but they didn't need to know all of that. "I can't be late."

"Oh, with Patrick?"

"No, I have other plans."

"This will only take a minute." He pointed toward the door again. Reluctantly, I climbed into the limousine. Mrs. Sterling was sitting on the opposite seat from the rear and was smirking like she had just won the latest designer wardrobe from Paris.

"Hello, *Brooke*," she said snidely, emphasizing my name like it was a curse word.

I didn't respond; I waited for Mr. Sterling to climb in beside me, then the driver closed the door. He waited outside to give us some privacy.

"What is this about, Mr. Sterling?" I asked, turning toward him. "I really only have a minute."

He stared at his wife for a few seconds, and she waved at him like he was her little puppy.

He cleared his throat. "Brooke, my wife and I are gravely concerned about the *situation* between you and Patrick."

I sighed. "Situation? You mean the *relationship* between us?"

"It's not a real relationship," Mrs. Sterling jumped in. "I tried to warn you before, but you wouldn't listen." She sat up in her seat, becoming irate. "I told you that he had another woman—many other women—but you're so dumb, it went right over your head."

"I may be a lot of things, but I'm not a dumb woman. Maybe you should look in the damn mirror."

Mrs. Sterling flung her hand over her chest, like she was on the brink of a heart attack. Then she glared at her husband. "Are you going to allow her to talk to me like that?"

Mr. Sterling held his palm up toward her. "Calm down, dear. Let me handle this."

"There's nothing to handle," I informed both of them. "Patrick is a grown-ass man. He's an attorney; he provides for himself; and he—"

"He provides for *both* of you," the wench said, interrupting me.

"Darling, didn't I just ask you to let me deal with this?" Mr. Sterling actually raised his voice to her. Damn, maybe the man did possess some balls.

"As I was saying," I said, rolling my eyes at her, "Patrick is more than capable of making his own decisions, and so am I. Whether or not we stay together, or break up, has nothing to do with either one of you. We didn't get together because of you and we won't fall apart because of you."

Mr. Sterling reached into his right breast pocket and pulled out a burgundy leather checkbook. "Let's keep this simple. How much is it going to take to make this *situation* go away?" He pulled out a gold pen and twisted it until the point popped out. "I'm sure that we can all find a way for you to be satisfied."

I glared at him for a moment while he started writing my name in the payee section on a check. Then he signed it.

He looked me in the eyes. "So, name your price."

"You have me all wrong, both of you," I stated with disdain. "There is no amount of money that will make me do something I don't want to do. I won't marry Patrick because of his money, even though he has asked me a hundred times. And I won't walk away from him because of yours. If I walk, it'll be because he and I can't work things out. Can't you comprehend that?"

"Look, bitch, take the damn check!" Mrs. Sterling grabbed the checkbook from her husband, ripped the check out, and handed it to me. "Fill it in, whatever you want, and then leave my son the hell alone!"

She shoved the blank check in my lap and sat back, like I was going to obey her orders. I picked it up and ripped it apart.

"I've had enough of you calling me out of my name." I sat up closer to her. "Let me tell you something. You think that you're so high-and-mighty because you live in a mansion and ride around in a limousine, but you're nothing. You think that your pussy is lined with gold and that you have Mr. Sterling wrapped around your little finger. Stop spending your time worrying about where Patrick is sticking his dick"—I pointed over my right shoulder to Mr. Sterling—"and start worrying about where he is sticking his."

"You really are the scum of the earth," she said to me. "And you're insane. We have a lovely marriage; always have. Now you want to make up lies."

I could feel Mr. Sterling shifting in his seat, worried about what might come out of my mouth next. He should have been worried.

"Oh, so you think you're the only woman your husband has fucked since you walked down the aisle damn near thirty years ago?"

"I *know* I'm the only one!"

I stared at Mr. Sterling, who looked like he was about to choke on his own saliva. Then I put my attention back on her. "Okay, you want to go hard. Let's go hard."

Mr. Sterling jumped in. "Dear, let's forget about this entire thing. Brooke is right. She and Patrick need to handle their own affairs." He sighed. "I don't mean *affairs*—their own personal matters."

"No, Mr. Sterling, let's talk about affairs since that seems to be your wife's favorite topic all the damn time." I smirked at him; he frowned, knowing where I was going. "Does she know about Roberta?"

"Roberta?" Mrs. Sterling stared at him. "Roberta Andrews? In Houston?"

"Oh, so you do know about her?" I laughed. "Bet you don't know everything though."

"Honey, let's get out of here. Brooke said that she needed to be someplace." Mr. Sterling yanked the door open, not bothering to tap on it for the driver to open it, as was customary. "We'll discuss this at home."

"Discuss what?" Mrs. Sterling was finally putting two and two together—about damn time. "How does Brooke even know about Roberta Andrews?"

"She's your best friend, right?" I asked. "Your college roommate? Well, let's just say that you're not the only person she's been sharing a room with. Your husband's been fucking her all along. From what I hear, he was fucking her before he ever crawled up between your thighs."

"This is absurd!" Mr. Sterling grabbed my arm and tried to pull me from the car. "Frank, let's get ready to go," he said to the driver, who hightailed it around to the driver's side to get in. "Brooke, just get out!"

"Patrick told me all about it," I continued, enjoying the hell out of ruining Mrs. Sterling's perfect image. I pointed at Mr. Sterling with my left hand, pulling my right arm away from him at the same time. "He used to take Patrick there, to stay at her home, when he was a child. Everyone knew they were a couple but you. They're still a couple. How do you like them apples? You call me dumb, but what kind of dumb broad doesn't realize that her man has been fucking around on her for decades? Tell me that."

I could see that my work was done. Both of them were sitting there with their mouths hanging open, staring at each other.

I began to climb out of the limousine. "You two work on your own *affairs* and leave Patrick and me alone."

As I pulled out of the parking lot in my Corolla a moment later, their limousine was still sitting there. I could only imagine what the conversation would be like on the way home.

amon

May 4, 2008

OVERNIGHT, Able Minded Dating became a success. I was overwhelmed. I don't know if it was all the press coverage or the viral campaign that I launched with commercials on YouTube or because it was such a different concept; it had to be a combination. We had more than fifty thousand members within the first twenty-four hours. Unfuckenbelievable!

I rushed home to tell Carleigh, having stopped to purchase a bottle of Dom Pérignon at the liquor store a few blocks away. I never drank alcohol, but considered it to be a special occasion. They only had one left in stock so I got lucky—or so I thought. As soon as I walked through the door, I sensed something was off-kilter. Carleigh's car was in the driveway, so I assumed she was there. I heard some voices coming from the backyard, then I heard Carleigh's laugh. She hadn't been laughing much since my accident.

I went closer to the rear sliding door to find Carleigh, Jordan, and *two men* sitting around one of our patio tables, drinking beer. One of them, the taller of the two, was sitting too close to my wife for comfort; grinning in her face like he wanted to use his dick to knock a hole in something. They didn't even notice that I'd arrived.

"So, Carleigh," he said in a deep, husky voice, "you still planning to spend your birthday in Vegas?"

"You bet," she responded giddily. "I hear it's hot as hell out there though. I've never been and I'm excited."

Jordan took a swig of beer and added in her two whorish cents. "We're going to turn Vegas the hell out. I can't wait to win a shit-load of money at the Bellagio."

The other man, who looked like he had already fucked Jordan once or twice, asked, "Isn't that the hotel from all those *Ocean* movies?"

"Yeah, man. The ones with George Clooney, Brad Pitt, and Don Cheadle," Carleigh's flirt partner replied. "Don Cheadle is the man."

I didn't know a damn thing about Carleigh planning to go to Vegas for her birthday. It was less than a month away and I'd made tentative plans to do something else. Now it appeared that she was planning to hang out with Jordan in Vegas. Now I don't believe in controlling a woman. She should spend quality time with friends and even travel with them from time to time. My issue is her making arrangements without giving me any consideration what-soever.

The bigger issue was the man trying to push up on my wife. Who the fuck was he and who was he to her?

Jordan said, "Where's Mr. Crippled?"

The two men laughed, and to my astonishment, Carleigh laughed.

"He's somewhere," Carleigh replied. "Probably out worried about those stupid-ass websites."

"Websites?" one of the men asked.

"He has these two dating websites," Jordan said. "One for online sexual predators and one for people like him."

Carleigh was about to say something when I walked outside.

"Hello, all," I stated with much sarcasm in my voice. "Carleigh, I didn't know we were expecting company."

Carleigh jumped up, looking guilty as hell. I couldn't help but notice the smirk on Jordan's face.

"Damon, hey, baby." Carleigh rushed over to me and gave me a kiss, not on the mouth but on the cheek. I noticed that shit, too. "We were just—"

"Discussing your birthday in Vegas." I eyed Carleigh with disdain. "When were you planning to mention your upcoming trip to me?"

Carleigh sighed and seemed embarrassed. "Can we discuss that later?" She turned to her *friends*. "Honey, this is Arnold." She pointed to the man who had been breathing all over her. Then she pointed to the other one. "And this is Gavin."

Gavin gave a slight wave. "What's up, man?"

"Everything's cool," I replied.

I could see both of the bastards staring at my prosthetic arm. They had obviously discussed it at some point.

I stared at the man with the punk-ass name. "So, Arnold, how do you know my wife?"

"She and I have some real estate dealings together."

"Really?" I rubbed my chin purposefully with my fake fingers to draw even more attention to them. I wanted everyone to realize that I felt comfortable with my situation. "That's odd, because I've never heard her mention you before."

Jordan decided to get smart. "Carleigh doesn't have to report in to you about every single thing that she does." Carleigh and I both glared at her, then she shrugged. "Well, shit, I'm just saying."

Carleigh started rubbing the small of my back. "I've known both Arnold and Gavin for years, baby. You remember that condominium complex that I sold a bunch of units for a few years back? Their company developed the building."

"Oh, so you're on the development side." I pulled slightly away from my wife. "I still have never heard of you."

I wanted to make it clear that Arnold was nothing; they were nothing. As far as I was concerned, nothing was ever going to come out of his advances. My natural instinct to stake out my territory had kicked in and I hated it, but had to do what came naturally.

I turned to Carleigh. "Can I see you inside for a moment?"

I heard her say, "I'll be right back," to them as she followed me into the house and down the hallway to my study.

Once inside, I shut the door and pressed her up against the wall with my body.

"Who is that man to you?"

"Nobody," she responded, too quickly for my liking. "Like I said, he's a colleague."

"In all this time, how come I've never heard of him or met him? Yet, all of a sudden, he's in our backyard drinking beer and disrespecting me by trying to get in your pants."

Carleigh pushed into my chest to create a distance between us, then went and sat down on the leather recliner.

"Arnold is not trying to sleep with me. Don't be ridiculous." She sighed. "Besides, even if he *did* want to sleep with me, it takes two to make that happen."

I stared at Carleigh, trying to sense whether she would actually go so far as to cheat on me. I decided that I didn't think she would go that hard, so I changed the subject.

"I'd made plans for us to go away for your birthday." She looked at me, surprised. "I was going to take you to New Orleans. We haven't been back there since we met. We never got to explore the city together, and I thought it would be nice."

"I had no idea."

"That's because it was going to be a surprise." I walked around my desk and sat down in my chair. "Ironically, I booked a room at the Harrah's Casino down there. Thought you might like it." I shook my head. "At least I was on the right track."

"Damon, I can cancel the trip with Jordan. It's no big deal."

"No, you go ahead." I grinned. "Have a good time."

"But, I—"

I held up my palm to stop her. "It's okay, honey. We can go to New Orleans some other time."

"Maybe we can go down for Mardi Gras. I realize that's some time away, but I've always wanted to go to Mardi Gras, and we can stay in the French Quarter and—"

"That's sounds great, baby. Let's do just that."

"What does *Mardi Gras* mean anyway?"

"It's French for 'fat Tuesday.'"

Carleigh laughed. "Damn, I never knew that. I mean, I knew about Fat Tuesday, but never realized that was the exact translation."

She was rambling. She always did that when she was nervous. But why was she nervous?

She started eyeing the closed door, like a child trying to escape a lecture from her parents. "Jordan and I are going out to a play tonight. Is that cool?"

"Are Arnold and Gavin going also?"

Carleigh seemed hesitant. "Honestly? Yes, they bought the tickets. It's not a date or anything like that, Damon. Just hanging out. We've all had a rough time lately and, you know, no big deal."

I was still trying to absorb that she had actually asked me if I wanted her to be honest with me. That led me to believe that something was wrong, but I didn't want to admit it.

"Damon?"

"You all go ahead and have a good time."

Carleigh got up and opened the door. She paused and turned to me. "So how's the new site coming along?"

I looked at her, and all of the excitement that I'd felt when I'd rushed home with the bottle of champagne—the one she didn't even notice sitting on the counter when we walked through the kitchen—had dissipated.

I shrugged. "It's going okay, so far. We'll have to see what happens over time."

"I'm sure it will do incredibly well." She came around my desk and kissed me, this time on the lips. I couldn't help but wonder if that was because Arnold was not there to witness it. "I love you, Damon. I can stay home, if you want. I'll just reimburse them for the ticket and tell them to go ahead."

"I love you." I gazed into her eyes for a brief moment, searching for a life rope. Even though she had spoken those words about staying at home, I could tell that she was lying. The thought of being around what she considered an "invalid" instead of being around normal people was killing her. "You have a nice time."

"But, I can—"

"I didn't see any other cars out front. Aren't they supposed to be riding with you?"

"Well, yeah, but Jordan can drive my car and—"

"Carleigh, please go and enjoy yourself. I have a lot of work to do, anyway, on both websites."

Carleigh slowly moved away from me, staring at me as she moved backward toward the door. She grinned, like a convict about to escape a prison, and with that I watched her saunter off down the hallway to join her *friends*.

Brooke

May 5, 2008

WHEN I showed up at Patrick's house the following evening, I knew that no bath would be waiting for me. He had left me a dozen messages, going off about my telling on his dearest father. At first, I did feel a little bad about it, but then I realized that I had nothing to feel bad about. They both asked for it by trying to get into my relationship with their son. I came out of the diner, minding my own business, and they were lying in wait like two predators ready to pounce. First rule of the wild: don't pull out your claws unless you're prepared to be mangled your damn self.

"You do realize that you've ruined my parents' marriage!" Patrick yelled the second that I came through the door.

I glared at him. "Oh, please! Your mother's not going anywhere, and neither is your father."

"You don't know that. Mother's very upset. She's threatening to sue him for divorce."

"Your mother's flapping her gums. She's not going to seek a damn divorce." I laughed as I kicked off my shoes near the door. "She'd be too ashamed. She puts on more pretenses than anybody on the planet, and she's not about to be known as a chick who couldn't keep her man satisfied."

Patrick folded his arms like a kid about to throw a tantrum. "You don't know her like I do."

"Thank goodness I don't, but I know enough. She'd probably let Roberta Andrews move in their place before she'd let your father leave."

Patrick followed me into the living room, where I plopped down on the sofa. I was dying to get the food smell off me, but he would have followed me into the bathroom, ranting and raving the entire time I was trying to bathe.

"I don't even think she was that surprised when I told her," I added. "Her gut has been telling her something was up all along; I could tell. She didn't know who the other woman was, or how long it had been going on, but she knew he was cheating."

Patrick sat beside me. "She didn't have a clue."

"Whatever, Patrick." I threw my legs over his. Normally, he would have rubbed them, but not that night. He seemed like he wanted to push them off his lap, but he didn't. "I'm not sure if she was more stunned that it finally came out, or that you knew about it and told me." I grabbed a toss pillow, placed it behind my head, and closed my eyes. "Either way, she'll be mad for a hot minute and then she'll be right back at her plastic surgeon getting her next Botox injection."

"Why would you do something like that, Brooke? How could you?"

I laughed and kept my eyes closed, adjusting the pillow to get more comfortable.

"What's so amusing?"

"You are, Patrick." I popped one eye open and squinted at him.

"It's amazing how I always end up being the bad person in any given situation involving your parents."

"That's not true!"

"It is *very* true." I closed my eye again and sighed. "Your father used to take you to visit his mistress as a child, and I'm at fault? If he hadn't done it in the first place, we wouldn't be having this conversation."

"My father was just being a man!"

I sat up and took my legs off his lap. I stared at him. "Oh, so now it comes out!"

Patrick realized the error of his ways and shrugged innocently. "I didn't mean it like that."

"No, don't backpedal now, Patrick." I sat up even straighter. "Like *you* said, he was just being a man. That's what a real man does, right? He maintains more than one woman and gets his dick wet day and night. He has women across the country—if he can afford it, across the globe—and can lay his head where he pleases, when he pleases."

"You're being ridiculous and reading too much into what I said."

"No, I'm not. Not at all." I stood up and looked down at him on the sofa. "So if it's not Mandy, *Mandawhore*, then who is it?"

"I'm not cheating on you, Brooke." Patrick stood up so he could look down at me, trying to get the clear advantage. "I learned my lesson. When you were in that accident, I could've lost you forever. No amount of sex is worth giving you up."

"You know, your parents actually did us a big favor." I found myself smirking, even though not a damn thing was funny about our conversation. "Ironically, that little scene they pulled at the diner has awakened me."

"What are you talking about?"

I took a step back and glared at him. To think I'd almost settled for a lifetime of misery and heartache. "I'd almost convinced myself that it was okay to turn the other cheek. That *eventually* you'd come to your senses and be faithful."

Patrick tried to take me into his arms, but I wouldn't allow it. "I am faithful, baby."

"Bullshit, Patrick!" I turned from him and started toward the master bedroom. "You're more careful now. You've stepped up your game. You may not be jiggling the keys to another woman's home these days, but you're fucking around on me. You can't help yourself."

Patrick was right on my heels as I entered the bedroom and walked into my closet. "What happened with Mandy was a mistake. A weak moment. It'll never happen again."

"I believe you, about Mandy. I don't think you'd be that stupid. She's too risky and too attached. She might show up here one day, or at my job, and burst your bubble." I hesitated as I changed into some jeans and a sweater and took a good, long look at him. "But you're fucking someone. Some socialite who thinks her pussy is collecting dividends as long as she's fucking you."

I pulled down a duffel bag and started shoving my limited belongings into it.

"What are you doing?" Patrick asked as he grabbed for the bag.

"What's it look like I'm doing?" I yanked the handle away from him and kept on throwing items into it. "Thank goodness I never moved all of my shit back in here."

Realization dawned on him. "You can't leave me."

"Watch me!" I yelled as I pushed past him and threw the bag on the bed.

"You have no proof that I'm fooling around, Brooke," Patrick said as he followed me into the master bathroom.

"Is that what it comes down to? Proof?" I started throwing my toiletry items into another bag that I'd brought with me from the closet. "I don't need *proof* for something that I know within my heart."

I paused and stared at his reflection in the bathroom mirror as I retrieved my toothbrush, mouthwash, and favorite dental floss. I had a fleeting thought about not having to worry about rinsing his nasty-ass cum out of my mouth anymore.

"The funny thing is that I'm not even mad at you. You're only doing what comes naturally and I shouldn't take it personally."

"Take what personally?" He caressed my shoulders and leaned down to kiss me on the neck. For a second I was weak. "I love you, Brooke."

I snapped back to my senses and moved away from him, heading back into the bedroom. "Your inability to keep your dick in your pants has nothing to do with me. I may not be willing to do a bunch of perverted shit when it comes to sex, but, dammit, I do enough."

"Is that why you think I'm cheating? Because I ask you to do some things that make you feel uncomfortable?"

"I think you're cheating because you can't help yourself." I zipped up the duffel bag and flung it over my shoulder. "All that shit you ask me to do; I finally get it. It's not about making you feel good. It's about making you feel powerful."

"Now you're really trippin'."

I left the bedroom, with both bags, and headed down the hallway toward the front of the penthouse. "If you can convince a chick to let you fuck her in the ass, cum in her mouth, kiss you with her own cum in your mouth, then that makes you *the man*."

Patrick grabbed my elbow and swung me around. I could see

the pain in his eyes. "Please tell me how we went from having a discussion about my parents to talking about us."

I ran my fingertips over his cheek. I was going to miss him . . . a lot. "Don't you see that we're one and the same? If we don't end this now, we'll end up exactly like your parents." I'd never felt more saddened in my entire life. I didn't want to leave, but I couldn't stay a moment longer. "We'll get married, bring some innocent kids into the world, and then ruin their lives."

"We're both loving people, Brooke. We could never ruin the lives of our children." Patrick got down on one knee and grabbed my free hand. "Marry me! Tonight! We can go to Atlantic City and find a quaint little chapel and leave out of there as husband and wife."

I pulled my hand away and traced the outline of his features with my index finger. Damn, he was a beautiful man. Why couldn't he just be faithful?

"There isn't going to be a marriage, Patrick. Not today, not ever."

I continued on toward the front door. Patrick got up and yelled behind me, "You'll be back, Brooke. I know you'll be back. You have no place else to go."

I refused to turn around. It might have caused me to lose my senses and run into his arms. I had the door open and was about to step out into the hallway when Patrick ran down the hall like a linebacker and slammed the door, pressing my stomach up against it.

"Hold up. This isn't about that bastard, is it?" he whispered into my ear.

"Bastard?" I asked, my lips nearly touching the cherrywood.

"Don't play dumb with me! You know who the fuck I'm talking

about! Are you leaving me for him?" Patrick continued to whisper, his voice full of anger.

I managed to get enough room between us to turn around and look up at him.

"If you are referring to *Damon,* who is ten times far removed from being a bastard, no, this is not about him. Damon is happily married, and unlike you, he would never cheat on her."

"And how do you know that?"

"Because I know." I moved around Patrick and faced the door. He was now standing against it like he was going to force me to stay with him. "Would you kindly move out of my way? I'd hate to have to call the police."

Mentioning the police made him move. Patrick didn't want, or need, that kind of drama in his line of work.

"I do love you, Brooke. We can make this work," he said as I opened the door.

"I love you, too, Patrick, but this can never work." I was staring at the elevator but I could feel his breath on my neck. "It's time for us to both realize that."

He waited there in the doorway while I pressed the button for the elevator. It ascended from the lobby, and I got on board. As the doors closed, I saw the hurt and anguish in his eyes. I imagined that mine looked similar.

"It had to end," I said to myself as I pressed the button for the garage level. "It had to end."

By the time I'd placed my bags in the trunk of my Corolla, I could no longer hold back my tears. I did really love Patrick, but he could never change, and we both recognized that. The level of deception that it had taken for him to mess around on me first with Mandy, and then with whoever else had followed her, was a clear indication that he was capable of separating love and dirty deeds.

Destiny had almost convinced me that dealing with his lies, as long as he came home to me after he fucked other women, was "normal." Well, what is satisfactory for a lot of women simply didn't sit well with me.

I was scared; afraid that I might end up alone for the rest of my life, even though I was not even thirty yet. What if the next man was worse than Patrick? Gave me a disease? Tried to beat my ass? Notice that I said *tried,* because that was some shit that I wouldn't stand for. He might make an attempt, but I would never lie down and take a beating—not for all of the dick on the Eastern Shore.

I climbed into the driver's seat and swiped at my tears with the back of my hand. Part of me expected Patrick to come running off the elevator, to make one last attempt at getting me to stay. But he didn't.

"What have you done, Brooke?" I asked myself. "Now what are you going to do?"

My cell phone started blaring. I still had that damn MC Hammer song on it. It startled me and I almost jumped out of my seat. I grabbed for it in my purse, assuming it was Patrick, and flipped it open without glancing at the caller ID.

"Patrick, it's over. Please just leave me alone."

After a moment of silence on the other end, I heard Damon speak. "Brooke, are you okay?"

I tried to mask that I was sobbing and sat up straighter. I turned the engine on and revved it while I tried to get myself together.

"Brooke, you there?"

"I'm here. Sorry about that, Damon. I was just getting into my car and assumed you were someone else."

"Did Patrick do something to you? What's wrong?"

"I'm fine." I sighed, then took a deep breath. "I'm good. It's all good."

"Brooke, I can tell you're crying. Where are you? I can come and meet you."

A smile suddenly spread across my face. Damon was such a good man. "I'm on my way to Destiny's, but I'm fine."

"You keep saying that, but I don't believe you." Damon sucked in air on the other end of the line. "I can be there in a half hour."

"Damon, there's really no reason for you to come over there." I tried to sound convincing. "Okay, I'll admit that Patrick and I had a little run-in, but it's not your issue. Just stay there with Carleigh and have a romantic evening or something."

"I can't have a romantic evening by myself. Carleigh's out with her friends . . . *again*."

Carleigh's a damn fool! "I'm sure she'll be back soon. She'll expect you to be there, waiting for her."

"Humph! I seriously doubt all of that."

I sensed something in his voice—anguish. "Are you okay?"

"I'm fine."

I laughed.

"What's so funny, Brooke?"

"How we're both *fine* and neither one of us is being truthful."

Damon laughed then. "Good point." He paused. "Listen, I could really use someone to talk to tonight. How about you?"

I hesitated before answering, "Sure, but Destiny's home tonight, and she's the nosiest woman walking. Can we meet someplace else?"

"Name the place and I'll be there."

I thought about it for a few seconds. "How far do you feel like driving?"

"To see you? To the ends of the earth."

I blushed, even though he couldn't see me. "How about to Annapolis?"

"That's a little bit closer than the ends of the earth, but sure."

I giggled. "Meet me at Mike's. You know where it is?"

"I know it well."

I glanced at the clock on my dashboard. "See you in about an hour?"

"One hour. See you then."

We hung up without saying good-bye. I glanced at the elevator one last time, but no Patrick. I wondered if he was upstairs crying or dialing up some other woman for a booty call.

Damon

Brooke was visibly upset as she walked into the bar at Mike's, a seafood-and-crab house overlooking the water. As she approached me with her head down and her arms crossed over her chest, I couldn't help but take in her beauty. Some of the people had stared at me when I entered. I was still getting used to people dealing with my prosthetic arm. I wore long sleeves most of the time, but it was still noticeable because I was not yet accustomed to carrying it naturally. It was still awkward for me, but I was getting the swing of it, no pun intended.

"Sorry that I'm a few minutes late," Brooke said as she sat down on the stool next to me.

I leaned over and kissed her on the cheek. "No problem." I handed her a menu. "They had an hour wait for a table, so I hope the bar is okay."

"This is fine. I'm not really all that hungry."

"You need to eat something. Just order something light."

"Yes, Daddy." Brooke smiled at me, and it lit up the dark room. "What do you recommend?"

"How about some clams or oysters?"

"Raw?" I nodded. "I don't do raw, even seafood," Brooke said. "Some kind of flame has to hit my food first."

I chuckled. "You'd better not ever have to survive in the wilderness. You'd be shit out of luck, unless you know how to rub two stones together and light some twigs."

"I don't ever plan to be in that kind of position." She reached out and pushed my arm, the fake one, then pulled back. "I'm sorry. Did that hurt?"

"No, it's not real. Remember?"

"I know that, but I mean, did I put any pressure on the other part of your arm when I—"

"Brooke, relax." I reached over with my left arm and touched her face. Her skin was so soft as she looked at me with her big, doe eyes. "I'm a big boy."

"I didn't mean to imply that you weren't." She glanced at the menu. "I think that I'll take some shrimp cocktail." I chuckled and shook my head. "What?"

"You just said that you don't eat raw food, but now you want to order shrimp cocktail?"

She laughed. "The shrimp is not raw. It's not fried, or broiled, but they do boil it. You don't know the difference between raw and boiled shrimp?"

"Damn, you're right. Sometimes I can't seem to think clearly when I'm around you."

Brooke seemed uneasy with my statement, but she blushed anyway.

After the bartender took our orders, I made small talk, trying to take her mind off of what had happened with Patrick. "How's school going?"

"It's going . . . *slowly*. It's going to take me a while to finish, doing it part-time and working full-time."

"You can do it. I have faith in you."

"Too bad Patrick doesn't."

So much for keeping her mind off Patrick.

"What did he do to you?"

Brooke shrugged. "Patrick and I have a way of doing things to each other, but this time, things can't be fixed."

"How many times have you said that?"

"I mean it this time. Things have gone too far."

"Did he cheat on you again?" I asked.

I was prepared to rip his fuckin' throat out! "Yes, or no. I think so, but I don't have any facts. I know it in my gut though. Patrick is what he is and that will never change."

"But you went back to him after he cheated on you before."

"I didn't *technically* go back to him." She paused and took a sip of her rum and Coke. "Who am I bullshitting? I did take him back. Not officially moving back in doesn't mean a thing. I was with him, totally committed, and it got me absolutely nothing but heartache."

"Do you love him?" I asked, dreading to hear the answer.

"Yes." She looked at me. "I do, but love is not enough. And the love that I have for him is based in toxicity. I can't love Patrick and be emotionally healthy at the same time."

Brooke and I shared a nice, light meal, then sang some karaoke. We sounded hideous, but it was a lot of fun. I walked her out to her car afterward.

"Are you sure you're okay to drive, Brooke? You had a few drinks and didn't eat much."

"I'm fine." She put her hand on my back as we were walking and rubbed it up and down. It sent goose bumps up my spine. "I'm going to go over to Destiny's and crash."

"That's a ways from here." I stopped in my tracks and took her hand. "Let me drive you."

"And leave my car here? That makes zero sense, Damon. I'd have to trek all the way back out here tomorrow to get it."

"I can bring you back."

"You're not my man, Damon."

But part of me wishes I was.

"And I'm not your responsibility," she added.

I ran my fingers through her hair. I could smell the almond-scented shampoo. "What if I want you to be my responsibility?"

Brooke giggled. "Now you're the one acting drunk!"

"But I don't drink alcohol!"

"Maybe you should," she said jokingly. "You're not thinking clearly."

I'm not thinking clearly at all because I want to kiss you!

She stared up into my eyes for a brief moment, then stumbled off toward her car.

"Brooke, you're not driving home. That's final." I caught up to her and grabbed her keys. She tried to get them, but I dangled them over my head.

"Give them back!" she ordered.

"No, not a chance." I put her keys in my pocket and pointed toward my car. "Let's go."

"But I don't want to come all the way back out here tomorrow, Damon. I have to be at work by noon or Hank is going to have a heart attack."

"You won't have to come back." I helped her walk to my car and opened the door for her. "I have an idea."

I drove to the Sheraton and got us a suite. Brooke didn't protest, and even if she had, I was still going to do it. Once we got up to the seventh floor and settled in, I called Carleigh while Brooke was in the bathroom taking a shower. Even though she was half out of it, she still wanted to bathe before bed. My kind of woman.

Carleigh didn't answer the house phone so I tried her cell. She didn't answer that either so I left her a message—a lie.

"Carleigh, it's me," I said into the phone. "I'm going to crash at Bobby's tonight. He's going through some things and he could really use a friend. I'll be home in the morning. Call me if you need anything."

The only similarity between what I'd said and the truth was that *Brooke* and *Bobby* both started with a *B*. I did feel guilty, but I simply couldn't leave her; not like that. Allowing her to drive was not an option. After all, we'd met because of someone driving recklessly. I'd lost my arm because of it. No one was ever going to take off out of a parking lot intoxicated or drugged on my watch.

Brooke came out of the bathroom a little while later, wrapped in a bathrobe provided by the hotel.

"Feel better?" I inquired.

"Much, much better. I was going to shower earlier, but then Patrick and I got into it before I could. I can't stand the smell of the food from the diner on me. I hope that I didn't offend you with my body odor."

I grinned as she sat down on the bed in the sleeping section of the suite. I was watching her from the sofa in the other room. "You always smell great to me. Besides, we were in a crab house, Brooke. That smell masks everything else."

"Good point." She glanced at me. "Don't you need to get home? I can catch a cab to get my car in the morning."

"I'm not going to leave you."

"But, what—"

"I'm not leaving. I left Carleigh a message. It's cool."

Brooke looked at the alarm clock on the side of the bed. "It's after one. She didn't answer?"

I lied, "She's probably asleep."

My lie must have been obvious. All Brooke said was "Oh."

She picked up the remote, turned on the television, and started flicking through channels.

"Anything good on?" I asked.

"Not so far. A bunch of infomercials. Is it just me or have hotels cut back on the premium channels?"

"They want people to purchase a lot of pay-per-view movies."

"Ah, gotcha." She cut the television off and tossed the remote on the bedspread. "Not that I stay in hotels on the regular."

"Patrick doesn't take you out of town? Isn't he loaded?"

"Yes, he's *very* loaded, but I work all the time. He's asked me to go a ton of places, but I've only been to New York and that was in high school."

"Brooke, please tell me that you're kidding." She couldn't be serious. "You haven't traveled in that long?"

"What's the big deal? If you've seen one city, you've seen them all."

Brooke's inexperience endeared her to me even more. "You should see the world someday. You have to the world. Maybe we can see it together."

What the hell, Damon!

Brooke stared at me. "See it together?" She got up off the bed and walked toward me. "Damon, I think we need to have a talk."

"I know where you're going and it's cool." I raised my left hand to calm her down. "Why don't you get some sleep? We've got to get up and out of here fairly early."

Brooke hesitated before saying, "Okay."

She went back and lay down on the bed, then turned off the

lamp on the nightstand. I had a blanket to bunker down on the sofa. I craved a shower, but was not ready for Brooke to see me without my prosthetic attached; she had seen it through clothing, but not my actual stub. I realized that she still felt guilt over what had happened, even though that was a ludicrous thought.

I pulled the blanket up over me and watched her fall asleep. She tossed and turned for a little while, then began snoring lightly. I stared at her, part of me hoping that the robe would come loose at the top and expose her breasts. I had *zero* business hoping that, but I couldn't control my thoughts . . . or my stiff dick.

I finally succumbed to sleep about an hour later, after giving much thought to both Carleigh and Brooke. I could no longer deny it: I wanted Brooke. But I couldn't hurt Carleigh; even if she was hell-bent on doing things to push me away. She hadn't even bothered to call me back. My message stated that I would talk to her in the morning. Still, she could have had enough concern for my well-being, or for Bobby's for that matter, to call and check up on us.

I had to try to make my marriage work. But how was I going to remain Brooke's friend and never give in to my growing desire to be with her? I could damn near feel my dick inside her. Inside her pussy; inside her mouth. As she tossed and turned, I lay there in the darkness, fantasizing about how good we could be together. Unlike Carleigh, Brooke always seemed not only supportive of my efforts, but excited about them. She had this genuine compassion that couldn't be faked or acted out like a Broadway play. While Brooke was stunningly beautiful, the thing that drew me to her the most was her heart.

I found myself quietly jerking off underneath the blanket, like some dirty old man in an adult movie theater jacking off at the screen. I wondered if her pussy was lukewarm or steaming hot. I wondered if her nipples stood at attention when they were sucked upon and if she liked to have her pussy eaten. I wondered if she would let me run the tip of my tongue down the crack of her ass, or if she would swallow my seed. If she loved to suck dick, only did it to appease a man, or didn't suck dick at all.

Damon, get a damn hold of yourself!

I took my hand off of my dick and turned my back to Brooke. What I was doing was wrong, very, very wrong.

I forced myself to go to sleep, but woke up with the same erection several hours later. I went into the bathroom and took a shower while Brooke was still asleep; I jerked off under the shower-head and finally found some relief. Then I woke her up and told her that we'd better get back to her car. She quickly dressed and we headed out.

She seemed well rested, and once we got into the elevator to head down to the lobby, I asked, "So, how did you sleep?"

"Like a baby." She smiled. "I always feel safe when you're around."

"That's because I would never hurt you."

We stared at each other for a moment, until the elevator doors opened for us to get off. She understood what I was saying. *If I was your man, you'd never have to worry about me causing you any harm.* I couldn't speak those exact words though. I couldn't be her man, as badly as I craved to be just that.

"You'd never hurt Carleigh either," Brooke said, reminding me of my wife. "Would you?"

I was honest. "Not intentionally."

I took her hand as we headed to the parking lot. No further words were spoken between us until we got back to her car and said good-bye.

Brooke

June 14, 2008

DON'T know whom I was more disappointed with, Patrick or myself. I couldn't believe that he hadn't come chasing after me even once since the blowup. And I couldn't believe that part of me wanted him to, so I'd know that he still cared. But I didn't really need him to show up at the diner and cause a scene or wait outside Destiny's apartment building to know that. I was sure that he cared for me, in his own sick, perverted way. Patrick was a victim of circumstances, raised to consider himself a cut above the rest and, therefore, able to get away with things normal men could not. Then again, some women were putting up with poor-ass, damn-near paupers cheating on their asses.

It was a Saturday and Hank had actually given me an entire weekend off. I don't know if he felt sorry for me or didn't want me moping around the diner depressing the customers. I had a sneaking suspicion that Destiny had something to do with it, and I was determined to get to the bottom of it.

I walked into the kitchen, where she was scrambling eggs with cheese and making wheat toast.

"You want some breakfast?" she asked.

"No thanks, but I would like an explanation." I sat down at the breakfast bar on a stool. "How come I have the weekend off?"

"How the hell should I know?!" Destiny reached into the refrigerator and retrieved a half gallon of orange juice. "Didn't you ask for it?"

"No, I *did not* ask for it." She poured some juice into a glass and guzzled it down, damn near choking on the pulp. As she cleared her throat, I added, "You've never been a good liar."

Destiny glanced at me out of the corner of her eye, put the glass down on the counter, then laughed. "Okay, whatever. I told that member of the troll patrol that you needed a break. He didn't want to do it, but once I explained how you suffered that nervous breakdown in high school from trying to do too much, he agreed to give you a couple of days off."

"I never had a nervous breakdown in high school."

"Shit, you know I know that." We both laughed. "But he doesn't need to know."

"Now you're going to have Hank thinking that I'm certifiably cuckoo."

"Better than you actually getting there." She came and sat on the stool beside me with her plate and started spreading apple butter on her toast. She pointed to her food. "Sure you don't want any?"

"I'm straight. Thank you." I sighed and shook my head. "This is so strange."

"What's strange?"

"Having a weekend off. What am I going to do?"

"Well, unfortunately, I have to work this weekend." Destiny was scheduled one weekend a month on her J-O-B. "What you need to do is get some rest."

"Rest. What the hell is that?"

"Then go check out some of the tourist attractions. D.C. is full of them, but, like most residents, we never go."

I giggled. "Good point. You ever seen the Constitution?"

"Not in real life." Destiny took a bite of her eggs. "But that's not what I meant. Going to look at an old-ass piece of paper is not exciting."

"Then what did you mean?"

"The *aquarium*. The *zoo*. The *wax museum*."

"Ooh, now I do want to go to the wax museum. I bet it costs a mint to get up in there though."

"Go online and check."

"I'll do that." I got up and paused to give Destiny a hug from the back. "Thanks, sis."

"For what?"

"For being you. Letting me bum here."

"You're helping out with the rent so you're not a complete moocher."

"Still, this has always been your private sanctuary. You refuse to shack with a man, and here I come."

"Shacking with men is overrated. No matter how good the dick is, it eventually gets old." She took a bite of her toast, which was seriously burnt. "I like what Harold and I are doing. If we want to spend time, we spend it. If we want to chill out apart, I simply bring my ass back here to the crib."

"You know what? I am going to go lie back down for a little while. Hell, I'd better grab this chance when I get it." I paused in the doorway to the kitchen. "Once I get up, I'm going to check out some of the sights."

"Maybe you can check out some of the two-legged, hung-like-a-mule sights while you're at it," Destiny said giddily. "Everyone needs to be held, Brooke. Even you."

"Patrick and I haven't been broken up that long."

"You planning on getting back with him?"

"You know I can't do that."

"Then it's time to explore other options." She paused. "And Damon is not an option."

I stared at her for a moment, halfway offended, but also knowing that my attraction to Damon couldn't be denied. I could never act on it though.

"You're right. No married man is an option."

"He doesn't seem like your type, anyway."

I folded my arms in front of me. "What do you mean by that? Because he's disabled?"

Destiny stared at me. "You know good and damn well what I mean, Brooke. It has nothing to do with his missing arm."

"If I recall, you were the main one talking about how fine Damon was in the gym way back," I said, sarcasm dripping from my mouth with every word. "Remember that?"

"I never said he *wasn't* fine. Just not *your* type."

I paused for a moment, glaring at her, then walked off to the bedroom so I could doze back to sleep for a while. Our conversation was pointless. Damon and I would not, could not, get together, so there was no need to discuss whether he was my "type" or not.

Sleep didn't come easily for me again. I was thinking about Damon, wondering what he was doing; how he was doing. We had spoken only briefly since that night at the hotel in Annapolis. Both of us were obviously uneasy about the implications of what could have happened had we not maintained control.

I heard Destiny leave for work about an hour later, turned my iPod on low, and eventually dozed back off.

• • •

"How'd you get in here?" I asked Damon as I sat up on the bed. His footsteps coming down the hallway had awakened me. "What's going on?"

He smiled at me with that incredible smile and moved closer to the bed. "Destiny let me in."

"I thought she'd left already."

Maxwell's "This Woman's Work" was playing on my iPod. That didn't help matters any; the song instantly put me in the mood to be touched.

"She came back. She forgot something."

Damon sat down on the edge of the bed. He ran his fingers through my toussled hair. "You look so beautiful when you first wake up. When you're sleeping, too. I noticed that at the Sheraton that night."

I tried to hold back a blush, but failed. "Thank you." His eyes penetrated mine and then lowered to my breasts, which were covered only with a sports bra. I cleared my throat. "You never answered me. What are you doing here, Damon?"

"I had to see you." He leaned in and kissed me on the cheek, then whispered in my right ear, "I've missed you so much, Brooke."

His fingertips started caressing my neck as he placed butterfly kisses on my earlobe. Then he moved over to my chin and kissed me there.

"Ummm," I heard myself moaning, my panties getting instantly wet. I had forgotten that I was nearly nude under the comforter and sheets. "Don't stop."

Damon kissed my cheeks and made his way to my lips. We shared a tender, loving kiss for the first time. His tongue was long and thick; juicy.

Our kiss lingered for several moments and I never wanted it to end. When it did, I immediately felt guilty and reared back slightly on the bed, pressing my back and ass against the pillows.

"We shouldn't have done that, Damon."

"Did you want to do it?"

"That's not the point. You're married to Carleigh."

Damon ignored what I said and started rubbing my left nipple through my bra. Both of them were already hard enough to cut Sheetrock; the kiss had damn near set me on fire.

"I want to be with you, Brooke."

"But we can't," I said in protest. "I can't have an affair with you."

"I'll leave her. Right now, today."

I couldn't hold back my emotions any longer, so I pulled him to me and buried my tongue in his mouth again. He lifted up my sports bra, baring my breasts, and feeling all over my nipples—my Sheetrock cutters.

Damon started sucking on them and I moaned in ecstasy. He threw the covers back off me and onto the floor and reached his fingers inside my panties. He started fingering me.

"You're so wet," he whispered. "I can't wait to taste you."

I wiggled on the bed, trying to contain myself and not believing it was really happening.

"I can't wait for you to taste me," I responded, helping him to get my panties all the way off.

I kicked them onto the side of the bed. He lifted his head from my breasts and his saliva glistened on my nipples as he lowered his head to my honeypot. I spread my legs wider and he eyed me lovingly as he prepared to take the plunge and . . .

I was startled by the ringing of my cell phone.

"I need to change this damn ringer," I said aloud, as I sat up.

Damon's name appeared on the screen. I yanked the phone open quickly. "Hey, you!"

"Hello, Brooke." I could hear a lot of traffic in the background on his end and assumed he was driving. "What are you up to?"

I bit my lower lip. "I was just thinking about you."

"Really? What were you thinking?"

I was thinking about you eating my pussy until I screamed! "It dawned on me that we haven't talked much lately." I reached down and felt my bra and panties—still intact, of course. "I know you've been busy with Able Minded Dating, so I didn't want to bother you."

"I can't believe we've been getting so much press," Damon said, then sighed.

"That's a good thing, right?"

"It's definitely a *very good* thing. I've had to do a lot of interviews, that's all. I'm not really the public-speaking type."

I laughed.

"What's so funny?"

"When you gave that speech at the Carolina Kitchen, I never would've known that."

"I was running on pure adrenaline that day. I was so full of emotions that speaking about the site came easy." He paused. "I guess that it still does. On second thought, I don't mind the interviews. I just have a lot of other things going on."

When are you going to realize that she doesn't deserve you, I thought, but didn't dare speak. Instead, I said, "Well, I'm glad you thought of me today."

Damon chuckled. "I did more than think about you. I'm sitting outside of the diner."

I was stunned. "My diner?"

"Yes. I went inside looking for you, but some guy named Hank said you were off for the weekend. He seemed to have a bit of an attitude about it."

I giggled. "I'll bet he did."

"Then he said something about making sure that you didn't lose your marbles."

I really fell out laughing then.

"What did he mean by that?"

"Destiny concocted a story about me having a nervous break-down in high school and told Hank that I needed some time off. She's so crazy."

"Well, she's also right. I'm sure you did need some time off." There was silence on the line for a few seconds. "I was trying to surprise you. I wanted to see what time you were getting off."

I stood up and walked over to the window, opening the shades. It was a beautiful day. "Oooh, I love surprises. Tell me more."

"Summer's playing in a wheelchair basketball tournament to-day, over at the Fort Lincoln Recreation Center."

"That's great!"

"You seemed to connect with her a little and I thought you might like it."

I glanced at the alarm clock on the nightstand. It was 11:13 a.m. "What time does her game start?"

"At one."

"That's pushing it a little for me."

"It's cool. I understand if you can't—"

"But I'll meet you there."

I could sense Damon smiling through the phone. "I can come pick you up."

"No, that's okay. It's out of your way and I can hop on the metro. The station's less than two blocks away."

"Sounds like a plan. See you there."

"See you."

I hung up the phone and gazed out of the window for a moment, wondering what the hell I was doing. Why was I continuing to place myself around a man whom I had obviously developed romantic feelings for? *Pure stupidity!*

I pulled out a pair of jeans and a T-shirt that had THEY MIGHT ALL LOOK ALIKE, BUT MINE IS TIGHT screen-printed on it. I felt like being naughty. Plus, I wanted Damon to think that I was on the prowl for a new man. Not to make him jealous—of course not. I wanted him to realize that nothing could ever happen between us. That was the story I tried to spoon-feed myself that day.

I went into the bathroom to hit the shower so that I could get to Fort Lincoln on time.

Damon

June 15, 2008

THE basketball courts at Fort Lincoln were packed. Friends, family members, and other spectators were crammed in beside each other. It was hard for me to save Brooke a space, but I was determined.

I had my digital camera and was snapping shots of Summer as she and her teammates—both male and female—warmed up on the court. They were on the east end and their rivals were on the west. All of them were in wheelchairs, but their upper-arm strength was incredible. It is amazing how people learn to adapt in the face of adversity. They were rushing around the court like NBA players, and I could see the expressions on some of the local kids' faces. They were amazed to see what was possible with determination.

A lot of the players had been injured while in the military. Others had suffered spinal diseases, been in accidents like myself, or had been shot during the local wars, mostly over drugs or being in the wrong place at the wrong time.

Summer was throwing the ball back and forth with a young man who appeared to be about her age. They were grinning and blushing at each other, and I couldn't help but wonder if love was in the air. When I'd first arrived, we had a few moments to speak before she had to get out there. She said that she had been on about five dates already with men she'd met on Able Minded Dating. Amazingly, she liked all of them—a couple more than most. She had become a "playette," and I was elated. I remembered when she felt that she would never find love. Now she was finding it in abundance. She said that one of the men, Calvin, was not disabled in any way. He had decided to check out the site because he was sick of stuck-up women who thought that they were God's gift to men. They had a second date scheduled the following weekend.

Steve and Bobby were there, but they were too busy scoping out women to sit in the bleachers. I couldn't take those two anywhere without their having pussy on the brain. The women were there to check out the game and not them. Then again, what did I know?

When I spotted Brooke walking toward me, waving, I was surprised by how much weight she had lost in a few weeks. She was so damn beautiful. As she got closer and climbed through the people on the lower bleachers to get to me, I frowned when I saw her T-shirt. It said THEY MIGHT ALL LOOK ALIKE, BUT MINE IS TIGHT. Maybe some of the women, Brooke included, were there to pick up men.

"You've lost weight." As soon as I said those words to Brooke, I regretted them. I knew how self-conscious she was about her body. She pouted, then sat down next to me on the bleachers. "You look great," I added solemnly. "Not that you didn't look great before."

"Thanks for noticing," Brooke said reluctantly. "Stress will make you lose weight faster than anything else, but I'm glad the weight is finally falling off."

"That's not the way to lose it. You should—"

"I realize that's not the way to lose it, Damon. But it is what it is."

I touched her knee and she started shaking, so I removed my hand.

"What I was going to say is that you should start working out with me. Can you meet me at the gym three days a week?"

She smirked, then giggled. "With my schedule?"

"My schedule's crazy, too, since I started the new site. We can work out really early or really late. Your pick."

Brooke smiled at me. "That's great! I didn't realize you were back in the gym on the regular."

"Yeah, it took me longer than expected, but it feels good to be in the mix again. And I still plan to get out of the daily grind completely soon, but not yet."

She tapped me playfully on the arm. "Check you out, Mr. Entrepreneur."

"How's school?"

"It's coming along. Seems to be moving slowly though. I wish that I could afford to go to school full-time and get it over with, but, oh, well."

"You'll be a pharmacy technician before you know it."

"Thanks. From your mouth to His ears," she replied, pointing up to the sky.

"I appreciate you coming out."

Brooke smiled at me. "I appreciate you asking me." She glanced over in the direction of Bobby and Steve. "Aren't those your friends?"

"Unfortunately, yes. They have no shame." I chuckled. "I keep telling them that if they stop acting so desperate, they might actually meet some women."

"Closed mouths don't get fed."

"Is that why you have on that T-shirt?" I blurted out.

Brooke eyed me for a few seconds, then looked away. "It's just a novelty T-shirt. I think it's funny. Besides, it could be talking about anything. You just have a dirty mind."

"So do you, if you know what I'm thinking."

She looked back at me and I found myself glued to her eyes. The sexual tension was thick between us—too damn thick.

Brooke looked out at the courts. "Summer looks like she means business out there." Brooke glanced at her watch. "They're running late."

"They're waiting on one of the referees. They made an announcement that they would be starting around one fifteen."

"Cool."

A silence fell between us for a moment.

"Would you like something from the concession stand?" I asked. "Bobby said they have a mean hot dog."

"No thanks. Maybe later, but don't let me keep you, if you want something."

I rubbed my belly. "I'm stuffed. I ate a huge breakfast at the diner."

"Oh my God, you let Hank poison you?! Please don't tell me that you had the corned beef hash."

"No, I had bacon, eggs, and grits."

She let out a sigh of relief. "Whew, thank goodness."

"What's wrong with the corned beef hash?"

"Let's just say the ingredients can get a little tricky from time to time. Hank always makes that the special for breakfast when he has a ton of leftovers from the night before. He mixes various scraps together and calls it corned beef hash. It's amazing how people don't know the difference between what he serves and the right thing."

"Well, I guess it's a good thing that I have never been a corned beef fan."

"That's a very good thing."

Her tone was suggestive, even if she didn't mean for it to be. Maybe I just wanted her to mean it. I was glad that she hadn't brought up Carleigh or asked where she was. In fact, I didn't know where my wife was. She had left the house at the crack of dawn, mumbling something about meeting a client who couldn't do the viewing any other time.

We'd made love the night before, if that's what you want to call it. Carleigh still acted like she was doing me a favor by giving me some pussy. She definitely was not into it the way that she used to be. We were still trying for a baby. I was hoping it would happen soon. Maybe it would reignite the spark in our marriage and maybe it would make me stop lusting after Brooke. I couldn't keep myself from spending time with her though. She meant something to me, but she couldn't mean *that*.

"Looks like they're about to get started," Brooke said, breaking me out of my trance. She stood up and yelled out, "Let's go, Summer!"

Summer looked in our direction and waved, then smiled as she wheeled herself into position. It was about to be on!

After the game, Summer's team went to Armand's Pizzeria over on Wisconsin Avenue. Collectively, we took up the entire place. Bobby and Steve tagged along and were trying to talk to some of the sisters and friends of the players. They really were an embarrassing pair.

Brooke walked up to congratulate Summer and hugged her. "Summer, you did great! Congratulations!"

"Thanks, Brooke. I'm glad you were able to make it," Summer replied.

"This is my first weekend off in heaven knows when so everything worked out for the best."

"Oh, you shouldn't have given up your free time for me."

"I couldn't think of a better way to spend it," Brooke replied. Both of them were so sweet. "You all kicked some serious ass out on that court. Thirty-two to thirteen. The other team might as well have stayed home."

We all laughed at that comment. Other people came over to speak to Summer, so Brooke moved away and came to sit with Steve, Bobby, and me at a corner table.

"What are we ordering?" Brooke asked. "Other than beer. I can tell you two are serious beer drinkers," she added, eyeing their guts. "Damon's such a fuddy-duddy, with his no-drinking ass."

"I like her more by the minute." Steve waved his index finger at Brooke and then grinned at me. "Single?"

"Why don't you ask me that?" Brooke said. "I can speak."

Steve gazed into her eyes. "Single?"

"Yes, but my situation is complicated."

"Aw, hell," Steve said, then chuckled. "Same shit, different day. Not the *complicated* thing again."

We all laughed.

Brooke said, "I'll admit that I'm carrying a lot of baggage, but technically, I am single."

I was fuming inside; the two of them were about to flirt right in front of me. Steve was about to say something when I yanked the menu that he was holding out of his hand.

"I'm starving. Let's decide what to order." I scanned the pizza toppings quickly. "With all of these people in here, there's probably going to be a backup in the kitchen any minute now."

Brooke got up from the table. "I'm going to the ladies' room. Be right back."

As she walked away, Steve yelled after her, "What do you like on your pizza?"

Brooke replied over her shoulder, "Anything but mushrooms and anchovies."

We all watched her disappear through the crowd and into the back to the restrooms.

"So how long have you been fucking her?" Bobby asked out of the blue.

I glared at him. "Watch yourself, man!"

"No, you watch *yourself.* It's as obvious as a six-legged dog that something's going on between you two."

"Bobby, Damon would never cheat on Carleigh," Steve said in my defense. "That's out of the damn question."

Bobby addressed Steve. "A few months ago, I might have agreed with you, but check out where we are. Brooke is here, Carleigh is not. When Damon launched his new website, same story. Why's she playing wifey if he's not making her feel that way?"

I was pissed. "Brooke is not playing *wifey!* She's my friend and I'm entitled to have friends; even female ones. Stop trippin' over nothing."

"Damon, I've known you a long time; both of us have. When you're infatuated with someone, it shows all over your face. The way you talk to a woman. The way you look at her. You look at Brooke the way you *used* to look at Carleigh, and that's fact. I don't give a damn what you say."

Steve acted like he wanted to say something but thought better of it. My cell phone started vibrating as the waiter was approaching the table to take our order. Steve and Bobby ordered a large pepperoni-and-sausage deep-dish pizza while I answered the phone.

"Hey, Carleigh."

"Hey, baby. Where are you?"

What do you care? "I'm over at Armand's on Wisconsin with Bobby, Steve, and Summer."

Bobby eyed me suspiciously, since I'd omitted Brooke's name.

"I'm not that far from there," Carleigh said. "I might stop through."

"No," I said much too quickly. "I mean, we're about to leave. All the pizza's gone."

"Oh, okay. So you'll be home soon?"

Brooke was out of the restroom and Summer was now introducing her to some of the other players.

"Damon, you there?" Carleigh blared through the phone.

"Yes, I'm sorry, baby. Steve distracted me with his usual antics."

She laughed. "Steve needs to get laid."

I chuckled. "Trust me. Both of them have been working overtime on that all day."

"What time will you be home?"

"I'm not sure." I was about to tell a bald-faced lie. "Bobby wants me to go with him over his parents' house for dinner. It's their wedding anniversary."

Bobby shook his head and Steve suppressed a laugh.

"Oh, that's nice," Carleigh said. "What time is the dinner? I could go with you."

"They already did a final head count, baby. It would be rude for me to bring you. You know how that goes. People always show up without responding to the invite and then someone has to share a steak or split a chicken breast."

I realized that my words sounded utterly ridiculous, but a ring of truth was in there someplace.

"Good point." Carleigh sighed into the phone. "Maybe I'll go see my mother."

"That's a great idea." I hated Carleigh's mother, but she was a welcome distraction at the moment. Carleigh couldn't know that I was hanging out with Brooke. She would've never understood. "Why don't you take her to her favorite restaurant?"

"Sometimes it's tough getting last-minute reservations at Art and Soul. I'll give it a shot though."

"Sounds good." Brooke was making her way back to the table. "You all have a good time and I'll see you later tonight."

"Okay. Love you."

"Love you, too."

I hung up my phone and noticed Bobby sucking his teeth.

"What?" I asked him.

"Nothing. My name's Bennett and I'm not in it. But whenever the shit hits the proverbial fan, I'll have your back."

"No shit is hitting any fan," Steve interjected. "My boy's faithful, despite what you just heard on the phone."

Bobby said, "Whatever," as Brooke sat back down.

"So what did you fellas order?" she asked.

Steve rubbed his hands together, like he was anticipating the pizza's arrival. "Pepperoni-and-sausage; a pizza made for champions."

"Summer and her team are the champions. You didn't play jack," I stated jokingly.

"Oh, picking up women can be hard work," Brooke said giddily. "Hell, he even tried to pick me up in here."

Steve seemed ashamed at her comment. "I was only being nice."

"I was only kidding," Brooke replied.

Steve glanced down at her T-shirt, which implied how tight her pussy was. "But that T is quite inviting."

Brooke spread it out over her newly flat tummy. "Only people with dirty minds would interpret it the way that you are." She paused. "Ain't nothing wrong with a dirty mind." She patted my hand. "Damon thought the same thing, so don't feel bad."

"Oh, did he?" Bobby asked, implying that I'd done something wrong. "Damon needs to keep his eyes adjusted elsewhere."

"I realize that he's married, Bobby," Brooke said. "You don't have to throw out not-so-subtle hints. Damon's virtue is safe with me."

Too bad, I wanted to blurt out. Brooke was looking sexier on that day than ever before, and it was not only the weight. It was like a weight had been lifted off her shoulders, even though she professed to be under a ton of stress. I was so glad that she had finally got rid of that Patrick bastard. He didn't deserve her.

Brooke looked at me. "You hungry? Those bacon and eggs from the diner wear off yet?"

I chuckled. "Those are history."

"Good thing you didn't eat that corned beef, or you'd be back there locked to the toilet right about now."

Brooke and I laughed at our inside joke as the pizza arrived and we all dug in.

Brooke

June 15, 2008

W<small>E</small> were at the Half Note Lounge in Bowie later that night. Not my idea. I thought that Damon should go home and be with his wife, but he insisted that she wasn't around and he wanted to make sure that I enjoyed my time off. He'd driven me back to Destiny's after Armand's so I could change. I used Destiny's master bathroom while he showered in the bathroom off the hallway. Damon had some extra clothes in his trunk.

"I'm always prepared, in case an interview opportunity pops up," he had told me on the way there.

Even though he *claimed* that he wasn't feeling all of the attention that he was garnering from Able Minded Dating, it was obviously stroking his ego. He had every right to feel proud of his accomplishments. He'd taken a bad situation and turned it into something positive—and profitable. So many people feel down in the dumps and simply give up on life, instead of fighting and being determined to work things out.

I had a lot of nerve, thinking that way. I was a prime example of someone ready to give up and let her fate ride on the unknown. Sure, I waited tables and was working toward my pharmacy-assistant certificate, but my life still seemed like it was on autopilot. My dysfunctional relationship with Patrick had defined me more than I'd realized. Once I was away from him, the pounds had fallen off. I didn't feel like eating much and I'd stopped drinking 80 percent of my calories. Anyone who is a soda fanatic can drop at least ten pounds instantly if they give it up. I was living proof of that. Between giving up soda and scaling back to one meal a day, I was down nearly thirty pounds, just like that.

I'd gone past my parents' place the week before to go shopping in my old closet. My ass was back in clothes that I hadn't worn since high school. I was never one to be trendy, so my basic wardrobe was still practical and didn't look out of place. That was a godsend; in no way could I afford to purchase new items. I was hanging on by a thread. I was sick of barely getting by and needed to figure out something—and quick.

"This place is jumping," Damon said of the restaurant, which featured live bands. "Hell of a band."

"They're my favorite. Not that I ever get to see them. I caught them a couple of times a while back." I gazed at him over the candlelit, white-clothed table. "Thanks for spending so much time with me today."

"It's my pleasure."

Bella Donna, an all-female band, was ripping up the stage with their renditions of all the latest songs, as well as some classics.

"This is the most that I've eaten in weeks," I said, staring down at my chicken salad. "I'm going to gain all of my weight back."

"You have to eat, Brooke." Damon cut into his chicken breast. "Like I said, I'm going to help you get your workout routine together. I promise."

"Never make a promise you can't keep."

He eyed me seductively. "I never do."

I wanted him to fuck me right then and there, on top of the table, in front of the band and the other patrons. I could blame my actions on the alcohol, like that Jamie Foxx song, but I had only had one mojito. Ever since I'd got so drunk in Annapolis, I'd cut back on my alcohol consumption. A wise person solves an issue before it becomes a major problem. I was not going to become an alcoholic, depressed or not. I'd seen the ramifications of that way too often.

We enjoyed the rest of our dinner and listened to the band. I caught Damon looking at me, instead of the band, numerous times. We were playing a dangerous game, but neither of us would back down from it. The couple of times that I went to the ladies' room throughout the evening, I checked out some of the other men in the club on the sly. The majority of them were not that attractive, and the few who were, were with strikingly beautiful women. Some people deny there is a man shortage, but there really is. After those who are married, gay, or in prison, half of the remaining ones are not trying to settle down, and the other half are either lazy, worthless, or a combination of both.

After the band finished up, Damon and I left. He was quiet the majority of the way back to Destiny's apartment. It reminded me too much of a date when both parties have to contemplate what is going to happen next. Nothing could happen next with us, though.

The sky exploded on our way there, and the rain came pouring out of the clouds like from an open, high-pressure faucet. As we pulled up to Destiny's building, Damon suggested, "Maybe you should wait here in the car until the rain slows down."

"I don't see any lightning, *yet*. A little water never hurt anybody," I joked.

"You don't want to ruin your dress." Damon turned the radio to WPGC 95.5; they were playing late-night slow jams. "I'm in no hurry."

"Damon, can I ask you something?"

He looked at me. "Sure."

"How can you not be in a hurry when it is close to three in the morning and you're a married man?"

He refused to respond at first. Instead, he cut the radio up a little bit. "That's my song," he said, refering to "He Is" by Heather Headley.

"That's usually a girlie song." I laughed. "That's the kind of man we're all searching for."

"And the kind of man that I'm trying to be." A sad expression overtook his face. "Brooke, my wife and I haven't been the same since the accident. It's so strange. Here you are, a complete stranger to me before that crazy-ass day, and you show more appreciation for my actions than my own wife."

"I'm sure that this has been hard on her."

"It's been hard on me! I'm the one who lost something!"

I reached over and caressed his cheek. "Actually, I think you gained something."

"What do you mean by that?"

I could see a tear forming in his eye, even with the limited lighting from the streetlamp and the windshield wipers swaying back and forth.

I took off my seat belt and moved closer to him, then kissed him on the side of the eye where I saw the tear.

"You can let it out, Damon. No one expects you to be a statue. You went through something horrible, something most of us can never imagine. Yet, you saw the beauty in it and decided to make a difference in the lives of others."

I rested my head on his shoulder and stared out the window, the pace of the wipers sounding melodic and calming as the song went off and the disc jockey started speaking softly. I turned the radio off.

"I see the beauty in you," he said. I clamped my eyes shut and allowed his words to saturate my skin and drill into my heart. "Even if you can't see it, I see it. I know that you worry about your weight, but being larger only means that there is more of you to love."

In the past, I'd been the queen of talking junk about women who got involved with married men. I couldn't comprehend the thought process and made them all out to be pieces of trash or fucking fools. How could they allow themselves to even be placed in that situation? That was what the old me used to say. Yet, there I was, with my head resting on Damon's shoulder, craving to feel his dick inside me, so hard and so deep that he might knock a hole in the bottom of my pussy.

"I care about you, Brooke."

Was he reading my thoughts!

"And I believe that you care about me."

I couldn't force myself to look at him when I said, "I do care, but I can't sleep with a married man, Damon. As much as I want to at this very moment, I can't."

"I don't expect you to, nor would I disrespect you like that." He took my hand, brought it to his lips, and kissed my fingertips. "Unless I can be the man that you need, unless I can come to you correctly, we can never go there."

"But you do want me, don't you?"

"More than any words could possibly express. My marriage is

hanging on by a thread. I realize that men say that all the time, but, in my case, it's true. We were having issues, even before I lost my arm."

"What kind of issues?"

He let out a heavy sigh. "I already told you that she was taking birth control behind my back."

I sat up and stared at him; the pain was visible all over his face.

"I tried to tell myself that I could get over that deception, tried to assure Carleigh that it was okay, but I've been fooling myself. It still bothers me." He kissed me lightly on the forehead, then gazed into my eyes. "How could she do such a thing? Deprive me of the right to have children, for so long?"

"I can't answer that because I could never do that. Not to you, or anyone else."

Then it happened. It was not intentional. I swear.

I leaned in and kissed Damon on the lips. Not the kind of friendly kiss that I might give an old classmate that I hadn't seen in years. The kind of kiss that I'd imagined a hundred times in my fantasies about him. He didn't hesitate to return my affections, despite everything that both of us had just said about not going there.

I needed it. I needed to feel that closeness to him, if only for a moment. When that moment was over, I silently got out of the car and ran for the entrance to the building without looking back at him. It would have been too painful; knowing that I wanted him to make love to me. It would have been too wrong; to allow it to actually happen.

When I got up to Destiny's apartment, I grabbed a towel from the bathroom, then walked to the window in my bedroom. Damon's car was still sitting there, the wipers going back and forth. The rain had slowed a little, but the pulsations of my heart were so loud that I could hear them in my eardrums.

I saw the light from his cell phone as he started dialing. I assumed that he was calling Carleigh, to tell her that he was on his way home. Instead, my cell starting ringing seconds later. I answered, but said nothing.

"Brooke, I'm sorry."

"You have nothing to feel bad about. I kissed you."

"But I wanted it."

"Both of us wanted it."

"I can't lose your friendship," he pleaded.

I sat down on the bed, in utter confusion. "I'll always be your friend. But we can never be anything more."

"I understand that." He paused briefly. "I'm going to go now. You try to get some rest."

"I'm so tired that I'll probably pass out before my head hits the pillow." That was a damn lie. I already knew that I would be up until sunrise thinking about what had happened. "You drive safely."

"I will. Can I call you tomorrow?"

I should have said that he could not, but I replied, "Sure."

"Can I see you tomorrow?"

Playing with fire! "Okay. What time?"

"I'll pick you up around noon."

"Okay, I'll be ready," I heard myself saying.

Damon hung up and I laid my head back on the pillow, staring at the ceiling. I heard his car pulling off from the curb and sucked in a deep breath. Destiny was not home so my music wouldn't disturb her. I spun the dial on my iPod and put "He Is" on repeat. Then I started my fantasy all over again.

Damon

June 15, 2008

WAS ten minutes early getting back to Brooke that Sunday, having told Carleigh that I had some business to attend to. She was not a happy camper. After asking me a dozen questions about why I came in so late, she had finally accepted that I was with Bobby at his parents' anniversary party. I told her that everyone had got toasted, except for me, and that Bobby's mother had insisted that he sleep it off a little before we got back on the road. Carleigh asked why I couldn't have driven, and I told her that I was too tired from sitting out in the heat at Summer's game earlier.

Even with one arm, I was in incredible shape and I could tell that Carleigh was skeptical. I was upset for various reasons. For one, she had been hanging out with that Arnold character a lot, and I was wondering if she was indeed fucking him. Second, I wanted to *make love* to Brooke, and that was not a good thought for a married man to have. But I could not stay away from her. I couldn't.

When I rang Destiny's buzzer, Brooke said, "Come on up," then buzzed the door open. The door to the apartment was open when I got off the elevator on the third floor. I rapped lightly on the door. "Come in," she said from someplace down the hallway. "I'll be right out."

I went in and sat down on the sofa. Having been there the day before to get dressed, I couldn't help but feel like we were somehow setting up house in someone else's place. Yet, my natural reaction was to reach for the remote and turn the television on to ESPN. A documentary was on about athletes who were drug addicts. They always had great subject matter. One time, I was watching one about professional ballers who had fathered children outside their marriages. The host was talking about how, even though Magic Johnson had come out nearly a generation earlier and confessed to contracting HIV by sleeping with numerous women, men were still playing Russian roulette with their lives and the lives of their wives. I mean, after all, how can all of them be fathering children if they were using protection? There may a slipup here or there, but, for the most part, they are running around screwing whoever, whenever.

"I'm ready," Brooke said, emerging from the back wearing a pair of black slacks and a white blouse. "I didn't know what to put on so I hope that I'm dressed okay."

I stood up. I had on black slacks and a white shirt. "If you're not, then I'm not either."

She giggled. "So, where are we off to?"

"Wherever you want to go." I shrugged. "I really just wanted to see you today." There it was. The tension. "Listen, about last night?"

"I think we should leave that alone." Brooke reached for her purse and pulled out a tube of lipstick. "We had a moment of weakness, but it's cool. I value our friendship and don't want to do anything to jeopardize it."

As I watched her put on her lipstick, I replied, "I agree. Listen, have you ever been to the wax museum?"

"Wow, it must be karma." Brooke blushed. "Before you called me yesterday, I told Destiny that I was going to look up the information for Madame Tussauds and go check it out."

"Then it sounds like a plan."

I followed Brooke out of the door of the apartment, and my eyes fell to her ass. What can I say? Instinct!

We arrived at Madame Tussauds Wax Museum at the corner of Tenth and F streets, NW, a little after one. Since it was a Sunday, a lot of the huge churches downtown had people flooding out of them, and it took a minute to find a parking space. After all the madness, we found a lot right across the street that neither of us had spotted at first amid all the confusion.

Once inside, things were much calmer. It was not that crowded at all.

"I wonder why more people don't take advantage of the local attractions," I commented to Brooke.

"I can't talk. I'm definitely one of the guilty ones." She was staring at a wax figure of George Washington. "For me, it's a schedule thing, coupled with a lack-of-money thing. Even though the admission is twenty dollars, that's still a little steep for me, compared to putting food in my stomach."

Brooke always made it a point to say how poor she was. I noticed that she never used to talk about that when she was with Patrick. Since he was obviously loaded, I guess she felt more secure about her spending then. Even though she didn't strike me as the type to mooch off him, at least she had a lifeline back then.

"You know, my websites are taking off so much that I could really use an assistant. You think you might be able to help me?"

Brooke paused beside the Denzel Washington figure and stared up at me. "I don't need your pity, Damon."

"Pity? It's not pity, Brooke." I pulled out my digital camera and waved for her to move in closer to Denzel. "Say *Denzel!*"

Brooke looked great for the photo, but she didn't seem happy about my job offer.

"Look, tons of people are joining the sites, and even though Able Minded Dating kind of runs itself, the Last Good Men site still has to have someone to approve the profiles and all that jazz. Plus, a lot of corporations want to place ads now, and it's getting overwhelming."

"Then hire someone who knows how to run a website. The only thing that I know about the internet is that I go on it. I check out gossip sites, eBay, even though I can't afford anything, and the latest important news."

"Gossip sites? You don't seem like the type that would be into those."

Brooke slapped me playfully on the arm. "Please, I have to get some excitement out of life some kind of way. Heaven knows that I don't have anything going on."

"So what's the latest?"

"Ah, see, you're nosy, too, Damon." We continued walking toward the sports-figures section. "Well, that rapper Taariq is dating Reaction and his girlfriend Ana Marie found out about it. They've been all over the place lately. Taariq is claiming that Ana Marie used to turn tricks, and Reaction is saying that she's pregnant. It's what they call a *hot ghetto mess.*"

"Sounds like it," I said, then laughed. "You're really into that stuff."

Brooke stopped in her tracks and stared at me. "What?"

"I'm just saying. I didn't peg you for the type."

"Look, if people want to put their business out in the streets, why shouldn't I listen to it?"

"True." I got excited when I saw the Muhammad Ali wax figure. I handed Brooke the camera. "Take my picture with Ali."

As she was snapping the photo, an older couple walked by. The woman said, "Want me to take one of both of you?"

Brooke said, "Yes," then handed the woman the camera. "That would be great."

The man stated, "That's the only thing about coming places as a couple. You never have someone else to take the pictures. Gloria and I have been going through that for fifty-six years now."

Brooke was standing on the opposite side of Ali, grinning from ear to ear, as the woman took our picture.

"Fifty-six years?" I said after I finished posing. "How do you two do it?"

The couple looked at each other with a love in their eyes as if they had just met. "I knew Randolph was the man for me the first time I laid eyes on him," Gloria replied.

Randolph chuckled. "Yeah, she did, even though I was engaged to someone else."

Brooke walked closer to them. "Really? So she stole you away from the other woman?"

"She stole my heart and I had no choice but to leave. I couldn't live a lie." He looked at his wife and took her hand into his. "Never regretted my decision for a single day."

Gloria looked Brooke dead in the eyes. "That's what's important in life, dear. Not having any regrets. If you care about someone, you need to tell them. You need to show them. Otherwise, you might never get that chance." Then she stared at me. "Every once in a while, God winks at you."

"What does that mean?" Brooke asked.

"It means that He'll let you know where you're really supposed to be, even if you are in the wrong place."

"We'd better get going, Gloria." Randolph glanced at his watch and then at us. "We're supposed to be having dinner with the grandkids."

I asked, "How many do you have?"

"Eight," Gloria replied. "Our life is full of love." She leaned forward and whispered something in Brooke's ear. Then she gazed at me and walked off, with Randolph behind her.

"You all have a nice day," Brooke called after them.

After they were out of earshot, I asked, "What did she say to you?"

Brooke blushed, then shrugged her shoulders. "It wasn't important." She walked over to Tiger Woods, who was about to take a shot on a golf course. "Take my picture with Tiger."

I decided to drop it—for then. We still had quite a few sections to walk through, and I had some other plans that Brooke knew nothing about.

"This is so beautiful." Brooke was sprawled out on the blanket at Hains Point, watching the planes fly overheard—both military and commercial. The water of the Potomac River was glistening, even though it was full of pollution. "I can't believe that I've never done this."

"Been here?" I took out the bottle of sparkling apple cider from the picnic basket I had prepared and started opening it. "This place has been around forever."

"I've never been here and I've never been on a picnic."

"Are you serious?"

"I mean, my parents took me on picnics once or twice of course, and I've been to my share of cookouts, but not a picnic. Not like this, with a . . ." She paused. We both knew she meant a romantic picnic with a man.

"Well, I'm honored to be the first."

My cell phone started vibrating in my pocket again and I knew it was Carleigh. She had been blowing it up, practically since I'd left home. I was not feeling good about myself or my actions; not at all.

Brooke was looking at me strangely. "Damon, is something wrong?"

"No, what makes you think that?"

"The *expression* on your face, maybe."

I grinned. "I'm starving; that's all. Let's dig in."

Brooke smiled. "What you got in there?" she asked, eyeing the picnic basket.

"I've got some blue cheese and pecan over spring-mix salad, some turkey-and-Gouda-on-rye sandwiches, and some mixed tropical fruit."

"Wow. Sounds gourmet. You didn't fix this stuff, did you?"

"Actually, I did. Something else you didn't know about me. I love gourmet cooking. One day, I'll have to fix you my specialty—beef burgundy."

"Damn, that sounds great." She picked up half of a sandwich. "And this smells delicious."

"Dig in." I sat there and watched her take the first bite. She definitely was feeling the taste. "I have plenty."

After we finished eating, I don't know what overcame me, but the next thing I knew, I was spilling my guts.

"Brooke, I want you to listen to me, and don't say anything."

She had been lying down, looking at the sky, but she sat up when I said that.

"No matter what comes out of my mouth, promise me that you won't comment until I'm done."

She reluctantly said, "Okay," and stared at me.

"I'm sure it's obvious to you that we're playing with fire. There's something going on between us, and it's growing deeper. Sure, it may have started out because of the accident. That's how we initially crossed paths, but, like they always say, everything happens for a reason.

"We saw each other in the gym before then and maybe we were supposed to connect then, but it wasn't the time. It wouldn't have had the same impact as what happened." I looked down at my prosthetic arm. "You were right when you told me last night that I'd gained something when I lost my arm. I gained a new outlook on life, on what's important."

Brooke seemed like she was dying to say something, but held it back.

"My wife always saw me as a trophy; something that she could show off to her friends. I was the perfect man, in her eyes, and that's the only reason she ever wanted me."

Brooke sighed and bit her bottom lip.

"After I lost my arm, I wasn't perfect anymore. She began to distance herself from me. She became ashamed of me. Now I think she's beginning to regret it, *maybe,* but she's already proven that her love for me wasn't unconditional. When you get married, it's supposed to be for better or for worse, in sickness and in health. When I said those words to her, I meant them. She was everything to me. I wanted to put the sunshine on her face every day. I wanted to protect her, to be her knight in shining armor. In a sense, I guess that I was being that knight when I pushed her out of the way of that SUV.

"I don't regret doing it. Like that couple said earlier, life shouldn't be lived shrouded in regrets." I reached out and touched Brooke's cheek. "I don't regret the way I feel about you, either. I love you, Brooke. I do."

She pulled her face away from me and started to fight back tears.

"But you and I both know that I'm not the kind of man who could cheat on his wife. I'm tempted, and for the first time in my life, I can understand how it's possible. How a good man, a really good man, could stray outside of his marriage. I used to look down on my friends who did it, even though most of them do it for the sex. I still don't agree with that. But what about when there are genuine feelings involved? When two people honestly fall for one another and one or both of them is already taken? What happens then?"

Brooke blurted out, "I have to say something."

"No," I said, holding a finger to her lips. "Let me finish, please."

She nodded and motioned for me to continue.

"Carleigh's not the best wife in the world, but I never expected her to be. I never believed that she was perfect, and I didn't marry her because I thought she was. I married her because I thought she was my soul mate. What's happening between you and me is not her fault, and she can't suffer for our actions.

"What I'm saying is, if Carleigh and I don't work out, I'll be making a beeline for your door. But that's not fair either, and I don't expect you to wait for something that may or may not happen. I can't simply leave her. She doesn't deserve that. While she did treat me badly right after the accident, she didn't walk away from me, and she could have. I've read a lot of stories about people who've become disabled and their spouses divorce them. She hasn't done that."

Brooke stood up and walked over to the railing by the river. Her back was to me and I could tell that she was crying, trying to prevent me from seeing it. I followed her and put my arms around her waist. She rested the back of her head on my chest.

"Brooke, you are so special, so damn special. You need a man who can give you everything that you need, and not only part of it. I wish that I could be that man. That I could be the one to greet you every day when you come home from your new *career* at the pharmacy. That I could be the one to run you a bubble bath every night, to wash your hair for you, and rub your feet. That I could cook for you, clean for you, make love to you, and make you feel special." I paused. "But I can't be that man."

She tried to pull away from me, but I wouldn't let her.

"I realize that I'm the one who's been asking to spend so much time together. I realize that I've fanned these flames, and that's not fair." I shut my eyes, hating to have to say the words that would come out next. "I don't think we should see each other anymore. If we don't stop this, I'm going to lose all self-control and we're going to end up making love, no matter how much we try to fight it. If I could, I'd be inside of you right this very second. When I'm near you, all I think about is touching you, tasting you, becoming one with you. We've got to stop this train before it wrecks."

When Brooke tried to pull away from me again, I let her go, now fighting back my own tears. She walked a couple of feet from me and turned around. Her eyes were bloodshot and she was wiping them with her sleeve.

"Please, just take me home," she whispered.

"Don't you have anything else to say?"

"You told me not to say anything."

"Until I was finished. Now, I'm finished."

"No, now *we're* finished."

It hurt to hear her speak that out loud, even though she was right. We had to stay away from each other. That was the only way to ensure that we wouldn't end up doing the unthinkable.

Brooke walked back to my car while I gathered up all of the picnic items. Then I drove her back to Destiny's apartment in complete silence. No talking, no radio, no breathing.

As I watched her disappear into the building, I wondered what life would be like without seeing her face, hearing her voice, watching her smile.

"You're doing the right thing," I told myself as I pulled slowly away from the curb.

Brooke

July 22, 2008

DESTINY walked into my bedroom, passed my bed, and opened the blinds. "I'm not taking one more day of this shit!"

I sat up. "What's wrong? Did something happen with Harold?"

She plopped down beside me. "No, I'm talking about you, heifer. I'm sick of you moping over that married-ass man."

"Don't go there." I put my index finger up to her face. "I don't want to talk about Damon."

"You need to get over him. He did the right thing, and you know it. You have no business being someone's mistress."

"This coming from the woman who always proclaims that we all have to get used to sharing dick?" I lashed out in anger. "At least he cares about me. A lot of women are sleeping with someone else's man and they don't give a shit about them."

"So you did sleep with him?" Destiny folded her arms across her lap. "Lying ass."

"No, I kissed him. Like I said." I wanted to kick myself in the ass for telling Destiny everything that had gone down between Damon and me. But I needed to vent and I didn't have anyone else to talk to. "Would I have slept with him? Probably. Definitely, if things had gone there, but they didn't. He made sure of that."

"And you need to get down on the ground and kiss his feet." She smacked her lips. "Okay, I admit that I know Harold fucks around, but I can handle it. I expect it; I accept it. You're not *that chick*. You couldn't handle Patrick's escapades, and he damn near worshipped the ground you walked on."

"He's been calling me lately." I sighed. "Patrick's trying to get back into the picture."

"Did you speak to him?"

"No, I never answer. I let his calls go straight to voice mail."

"And he leaves messages?"

"Yeah, asking me to call him back. He wants another chance. Blah, blah, blah."

"Blah, blah, blah, nothing." Destiny stood back up and walked toward the door. "Patrick loves you. He's willing to provide for you, even marry you. Men like him don't come walking into our lives every day. You never realized how lucky you were to have him. You need to rethink what you're doing."

She left out and slammed the door. I got up and put on a bathrobe, then glanced at my pile of textbooks in the corner. I was falling behind, but I was determined to achieve something in my life. I sat down at my desk and opened up a book on prescription pills. My mind kept wandering to Damon, which it always did. I missed him. When he told me that he loved me that day, I wanted to say the words back to him so badly. I'd tried to sugarcoat my feelings, pretend like they were innocent and friendly. But I did love him, more than anything.

They say that love is the best emotion in the world. But what about when you are not free to love? Damon did the right thing by saying that we should not be around each other. We were dating, regardless of what we made it out to be. I am sure that he had started lying about his whereabouts to his wife, and he was not the type of man to feel comfortable running around behind a woman's back. That was a positive trait about him, and I didn't want to ruin it. He was a good man, one of the last good men. I only hoped that Carleigh appreciated what she had.

Tony was on the prowl again during the dinner shift. This time, his mark was openly gay, like him, but he was on a date with his man. Tony didn't give a flying shit though. He was going to get him some.

"Look at the two of them over there, all lovey-dovey." He was staring at the two men in a corner booth. Both very attractive. "The one in the blue shirt has been checking my ass cheeks out since they came in here."

"How do you know he's been looking at your ass?" I asked Tony as I cut a piece of pecan pie for a customer. "You have eyes in the back of your head?"

"Don't need them. I can sense it. When a man wants a piece of me, my ass starts twitching in anticipation."

I decided to be nosy. "Can I ask you something?"

Tony was putting two glasses of soda and two glasses of water on a tray. "Sure, give me a second though."

He took the tray over to a family of four and took their order. As he was passing the table with the two men, he paused and said to the one in the blue, "Can I get you *anything* else?"

The other man, in black, jumped in. "We're fine. Thank you." The sarcasm in his voice was heavy. "When you get a chance, just bring us the check."

Tony was rolling his eyes as he walked back toward me. I'll be damned if the one in the blue was not boring a hole in Tony's ass though. Tony knew his shit.

"He is staring at your ass," I informed him, as soon as he made it back to me. I'd dropped off the pecan pie to my counter customer while Tony was gone.

"Chile, I know what's up!" Tony flung his head back over his shoulder and winked at the one in the blue. He blushed in return. "What did you want to ask me?"

"This may be none of my business, and goodness knows I have no practical reason for wanting to know this, but . . ."

"Spill it already."

"I hear you talk a lot about men wanting your ass, so does that mean that you're a bottom?"

"Indeed." Tony turned around and started popping his ass up at me. "Bottom's up."

"You're wild." He turned back to me. "So you never do the giving?"

"I have but it's really not my thing."

"So when a man decides that he's gay, how does he—"

"Men don't *decide* shit. I get so tired of people assuming that we wake up one day and *decide* to fall in love with dick. You're either gay or you're not gay. I don't believe in any of that bisexual nonsense either. Some *gay* men sleep with women, but they're still *gay*. There's no such thing as partiality or going both ways."

"I feel you, but what I'm asking is, how do you determine whether you want to be a top or a bottom? Do you experiment with both and then make a choice? Do you do both an equal amount of the time? When you have a lover, do you do each other? How does that work?"

Tony looked at me like I was crazy. "What? You dating a gay man or something?"

I frowned. "I'm not dating anyone. Nobody wants me."

"Aw, hell, not a pity party." Tony ran his fingers through my hair. "Look at you, Brooke. You're gorgeous, even when you walk around here acting like the sky has fallen. You've just been dealing with the wrong assholes, that's all. The right man will come along." He paused and cleaned out some dirt from his fingernail. A nasty act, considering he was serving food. "What about that tall drink of water who came in here looking for you a few weeks ago, when Hank the Stank gave you some time off?"

"Oh, Damon's married. He and I used to be friends, but we're chilling now."

"Used to be friends, huh?" Tony seemed skeptical. "Uh-huh, whatever."

"Can we get back to my question?" I popped him lightly in the chest, and he acted like Tyson had just punched him. "Stop over-reacting and tell me the deal."

"Well, in my case, I always wanted something thick and long filling up my insides. I've never been into being the one who has to stick and move." The man in the black got up from their table and was walking toward us. "I want someone to do me like they're try-ing to knock a hole in something and—"

"Excuse me," the man in black said. "We're *still* waiting on our check."

Tony put his hand on his hip. "I'll be right there. My business associate and I are discussing a corporate matter."

The man seethed and walked off.

"He'd better fucking wait. He'll get his check when I say he'll get his check."

"'A corporate matter'?" I laughed. "'Business associate'?"

"Well, the shit sounded good." Tony giggled. We both noticed the man in black get up again and head to the bathroom. "Oops, time to make my move."

Tony rushed off to talk to the man in the blue while his man was gone and added up their check there at the table. I could see their flirtatious nature from where I was standing. One of my customers waved me over for some more napkins and another soda.

By the time I was done taking yet another order, the two men were gone and Tony looked disgusted.

"What happened? He turned you down?" I asked.

"No, he wanted some of my stuff, but he's a bug chaser."

"A what?"

"Can you believe that some *people* want to catch HIV so bad that they ask other people to give it to them?"

"He asked you if you were positive?" I was shocked. "So you could give it to him? That's absurd!"

"What's really crazy is that some people have bug-chaser parties. They'll be like fifty men there, and two or three will be the *givers* and all of them come hoping to catch it."

"You're making this shit up, Tony!"

"No, I'm not."

"But why would anyone want to catch HIV?"

He shrugged. "A lot of people figure that they'll end up getting it anyway, so why not orchestrate their own destiny. Some are grieving over losing a lover to the disease. Some are just plain crazy. Like people who play Russian roulette, or let poisonous snakes bite them and shit."

"So why did he want it?" I asked, nodding toward the now empty table.

"Do you think I asked? Fuck if I care. I'm clean and I'm staying clean. I get tested every other month."

"Why so often?"

"Brooke, in many ways, you're like a naive little girl, so allow me to educate you. This world has gone to shit. People are fucking like there's no tomorrow. People are going around screwing with reckless abandon. Straight, gay, it doesn't matter. You'd better be careful. Hell, a lot of the men who go to bug-chaser parties are married. Peep that."

"Are you serious?"

"Stop asking if I'm serious. You know me. What reason on earth would I have to lie about anything?"

Tony had a point. He was the most open and honest person that I knew. You could either accept him as he was or go on about your business.

"Just like you have no problem telling someone to kiss your monkey, people can kiss my ass if they don't like me."

I laughed. "You know, since I broke up with Patrick, I don't think I've had to tell one single person to kiss my monkey."

Tony grinned. "Well, the night's still young. Here comes Hank."

Hank was coming back into the diner from who knows where and might as well have had the word ATTITUDE stamped on his forehead. Both Tony and I started pretending like we were superbusy to avoid his wrath. He had been looking at me strangely ever since Destiny told him that I'd had a nervous breakdown in high school. It was like he was waiting for me to go postal or something. Damn shame!

It is amazing how you can conjure up people by the mere mention of their name. When I left the diner that night, Patrick's Bentley was parked beside my Corolla.

"I figured if you won't take my calls, I should come by." He was standing by my driver's-side door. "We need to talk, Brooke."

I tried to pretend he was not there and maneuvered around him to unlock my door.

"Oh, so you're going to act as if I'm not standing here?"

"Patrick, I got your messages. You know I got them. Since I didn't call you back, doesn't that tell you something?"

"I can't live without you, Brooke. I've tried and I can't do it."

I looked at him and he was gazing into my eyes. I could see the pain and anguish in his.

"You should have thought about that before, Patrick. Getting back with you would only mean setting myself up for the same hurt and disappointment."

He started caressing my neck, my weak spot. "Just one more chance. Let me make love to you tonight; let me show you how special we can be."

I should have pushed him away from me and headed straight back to Destiny's place. But nothing was waiting for me there—no one. I thought about Damon and how he was probably at home, at that very moment, making love to Carleigh. The mere thought of the two of them together sent a stinger through my heart.

The one thing that certainly couldn't be denied was that Patrick cared about me. I recalled what Damon said about not expecting Carleigh to be perfect. Yet, part of me expected Patrick to be that very thing. I needed to be held; I needed some tenderness; and I could either go out and find it in the arms of a perfect stranger or return to a familiar place.

The things Tony had said to me earlier didn't escape me either. He was right. Having sex with anyone was risky, but at least I'd been with Patrick for a long time. Sure, he had been inside another woman—I saw that with my own eyes—but at least he cared. I never believed he would go as far as infecting me with something.

I was depressed, horny, and confused, which is why I said, "Let's go back to your place."

Patrick grinned and took my hand, leading me to the passenger's seat of his car.

Patrick and I bathed together when we arrived at his penthouse. As he stripped down, I took in every inch of him. I'd almost forgotten how handsome he was. Smooth skin; great body; juicy dick. I was already in the garden tub, with the whirlpool jets going, and playing with my little rubber ducky that I'd left there. I don't think Patrick had ever figured out that it was actually a vibrator that I used when I was alone. What he didn't know couldn't hurt him. As freaky as Patrick was, he felt competitive when it came to sex toys. He felt that he was breaking me off well enough that I should not need—or even want—to masturbate. What men fail to realize is that orgasms for women are usually greater during masturbation. That is why a lot of women feel like they never achieve orgasms with their men. I have a theory. I believe that they actually do have them, but they expect them to be earth-shattering and toe-curling and expect to experience aftershocks, like they do when they play with themselves. Instead, the orgasms are *minor* and they spend too much time stressing over why they didn't explode or squirt like a fountain. As long as sex is enjoyable and the man is not complaining, women need to ease up on that whole orgasm thing. All that "cumming at the same time" only happens in romance novels.

We exploded in unison!

I held off from cumming until he exploded inside me, and then I came all over his dick!

Our juices mixed together at the same exact time!

Whatever! Blah, blah, blah, blah!

I liked to read the kind of books where women were serious about their shit and didn't care whether their men got their nuts off or not. A new author was on the scene named Cairo. I was shocked to find out that a man had written *The Kat Trap* and *The Man Handler*. Those women in his two novels were slaying dicks and taking names. I was anxiously awaiting his next two books, *Daddy Longstroke* and *Deep Throat Diva*. Now those were some titles for your ass.

My mind was wandering, even though Patrick was stepping into the tub. Bad sign! All of my thoughts should have been on him, but I was playing a game and I realized it. Yes, Patrick cared, in his own convoluted fashion. Yes, he desired me and wanted to make me happy, or so he thought. Yes, I was used to being around him and had a certain level of comfort when I was near him—until he started calling me out of my name or acting like I was beneath him. But mostly, I just needed to be fucked to get my mind off Damon.

He's probably at home fucking Carleigh right now, I thought as Patrick's dick lingered in front of my face.

Without his even having to ask for once, I engulfed him in my mouth and greedily began to milk his dick, contracting my cheek muscles and tasting his pre-cum as it trickled down my throat.

Patrick moaned. "You missed Magnum, didn't you?"

Stroking his ego, I replied, "Um, yes, I missed Magnum so much, baby."

As I continued to suck him off, I used one hand to caress his balls and the other to form a vise around the lower part of his dick.

"Damn, Brooke, did you skip dinner?" Patrick asked, then chuckled, grabbing the back of my head to maneuver his dick in and out more smoothly.

I hated it when he did that, but decided not to complain for once. Men don't get it. When women suck dick, we want to be left to our own acquired skills, instead of being directed like a hired worker. That is the true enjoyment—the only enjoyment—that women get from sucking dick; believing that our skill set is stronger than the next chick's. We want to bring a man down to his knees with our head game; not be made to feel like any other woman could do the same exact thing. Men really need to get a clue.

Patrick got more head time from me that night than at any other moment in our relationship. I sucked him, and sucked him, and sucked him, until he exploded in my mouth.

Damn, I thought. *I'm trapped in the tub!*

I yearned to be able to brush my teeth and gargle his seed out of my throat, but that would only have started an argument and ruined the moment. This was the first time that I was not in a position to rinse my mouth after sucking his dick. That didn't escape Patrick either, and he decided to take advantage of it. He got down on his knees, straddling my legs in the tub, and buried his tongue in my mouth before I could lodge a protest. I thought about the night that I'd seen him with Mandawhore and realized that it was truly important to him to be able to kiss me after he had ejaculated. It was disgusting to me, but I endured it. *Endured;* not a good word to use about having sex.

When Patrick finally gave me a second to breathe, I blurted out, "I want to ride that big dick of yours."

That got to him, like I knew it would. He grinned like a little boy and sat back on the opposite end of the tub. I reached under the water and gave him a hand job. It didn't take long for him to achieve another erection; an even harder one this time. Not wanting to risk his trying to kiss me again, I sat down on his dick with my back to him. Then I handed him a bar of soap.

"Wash my back for me."

"I'll wash anything you want."

Patrick lathered up his hands and rubbed them all over my back, then my ass, and my breasts as I continued to go up and down, and from side to side, on top of him. It did feel good, fucking him. Then again, it had been so long since I'd fucked anyone else. I closed my eyes and pretended that Patrick's dick was Damon's dick. I wondered if Damon would fill up my pussy more. I suspected that he would, based upon what I'd scoped out and felt rub against me once or twice.

I imagined Damon licking my back; spreading my ass cheeks and blowing on my anus; grabbing my breasts from behind and teasing my hardened nipples. I was about to climax when Patrick ruined it for me.

"Penny for your thoughts."

I winced. Thank goodness he couldn't see the expression on my face as my eyes popped open.

"I'm just thinking about how much I've missed this big, juicy dick of yours," I lied. "How much I've missed you."

"Then let's get married," he whispered, making an already difficult moment even more tense. "By this time tomorrow, you can be Mrs. Patrick Sterling."

I relaxed my pussy muscles and sucked in a breath.

"Marry me, Brooke. I promise that I will be the man that you need, the man that you deserve. I'll give you everything you've ever wanted. You'll never need or want for anything, ever again."

I didn't respond.

"Brooke . . ." Patrick pushed me off him and tried to turn me to face him. "Talk to me. Please, baby. What's wrong?"

I gazed into his eyes, seeking the right words. "Patrick, you talk about my needs and wants like you understand me. You don't understand me. Not really."

"I do understand you, Brooke. I love you."

"I believe that you love me, but love isn't always enough."

"So what are you saying?"

"I'm saying that you're rushing me into making a hasty decision that I'm not prepared to make. We haven't been together for a minute, Patrick, but I came here with you tonight. It's a start, but this is not the endgame. You can't fuck me in the tub one time and think that I can forget about everything that happened. You can't seriously expect me to marry you when we have so many problems."

"Nobody's life is perfect, baby."

"I understand that, but I'm not going to make a bad situation worse by exchanging vows that I'm not sure you'd mean." I paused. "Or that I'm not sure that I would mean."

The look of dejection on Patrick's face got to me, and I felt bad. Not bad enough to retract my words though.

"Let's enjoy each other, tonight. We don't have to read too much into this."

Patrick stunned me when he said, "I've seen you with him."

I knew whom he was talking about, but played dumb. "With whom?"

"Don't play dumb," he said, reading me like a book. "Damon Johnson."

"Damon's my friend. You know that. You also know that he's a married man."

"If I'd been there that day, Brooke, I would've saved you. I *should've* been there, but you'd shut me out, yet again."

"I shut you out because I watched you make love to another woman through a window, Patrick. Don't try to make yourself out to be innocent." I tried to climb out of the tub, but he held me to him. "Let me go."

"No, not this time. That's your solution to everything. Running away. Not this time. We're going to talk about this."

I sighed. "Fine, but I'm shivering. Can we get out of the tub and talk?"

"Sure, if you promise me you won't throw on your clothes and haul ass out of here."

"I promise."

Patrick gazed into my eyes, probably trying to determine if he could trust me. Not a good sign. I was not going to leave without carrying through with the discussion.

"Okay, let's get out," he finally said, and released me from his grasp.

Patrick and I were sitting at the dining room table, sharing a bowl of kettle popcorn and drinking ginger ale. I'd brushed my teeth, of course, and felt a million times better. I still felt somehow violated by kissing Patrick with his seed in my mouth. He hadn't forced me though, so I was tripping. Still, it gave me a good starting point for our discussion.

"Patrick, I don't think we're sexually compatible."

He chewed the popcorn in his mouth and took a sip of his soda before responding. "We had incredible sex in the bathtub tonight."

"It was *good* sex, but I didn't want you to kiss me with your semen in my mouth. You knew that, right?"

"You're making a big deal out of nothing."

"Then there's the anal thing."

"I didn't try to fuck you up the ass, Brooke!" He was getting irate. "I *blew* in your anus; that's it."

"That's all you did tonight, but can you honestly say that if we got married, you wouldn't expect me to let you fuck my ass?"

"It's not a deal breaker for me."

"But you'd want it, right?"

"Maybe once a year, or something. Like I said, it's not a deal breaker."

"What if I don't want to be fucked up my ass once a year, or even once a decade? What if it makes me feel disgusted and it hurts like hell?"

"A woman should be willing to do anything to please her man. That's a given."

I snickered. "A given, huh? No, it's not a given. A woman should be willing to please her man as long as it doesn't make her feel uncomfortable."

"That's bullshit! Women know that what they won't do, someone else will!"

"Is that where Mandawhore comes in?"

Patrick slammed his ginger ale down on the table, almost breaking the glass. "You're never going to drop it, are you?"

"I don't know if I can . . . *drop it*."

"We'll never work this out if you can't forget about her. She's history; I told you that."

"She was also history the first time, when she dropped you and married someone else." I paused and watched him pout like a child. "Admit it; there's something about her that you can't stay away from. She's like your Achilles' heel."

"The hell she is. If I have an *Achilles' heel,* you're it. I can't stay away from you. I love you, Brooke, and as soon as I get you down that aisle, all this nonsense is going to come to a halt."

"You honestly believe that a marriage certificate is like a magic wand? That's not the way it works, Patrick. If we got married, and that's a big-ass if, we would still be the same two people, except we'd be legally bound together. We'd have the same problems; the same insecurities; the same dysfunctional relationship."

Patrick took my hand and kissed the inside of my palm, pleading with his eyes. "Think about it; that's all I'm asking. I understand that you don't want to rush, but, technically, we've been together long enough to know what we want. I'm very clear on what I want . . . and I am *sure*."

I imagined Patrick reciting marriage vows to me in a chapel someplace.

I, Patrick, take you, Brooke, to be my wedded wife, to have and to hold from this day forward, for better for worse, for richer for poorer, in sickness and in health, to love and to cherish, till death do us part: according to God's holy ordinance, and thereto I pledge you my love and faithfulness.

Or he could really go hard and say something like:

I take you, Brooke, to be my wife, loving you now and as you grow and develop into all that God intends. I will love you when we are together and when we are apart; when our lives are at peace and when they are in turmoil; when I am proud of you and when I am disappointed in you; in times of rest and in times of work. I will honor your goals and dreams and help you to fulfill them. From the depth of my being, I will seek to be open and honest with you. I say these things believing that God is in the midst of them all.

All of it would have been complete bullshit!

Patrick had constantly made it a point to put me down. He hadn't been open and honest with me. He had worn his disappointment in me, my job, and my background on his sleeve. No, there would be no marriage, only pure, unadulterated fucking.

"Let's go back to bed," I suggested. "We can make love all night and talk about this some more in the morning."

Patrick grinned like the cat that had swallowed a few canaries. "Sounds good."

I stood up and led him into the bedroom so that I could drown my misery by letting him give me some stiff dick. I had zero intention of being there to discuss jack shit when he woke up in the morning.

Damon

August 1, 2008

I THREW myself back into my marriage, determined to forget about Brooke, but, at the same time, realizing how impossible that would be. Carleigh was trying her best to be the ideal wife. She was coming home early every day. She was cooking, even though I really preferred to burn in the kitchen. She was refraining from bringing up her mother, whom she knew that I couldn't stand.

When I arrived home on Friday evening, she had the dining room table set with candles, and the aroma coming from the kitchen made my mouth water.

"Something smells good," I told her as I walked into the kitchen and found her rinsing lettuce over the sink.

"Dinner's almost ready." She shook the water off the lettuce, placed it in a bowl, and started chopping up tomatoes, cucumbers, and fresh mushrooms. "I hope you're hungry."

Even though I'd eaten a late lunch with Bobby, I replied, "I'm starving. I was hoping you'd cook."

Carleigh turned to look at me and grinned. She was truly a beautiful woman. "You shouldn't have to come home after a long day and fend for yourself, honey."

"What did you make?"

"I decided to keep it simple. I made a lemon-and-chicken casserole."

"Ooh, you know how I love anything lemon."

"Then you'll love the *lemonade*." She pointed to the refrigerator. "There's a pitcher in the fridge."

I grinned. "I'll be right back. Let me go wash my hands and change right quick."

When I entered the bedroom, I noticed that Carleigh had the bed ready for some "good good." I could always tell when she expected sex, and she was definitely anticipating some that night. She had scented candles burning, the bed was turned down, and I could smell the linen spray she liked to use.

Even though we had been spending a lot of time together, I'd yet to make love to her since I'd broken things off with Brooke. "Broken things off" seemed like a bad way to look at it, but I was dating her. I may not have succumbed to my desires, but I was emotionally tied to her. Some people don't think that having emotional ties to another person constitutes cheating, but that is complete bullshit.

I took off my suit and changed into some sweatpants and a long-sleeved T-shirt. I didn't want Carleigh to have to stare at my arm during dinner, even though it was a part of me that was never going away.

When I got back into the kitchen, Carleigh had stripped down to her lingerie. *Whoa, she isn't playing!* She had on a purple satin bra and panty set, and her body was looking tight.

"Got too hot in here?" I joked as I sat down at the kitchen counter and watched her prance around in her four-inch heels. She was putting on a show, and I didn't want to be an inattentive audience. "Want me to turn the air on?"

"Actually, I was hoping you'd turn up the heat." She winked at me over her shoulder and continued to toss the salad she was making. "Your mother called a little while ago."

"Oh, cool. I spoke to her briefly earlier but she had to go to her bridge club meeting."

"She really likes playing bridge, huh?"

I chuckled. "She and her friends play that game like their mortgages depend on it."

"Speaking of mortgages, can you believe I actually sold a house today?"

"Wow, that's great!" I clapped for Carleigh. "Big house or little house?"

"*Big* house. In today's market, the asking price dropped about a third, but, still, I'll take what I can get at this point."

"How much was your commission?"

"Fifty-one thousand."

"Damn, girl, you just made my dick hard." We both laughed. "You know I'm playing, but I am proud of you. I'm sure this means a lot to you."

"It makes me feel like I'm not a complete failure."

I got up from the counter and walked up behind her, placing my real arm around her waist. "You could never be a failure; not in my eyes or anyone else's."

Carleigh turned and kissed me on the lips. "You always say the right things to make me feel better."

"I saw the bedroom," I said, running my fingers through her hair. "Looks like you want me to make you feel a whole lot better."

She gazed lovingly into my eyes. "I do. I need that. I've felt like there's been such a distance between us lately."

That's because I've been dating Brooke, I thought, then forced a grin. "Well, I've been so boggled down with the sites, but, from now on, I'm going to be around so much that you'll probably get sick of me—*quick.*"

"Ummm, never that."

Carleigh picked up a cucumber slice, placed it in my mouth, then kissed me. It felt good to be flirting with my wife; kissing my wife.

After we finished dining by candlelight, Carleigh made her next move.

"How'd you like the casserole?"

"It was incredible." I rubbed my stomach. "I'm stuffed."

"Aw, I was hoping you'd have room for dessert."

My eyes perked up. "Dessert? You made dessert?"

"Don't seem so shocked, Damon. I've baked a few cakes."

I tried to suppress a laugh, but fell out laughing anyway.

Carleigh waved her finger at me. "Don't bring up my pineapple upside-down cake." She picked up a dinner roll. "Or I'll fling this upside your big-ass head."

"I wasn't going to bring that up." I held up my palms defensively. "But now that you did, remember how we couldn't get that smell out the kitchen for two or three weeks?"

Carleigh threw the roll at me and I caught it.

"I'm gonna get you now," I said, then jumped up from my chair, as did she.

I chased her around the table. "Damon, leave me alone!" she screamed out in delight as I tackled her and started tickling her. "Damon . . . stop!" She was laughing so hard that she could barely get the words out.

"Say you're sorry for throwing bread at me," I demanded, still tickling her.

"I'm . . . I'm . . . I'm sorry . . . now quit!"

I let her go and we both lay on the floor, staring up at the ceiling and breathing hard.

Carleigh climbed on top of me and started kissing me. I wrapped my arms around her waist as she straddled me. After a long, prolonged kiss, she lifted up my shirt, planted butterfly kisses all over my chest, and started grinding her hips on my dick.

"What about dessert?" I asked, when we came up for air.

Carleigh grinned. "Why don't we eat it in the bedroom?"

Five minutes later, we were in our room making human ice-cream sundaes out of each other. Carleigh had brownies—that she had actually baked—vanilla ice cream, chocolate syrup, chocolate sprinkles, whipped cream, and cherries.

I did her first and she was delicious. She was completely nude and lying on a towel. I spread chocolate syrup on her thighs, her lower legs, and her feet. Then I put whipped cream and sprinkles on her breasts. I strategically placed four cherries around her belly button and put a nice, big scoop of ice cream right on top of her vagina. Then I proceeded to lick and eat it all off her.

The sensation of the ice cream on her pussy made her shiver as I started with her breasts. I licked the whipped cream off slowly and methodically, enjoying how she moaned with delight. Then I suckled on her breasts, one at a time. I don't know what it is, but I've always been a serious breast man. Most of my friends were all about the ass and thick legs, but give me breasts any damn day.

"The ice cream's melting. My pussy's so damn hot," Carleigh told me as I continued to work on her breasts.

I came up for air, grinned. "I'd better pick up my pace then."

"Your pace is perfect. I was just saying . . . Oh, shit, Damon," she practically screamed as I lapped up the cherries around her belly button.

I stuck the tip of my tongue inside and she winced. Carleigh was so ticklish; it was extremely cute. As I consumed the last cherry, I pulled her thighs apart and fingered her clit. The ice cream that was sitting on top of her mound was melting and trickling down, mixing with her juices.

I moved farther down but skipped over her pussy and licked the chocolate syrup off her left leg. I started at the thigh and went all the way down, until I was on my knees at the foot of the bed, sucking her toes, one at a time.

"We need to do this more often," I said, pausing to stare Carleigh lovingly in the eyes. "This is the best dessert I've ever had."

Carleigh gave me a look that I hadn't seen in ages; one that made me feel like she appreciated both me and our marriage. Then . . . she pouted.

"What's wrong?"

"How come you didn't use any of my brownies?" She propped up on her elbows to eye me suspiciously. "You think they're going to taste nasty, don't you?"

I chuckled. She knew me too well. I put down her leg, grabbed a brownie off the plate on the nightstand, and took a huge bite. "Scrumptious!" I proclaimed. "Just like you!"

I kissed her with part of the brownie still in my mouth. When we came up for air, I said, "See how good good they taste?"

"Your loving is good good." She looked down at the ice cream on her pussy, which was more like soft-serve now. The heat from her was melting it like the sun. "Get back to work."

"Oooh, feisty. I like that."

I laughed and proceeded to lick the chocolate off her other leg and the rest of her toes. It was finally time for the main course, and I wasted not a moment burying my entire face in her pussy. I ate her like she was both my first and my last meal. Carleigh grabbed on to pillows, the sheets, the headboard, the edge of the nightstand; any and everything to try to keep herself from catapulting from the bed. My "head game" was right on point that night—if I proclaimed so myself. It had been a long time since I'd felt so comfortable with my wife, in my home.

When it was Carleigh's turn to make a human sundae out of me, she did an overwhelming job as well. She put whipped cream all over my dick and cherries all over my balls, crumbled pieces of brownie all over my chest, and made a trail of small spoonfuls of ice cream down the middle of my stomach. She consumed all of it and sucked my dick like it was giving her life.

For the first time since the accident, it didn't seem that she was uncomfortable at the sight of my arm. In fact, she was the one who took my prosthetic off because she knew that it sometimes still caused me slight pain. Then she *shocked* me.

"Turn over. I want to lick your ass," she stated nonchalantly.

In my entire life, I'd never licked a woman's ass, and no woman had damn sure ever licked mine. I was not sure how I felt about her saying that, but two things were for sure. I was not going to turn down her proposition because the chance might not ever come around again, and I was curious about whether it would feel as good as I had heard.

As I turned over, I held back a laugh. I didn't want Carleigh to think that I was amused by her. I was remembering how Steve always bragged about an ex-girlfriend of his, Raquel. This was way back in the day; Steve hadn't had a bona fide woman in years. Anyway, he used to tell Bobby and me that Raquel was a big freak who loved to toss his salad. The mere thought of it used to make me wince because Steve was not the cleanest man on the planet. His breath was often tart, his armpits would offend my nostrils from time to time, and I couldn't begin to imagine what his ass must have smelled like . . . nor did I want to imagine it.

On the flip side, I tended a bit toward overkill on my personal hygiene, but at moments like this it all paid off.

Carleigh first spread whipped cream on my ass cheeks, then licked it off. Then she poured chocolate syrup down the crack, held me open with her hands, and used the tip of her tongue to tickle my anus. I found myself thrashing on the bed; it felt great as she made sure she got every drop of that syrup. She stuck one of her freshly manicured nails into my anus and I shuddered.

"They say that a man's prostate is his greatest sexual organ," I barely heard her whisper. "Even more so than his dick. Is that true?"

I tried to regain some composure so I could respond. "Um, I'm not sure about all of that, but what you're doing feels incredible." I could feel a nut building up in my balls and I was ready to explode. I'd already come once when she was blowing me, and I didn't want to risk not being able to get hard for a third time to fuck her and give her some of my good good. I turned over on my back, and seeing Carleigh's face covered with chocolate syrup and knowing it came out of my ass was extremely sensual. "Why don't you come ride my dick? We might be able to make a baby tonight."

Carleigh giggled and climbed on top of me, putting my dick inside her hot, welcoming pussy.

"I can't wait to have your baby, a little Damon to run around here," she whispered as she began to ride me slowly.

I reached up and pulled her head backward by her hair. "I want two babies, a boy and a girl."

"Whatever you want, baby."

Now that's what I'm talking about, I thought, as Carleigh gripped my dick and started milking me with her inner muscles. I could feel myself explode inside her about ten minutes later and wondered if my seed would finally be planted.

Brooke

September 12, 2008

OFTEN thought about Damon and had to refrain from calling him a hundred times a day. The first anniversary of our accident had passed, and even on that day I somehow kept myself from calling. He had become such a significant part of my life, and a part of me was missing. I understood why he had to stay away from me, I really did, but it didn't make matters any easier on me.

Patrick and I were taking things slowly, despite being lovers again. I refused to make a serious commitment. His parents were still his parents and were always going to be his parents, so that presented a major problem. Neither of them would ever forgive me for destroying the facade that they had built in their marriage. Patrick didn't want to discuss that I'd outed his father. It was a bone of contention for him, and even though it was not his fault that Mr. Sterling had taken him around his mistress, acting like she was his stepmother when he was still married, Patrick regretted having ever confided in me about it.

That's the thing about secrets. The only true secret is one that *no one* else knows about but the people involved. Take my true feelings for Damon. They were my little secret; there was no point in others knowing that I was head over heels in love with him. Nothing good could come from it, which is why I denied my emotions to Destiny every single time she asked.

Destiny was getting ready for a date with Wesley, a man she had met on Damon's Last Good Men site. They had been out once before. Well, not technically. She had met him at a Starbucks so they could both get a visual of each other, but that had only lasted about ten minutes. She was on break at work and couldn't stay. However, she came back and told me that he was "so fine that I want to suck his dick until I can tell him his blood type." *Now that is some hella fine right there.*

"So, where are you and Wesley going tonight?" I asked, flipping through the latest issue of *Newsweek*. They had a great article on the Obamas. I envied them as a couple.

Destiny was sitting on the sofa, opposite from the armchair that I was sprawled in, working the straps on her heels. She had on a formfitting white dress that showed much cleavage, and her hair was up in a bun.

"I believe he's taking me to a restaurant in Adams Morgan called Bossa. Then we're going to see the Punany Poets perform at the Black Box."

"Oh, that's a cute little theater."

"You've been there?" Destiny seemed surprised. "Wow!"

"What do you mean 'wow'?" I rolled me eyes at her, then flipped to the next page. They had a photo of Michelle Obama reading to some kids at an elementary school.

"You don't get out much, Brooke, even with Patrick."

"Well, his law firm had a private function there a couple of years ago, and I actually went." I paused. "You make me sound like a hermit."

"Between slaving for Hank at that rusty-ass diner and school, you are a hermit, damn near." Destiny glanced at the magazine. "You know, Obama is making other men look bad."

I closed the magazine and glared at her. "What do you mean by that?"

She held her palms up defensively in my direction. "Ease up. I mean that in a good way. He's destined to become the most power-ful man in the United States, one of the most powerful men in the world, and he still has date night with his wife. He even takes her out in different cities. If Barack can make quality time for Michelle, and their kids, other men have no excuse."

I snickered. Every once in a while, Destiny came up with a gem of wisdom. "That's a damn good point. You should do a blog on that topic."

"A blog? You're tripping. I don't know how to do a blog, and no one gives a shit about what I have to say anyway."

"I give a shit and blogging is simple. Everyone's doing it. It's the best therapy in the world, really." I sighed. "I even have a blog."

Destiny eyed me suspiciously. "So you feel like you have to type your thoughts on the internet instead of talking with me, or other people you actually *know,* about them?"

"Now you're being overdramatic. I blog about funny shit that Tony does at the diner, how amazed I am that so many men are on the down-low, how much of an asshole Hank can be, how tough school can be, that kind of stuff."

"I'm so sick of hearing about that down-low shit." Destiny sat back on the sofa, glanced at her watch, and sighed. "Men today have it hard because too many women assume they are fucking other men."

"Destiny, I hear you, but you should see some of the men that Tony picks up at the diner. In a million years, I would never peg some of them as rump wranglers. They come in there *with women* and act like they are head over heels in love and then let Tony break them off in the bathroom or slip them his number. It's a damn shame, I tell you."

"Are you serious?" Destiny asked in amazement. "Tell me you're making this crap up!"

I shook my head. "I see it with my own eyes, all the time. Being on the down-low is nothing new. It's just a more familiar term to-day. There was a song called 'Boys in the Boat' in the thirties that used that term, but that song was about lesbians."

"Get out!"

"No, for real. Someone named George Hannah made it. People use it more now to talk about how men have sex with other men and then bring diseases home to their women." I paused. "It's a scary-ass world out there." Destiny was staring at me, making me feel uncomfortable. "Why are you looking at me like that?"

"Because you spend way too much time on the internet. That's become your best fuckin' friend."

"That's not true, but I do enjoy surfing. We're in a great age. Instead of having to look things up in an encyclopedia, everything is readily available on the Web. Think about it, if it were not for the internet, none of us would even look up one-hundredth of the stuff we learn about on there. That's how I keep up with the news and the latest gossip."

"And that's how you express your feelings, on your blog."

"I vent about life."

"Your feelings, just like I said. Why can't you talk to me?"

"Destiny, I talk to you all the time. Don't go there. I know you're always here for me."

"So why the blog?" She seemed offended that I had a blog.

"I blog because it relieves stress. It's like keeping an online diary but the names and places have been changed to protect the innocent, and to keep my ass from being fired." We both laughed. "I have about thirty followers. Not sure where they came from or why they would want to follow my boring behind, but they do. It's no big deal."

"You need to do a blog about how to pretend you love one man when your heart belongs to another."

A frown immediately overshadowed my face.

"Never mind," Destiny said. "I know you'll never admit your feelings for Damon."

"I haven't even *spoken* to Damon."

"That doesn't mean shit. I haven't spoken to Harold in two weeks and I love him just as much as I always have."

We fell silent. Destiny was thinking about what had gone wrong with her relationship with Harold. Actually, his actions—cheating on her—were nothing new. Destiny's refusal to accept it was new. She had surprised me when she came home one day and announced that she was "sick of his shit."

I could tell that she was having a hard time dealing with the breakup, even though it was about time she put her foot down. She was hoping to drown her sorrows by allowing another man— probably Wesley after the sensuous Punany Poets performance— to knock a hole in her pussy. I couldn't fault her for that; I was fucking Patrick on the rebound from Damon, even though he was never officially my man.

"Harold can kiss your monkey," I said, trying to make light of a heavy situation. "I'm so glad that you're dating someone else. I can't wait to meet Wesley."

"Shit, now you've got me scared to go out with him."

"Why?"

"What if he's on the down-low?"

I chuckled. "I'm sure he isn't."

Destiny sucked her teeth. "Brooke, two minutes ago, you were talking about how men come in the diner with their chicks and then want to break Tony off. Now you're so sure about Wesley. Please, I'm not sure about a damn thing."

"Most men still love pussy, Destiny. Relax and have a good time tonight. Going out with him doesn't mean you have to fuck him, even though, knowing you, you will."

Destiny tried to seem upset, but ended up bursting out laughing.

"You've got a lot of nerve, hooker. How long did it take you to give up those drawers to Patrick again?"

"Twenty hours and forty-seven seconds from the time I laid eyes on him," I said sarcastically, then giggled. "That's why I know you're going to fuck until the sun comes up. It takes one to know one."

"Wesley's ass is borderline late, and you know something else about me. Fifteen minutes late and he'll be standing downstairs looking like BoBo the Clown because Homey don't play that."

"You and that damn *In Living Color*." Destiny had the entire DVD collection of that Keenen Ivory Wayans show. It was a good stress reliever and funny as all get-out when you were drunk or high and watched it. "What times does the show start at the Black Box?"

"Eleven."

It was only a little past nine. "You still have plenty of time to eat and make it there."

"I wonder if Wesley eats pussy," Destiny blurted out. "Harold eats a mean pussy. I'm not sure if I can date a man who doesn't get the munchies."

"I'm going to speak that into existence for you."

"You're crazy!"

"Seriously, if you speak something into existence, it will happen."

"What are you going to speak into existence for yourself? That you can force yourself to care about Patrick again, or that Damon leaves his wife for you?"

"I do care about Patrick, Destiny. I may not think the earth revolves around him like I used to, but I still care. Otherwise, I wouldn't be dealing with him at all."

"And Damon?"

"What about Damon?" I hoped that she would drop the subject, or that Wesley would ring the buzzer downstairs. After a few seconds, I gave in. "Damon's not leaving his wife, nor do I want him to leave her. I want Damon to be happy. He deserves it."

"And so do you."

"Not at the expense of someone else's misery, I don't."

"Do you think he would leave her if you asked?"

"I don't know and I'll never know because I'll never ask. Can we let this go?"

Saved by the bell!

The buzzer from downstairs started going off and Destiny jumped up from the sofa, excited, and ran to the intercom. "Wesley?"

"Yes, love. It's me," he said in a thick British accent.

"I'll be right down."

Destiny blushed and ran down the hallway to get her purse. I was relieved; the topic of Damon's leaving his wife upset me. I felt like such a bad human being. Part of me still yearned for his touch. Life was cruel.

Destiny reappeared, headed for the door, but paused. "Brooke,

I'm not one to suggest that you become a home wrecker, but I don't want to see you settle for Patrick as some sort of consolation prize. Didn't you say that Damon and his wife are having problems? If she doesn't appreciate him, or the fact that he saved her life, then she's a coldhearted bitch and doesn't deserve him anyway."

I stared at Destiny, at a loss for words.

"I'm not suggesting that you carry on some affair behind her back. I'm *telling you,* you need to go to that man and confess how you really feel. Unless you do that, you'll always wonder what could have been." She sighed and held the door open, fingering the frame nervously. I could tell that, even though what she was saying made her uneasy, the words were coming straight from her heart and were meant to make me think more clearly. "I don't want you to have any regrets. Yes, he married her, but that was before he ever laid eyes on you. Maybe he was simply *loaned* to her temporarily; maybe you were *loaned* to Patrick. I've known you since forever, and I can see right through your facade. You love Damon, and we both know that."

Destiny left and I exhaled the breath that I'd been holding in the entire time she had been talking. A moment later, I tossed the magazine on the coffee table and rushed to the window in time to see Destiny getting into Wesley's car. He was driving a Benz. *Nice!* I couldn't get a great look at him but I could tell that he was handsome. They looked cute together. I was happy that she was opening her mind to the possibilities outside of Harold. At the end of the day, she would probably go back, like I did to Patrick.

Patrick! I had no idea what to do about him. He was expecting me at his place by midnight, the booty-call hour. Time after time, I was succumbing to his sexual advances, all the while fantasizing about Damon. I thought about what Destiny had said. No, I was definitely not a home wrecker, and I couldn't open up to Damon about my true feelings. What if he did leave Carleigh for me? I would never have a clear conscience. If he and I were going to end up together, their marriage would have to end for a reason other than me. I felt horrible, like a person waiting on a heart transplant. For me to truly live, their marriage would have to die.

Damon

October 7, 2008

'D never felt like I had the gift of discernment. I'd heard many people speak of it, particularly people from the South. How they could sense something about a person or a situation. How they could feel an event that was about to happen. That had never occurred with me . . . until the Tuesday morning when everything in my life changed.

I'd forgotten my briefcase in Carleigh's car. We had ridden together on that Monday because we attended a play after dinner at the Warner Theater in Washington, D.C. She was still asleep, so I took her keys off the kitchen counter and went out to the garage to get it. I opened the passenger-side door and reached over to the backseat for my briefcase. Then I spotted it. A foil packet on the floor in the back, halfway tucked under the seat. It was like it had fallen from the driver's seat and slipped down through the crack between the seat and the armrest, landing back there. I didn't want to believe it. My eyes had to be playing tricks on me.

I took my briefcase and closed the passenger door. I was almost back in the house when I froze in my tracks. I had to go back and see it; there had to be an explanation. A *reasonable* explanation.

A few moments later, I was sitting beside Carleigh on the bed. She was sleeping soundly. We had made love the night before. It had been intense and we had made a connection—or so I thought.

Carleigh stirred in her sleep, then gradually opened her eyes. She must have sensed my presence. She turned her head slightly and saw that it was past nine on the alarm clock.

"Damon, you're going to be late."

I didn't respond; just stared at her.

"Why are you looking at me like that? What's wrong?"

"I was thinking. Maybe we should take a pregnancy test today."

Carleigh giggled. "For what? My period's not late." She touched my hand. "Don't worry. We'll get pregnant soon enough. It's going to take some time."

"It's going to take even longer if you're still taking these." I threw the empty birth control packet on the bed. Carleigh looked like she was about to faint. "Care to explain?"

I don't know why I ever bothered asking such a silly question. I yearned for her to come up with something that made sense, but it was all going to be a lie.

"Where did you get that?"

"Oh, don't answer my question with a question, Carleigh." I stood up and started pacing the floor. "I can't believe you'd do this to me, *again*."

"That's not mine! Where did you get it?"

Okay, I'll play along! "The packet was in your car, on the back floor."

"Oh . . ." Carleigh giggled. "You're so silly, Damon. Those are old. I haven't been taking birth control since we went on that Virginia getaway."

"Really?" I glared into her eyes. "So they've been in your car ever since?"

"Yes, baby. They were probably crammed under the seat or something, fell out of my purse, and slipped out. I mean, think about it. How often are you in my car? I never look in my backseat, so those could have been there for a couple of years."

"But I clean out your car, Carleigh. I detailed your car last week."

She was speechless and struggling to think of another lie.

"I vacuumed and cleaned every inch of your car, *last week!*"

She lay back down and propped up a pillow so she could turn on her side. "You're being ridiculous. I don't have to listen to this nonsense. I am not on birth control. Maybe there's something wrong with you. Ever thought of that? I might not be able to get pregnant because of you."

I needed to hit something, but it wouldn't be Carleigh. Instead, I punched a hole in the bedroom wall. That got her attention.

She leaped from the bed and stared at me. "What the fuck was that all about? Now we've got to fix it."

"The wall can be fixed. This marriage can't."

She was breathing heavily as she continued glaring at me.

"You've told your last lie to me, Carleigh. *Your last fuckin' lie!*"

I walked out of the bedroom and she followed me in her black silk teddy. "Damon, where the hell do you think you're going?"

"Away from here! Away from you!" I yelled over my shoulder.

"You can't walk out on me!"

She grabbed my prosthetic arm and swung me around. Then she acted repulsed that she had touched it.

"You still can't deal with the fact that my arm is gone, can you?" She sighed and stared into my eyes, still breathing heavily. "It's gone, Carleigh. I can't get it back. But that doesn't make me any less of a man. If anything, it makes me more of a man because I stood up for you. That doesn't matter to you though. All you can see is my flaw. The perfect man is no more."

"That's not true, Damon."

"Yes, it is true." I leaned against the wall in the hallway and slid down to the floor, holding my head in my hands. "You're shallow, and there's nothing you can do about it."

She came and sat down beside me, trying to get me to look at her.

"Damon, we can work this out."

"No, it can't be worked out. Twice you've made the decision that I shouldn't be a father. You've deceived me and I can't trust you ever again." I did look at her then. "You can't even admit it now. We both know that you've still been taking birth control. Yet, you're prepared to sit there and attempt to tell me bald-faced lies. What does that say about our marriage, Carleigh?"

She didn't say a word. She sat there shaking her head and fighting back tears.

"You can't dictate my life, not like that. I want children. I've always wanted children and you know that. My mother has been waiting on a grandchild the entire time we've been married. I'm her only child, so you think it's cool to deprive her of ever having that as well?"

"I'm sorry, Damon. I won't take them anymore," Carleigh whispered, as if that would make a difference. "Let's go back to bed and make a baby right now. I can even go get some of those drugs so we can have twins. I'll do whatever you want. Just don't leave me."

"Why shouldn't I leave? Then you won't have to be ashamed of me around your friends. Your mother can stop encouraging you to do better." She drew in a deep breath. "Don't play dumb. Even before I lost my arm, she never thought I was good enough for you.

Now you can go find a man who's worthy. Maybe your *friend* Arnold can pass the miserable old broad's test."

Carleigh had the audacity to get angry at me then. "Don't talk about my mother like that!"

A lightbulb went off in my head. "Are you fucking him?"

"Fucking who?"

"Are you fucking Arnold?"

"Don't be ridiculous, Damon."

I started laughing. Not sure why. Maybe it was easier than crying. I never thought that Carleigh would cheat on me, but after my feelings for Brooke, I now understood that anything was possible.

"What's so funny?"

"I wanted to sleep with Brooke. I did. I wanted her, but I told her that we couldn't be around each other anymore. That I had to be faithful to you, *my wife*."

"You fucked her!" Carleigh exclaimed. "You've been cheating on me and now you've got the nerve to accuse me!"

"It's amazing how I'll say one thing and you'll hear another. Like that time you came after me with that knife, after I outed Jordan's scandalous ass. She tried to fuck me and you heard the complete opposite." I stood up off the floor. "No, I didn't make love to Brooke, but I wanted to. I didn't because I respected our marriage vows and was determined to make things work." I looked down at Carleigh. "Now I realize that I gave up the wrong woman."

"She'll never love you like me," Carleigh whispered.

"Honestly, I doubt that she'll even give me the time of day, at this point. I should probably leave her alone. I can't run back and forth into her life. It's not fair."

"Then stay with me." Carleigh grabbed my leg and tried to pull me back down with her. "I'll change, Damon. I promise."

"You apologized for the birth control before. You knew how much a baby meant to me. I can't forgive you." I paused. "I can forgive you, I guess, but I can never be with you. Not ever again."

"We can go to therapy."

"Therapy can't fix this. You've robbed me of years of fatherhood, Carleigh. How is therapy going to help?" I pulled her hand off my leg. "Maybe Arnold doesn't want children. The two of you can ride off into the sunset together."

Carleigh stood up and stared into my eyes. "If I tell you the truth about Arnold and me, can we work this out?"

I clamped my eyes shut. *She did fuck him!* "It doesn't matter what happened between you two. Not at this point. I'd rather not hear about your dirt."

"It only happened once. Just once." Carleigh ran her fingertips over my chest. "It was a moment of weakness and I should've known better. You've been so distant since your accident and you spend so much time on those websites. Then you started staying out late, probably with *her,* and I didn't know what to do."

"You started staying out first. Remember that?"

"Because it seemed like the life was sucked right out of you after the accident. You blamed me for—"

"Carleigh . . ." I grabbed her hands into mine and gazed at her. "Believe me when I say that never *once* did I blame you. The woman behind the wheel caused all of this. And she's paying for her mistakes."

"So you can forgive her, but not me?" Carleigh asked with much sarcasm. "That's just lovely."

"Like I said before, I can forgive you. It's going to take time, but I can do it. What I can't do is continue to live a lie, in this house, with you."

"I guess you want me to move out!"

"No, you can keep the house. I'll move."

She faced the wall and started banging on it with her fists. "You shouldn't have to move out of your own home. I'm the one who fucked up."

I found myself rubbing her lightly on the back. "I don't hate you. And this was *our* home; the place for us to build a life together. I couldn't stay here without you. If you want, we can sell it and split the equity, or you can stay. That's up to you."

She turned to face me. "I can't believe we're even standing here discussing this. We made love last night and now this. Things changed so fast!"

"That's the strange thing about life, but it's also what makes it exciting. None of us ever knows what tomorrow brings."

"I never thought it would bring this; that's for damn sure." She grabbed at me, overwrought with emotions, but I pulled away. "I don't want to be with Arnold, and I don't want to be alone. Please stay. We can make this work. I'll do whatever it takes."

"You'll be fine," I whispered to her. "You'll be fine."

I started down the hallway and Carleigh yelled after me, "You're going to be with her, aren't you?"

Without turning around I replied, "I don't know."

In truth I didn't know what would happen between Brooke and me. I had to reach out to her, to see where she was in life. After the way I'd dismissed her from my life, she had every right to ignore me. But I had to try. I had to try.

Brooke

October 31, 2008

ETRIFIED. That is the only way I could describe what I felt as I stood on the other side of Damon's hotel room at the Grand Hyatt in Washington, D.C. When he had called out of the blue, I didn't know what to think. At first, I was not going to answer, but I caught the call right before it went to my voice mail. He hadn't said much, just that he needed to see me right away and where he was. Then he said, "If you don't want to come, I'll understand." He hung up without another word.

I'd paced the floor at Destiny's for a good two hours, thinking about Damon and also thinking about Patrick. Even though the words had gone unspoken, I could read between the lines. If I went to that hotel room, Damon and I would make love. Then a part of his spirit would remain with me forever, even more so than it did already.

There were no other options for me. I loved Damon, so I went to him.

I rapped lightly on the door. He must have been lying in wait because he yanked it open before my hand was back down at my side.

He smiled at me and looked me up and down. I was wearing a simple black dress and it fit me nicely. I was still not exercising on the regular, but that good old stress had continued to work its magic.

"Come in," he said, then moved to the side.

The room looked as if he'd been in it for a while; not just a night. There were several bags, his computer, and papers. I wondered what was really going on.

"I'm glad that you came." He walked over to the minibar and unscrewed a bottle of orange juice. "You thirsty?"

"No, I'm fine. Thanks."

He joined me on the sofa, after I'd taken a seat. For a few moments, we simply stared at each other, both of us struggling for words.

"So how has life been treating you?" he finally asked. "You look great."

"Life has been . . . life. What more can I say?"

"I don't want you to think that I called you here to play games, Brooke."

"You'd never play games with me, Damon. You're a good man."

He set his juice down and clasped his hands together. "I try to be . . . a good man. It doesn't seem to make a difference some of the time."

"That doesn't mean you should ever change." I took his hand. "Don't ever change."

"Are you back with him? Patrick. You're seeing him again, aren't you?"

"Is it that obvious?" I shifted in my seat. "I'm not living with him, or anything like that, but after . . ."

"After I hurt you."

"You didn't hurt me intentionally, Damon, and I understand that. In many ways, I set myself up to be hurt. Despite the connection that I felt to you, I shouldn't have let my feelings grow so deep. I was more disappointed than anything, but that was to be expected. You're a married man and I'm not cut out to be a mistress."

"No, you're not, nor should you be one."

I sighed and crossed my legs. "What are we doing here? Why'd you ask me to come?"

Damon sat back and stared at the ceiling for a moment. "You should go. I have no right to do this to you."

"Do what?"

"You're trying to work things out with him, and it's not fair for me to ask you to give that up; not after the way I treated you."

I was totally confused. "But you're working things out with Carleigh." He stared at me and I read between the lines. "Aren't you?"

Damon shook his head. "No, I left Carleigh three weeks ago." He glanced around the room. "I've been here ever since."

Speechless, I put my elbow on the armrest of the sofa and sheltered my eyes with my hand until . . .

. . . he touched me. He touched my leg and it sent a shiver down my spine.

"She cheated on me, and she continued to take birth control behind my back. She made the decision for me to be childless, and I can't forget about that; not again."

I grabbed his hand and held it tightly, looking him in the eyes. "I'm so sorry, Damon. How'd you find out?"

He winked. "God winked at me."

I decided not to push the issue, even though the nosy side of me craved to know how he had discovered what Carleigh had done.

"I couldn't leave her before, but now I'm done. I'm free . . . and you're not."

I leaned my head on his chest and could feel his heart beating. I wanted to climb inside him and live there forever. We sat in silence for a few moments, holding hands and thinking about the implications of what would—or would not—come next. The ball was obviously in my court, and I adored that Damon was not trying to pressure me to make a decision.

In fact, he said, "Brooke, you should go. You should go and be with him. Go be with Patrick."

I sat up and looked at him. "You don't mean that."

"I want you to be happy, and if he makes you happy, then you should be with him. I have no right to even do this to you. I shouldn't have called. I should've left well enough alone."

"You don't mean that either." I lifted his hand and kissed his knuckles. "You're trying so hard to do the right thing, and I appreciate that, but you don't mean any of the shit you just said."

A tear began to cascade down his right cheek. I leaned up and kissed it away. Then I kissed him on the lips. Once. Twice.

He parted them and I slipped my tongue inside, exploring his essence, yearning to feel closer to him in every way. Our kiss intensified, full of emotion, full of lust, and everything in between. He pushed me back onto the sofa and I spread my legs so he could grind his dick against me. Even through our clothing, I could feel it hardening, throbbing, aching to be inside me.

I unbuttoned his shirt and yanked it off his shoulder, then ran my fingertips down his arm. When I touched his prosthetic one, he almost pulled away. I broke the kiss and gazed into his eyes.

"I need you to lay your hands on me, Damon." I caressed the fake arm. "Both of them."

Damon picked me up as I straddled my legs around his back and carried me to the king-size bed. It had a fancy paisley comforter and plush pillows. He took his time and slowly removed my dress. Then he stared at me, all of me, naked except for my black satin bra and panties.

"You're so beautiful," he said, before kissing my belly button and pulling my panties over my thighs. "I want to taste you."

"I want to taste you, too," I heard myself say, even though sucking dick had never been my choice; more like a chore. I was serious though. I craved to have his dick in my mouth. I wanted to satisfy Damon in every way.

Damon spread my legs and started sucking gently on my clit. I almost exploded from that alone. Then he pushed the tip of his tongue inside me and I shivered. He engulfed my pussy with his mouth, and I leaned up on my elbows so I could see him; see him enjoying me.

"You want to know what that woman told me that day?" I whispered.

He stopped and looked at me for a moment. "What woman?"

"The older woman at the wax museum that day. Remember that she whispered something to me?"

"What did she say?"

"'Love sought is good, but given unsought is better.'"

"Huh?"

I giggled. "That's what I thought, too, until I looked it up. It's a quote from William Shakespeare. It's from his play *Twelfth Night;* a comedy, kind of like my life. More than four hundred years ago and he understood that."

Damon sat up, moved farther up on the bed, and gazed into my eyes.

"I didn't mean for you to stop what you were doing," I chided. "That felt great."

He laughed, then seemed to be in heavy thought. "That's deep, what she said. What do you think she meant by it?"

"I've pondered over it since that day. I believe that she sensed we were not really together, that one or both of us was tied up with someone else. Maybe it was because you were wearing a wedding ring and I wasn't." That caused me to look at his hand, and it dawned on me that his ring was gone; only the tan line from where it had once been remained. "I interpret the quote to mean that we can't control our own destiny, no matter how hard we try. We can seek out the perfect person, in our eyes, and it can be a hit-or-miss situation, but if we fall in love unintentionally, then it must be the real thing."

"This is definitely the real thing." Damon took my hand. "I have a quote for you."

"Oh, really?"

"Yes. 'To get the full value of joy, you must have someone to divide it with.' "

"Who wrote that?" I asked, impressed that he was reciting quotes.

"I have no idea; maybe me." We both laughed. Then Damon kissed my hand. "Brooke, I love you, and I'm going to love you forever. I realize that these were not the ideal circumstances, but that old woman was right. This love *is* better."

"Indeed it is."

I buried my tongue in his mouth, shocking myself, and savored the taste of my pussy on his tongue. His kisses were the kisses that were meant for me; there was no doubt there. *He* was meant for me.

I pushed Damon onto his back and started caressing his upper arm. He seemed a bit uneasy and I knew why.

I whispered in his ear, "Don't worry. I love all of you."

He helped me to get his shirt all the way off and I looked at his prosthetic arm. For me, it symbolized his manhood; what he had sacrificed for both Carleigh and me. I fingered it, where it attached to his remaining muscles. He winced a little.

"Is it causing you pain, Damon?"

"No, I'm okay. I only want to be with you."

"Take it off."

"My arm?"

"Yes, I want to see you. *Really* see you."

After briefly hesitating, he unclasped it and slid it right off. I touched his arm, at the place where it had been severed, then leaned down and kissed him there. He shuddered and I couldn't tell if it felt good or bad.

"I'm not hurting you, am I?"

"No, actually, I like that." I saw a tear forming in his eye. "You really do accept me as I am."

"I adore you as you are."

I unbuckled his pants, unzipped them, and pulled them down around his ankles. I unlaced his shoes and took them off, then removed his pants completely. His dick, astonishingly bigger than I'd even fantasized about, was stretching the fabric of his boxers to their limit. I decided to relieve it.

"Let me rescue him," I whispered, pulling Damon's boxers down and off. I sat there, staring at his dick, *my dick,* then could not take it another second.

I started with his balls, lobbing them up and down on my tongue, teasing them before I captured them in my mouth and sucked on them like sweet grapes. Damon moaned and ran his fingers through my hair.

I planted small kisses on the shaft of his dick as I worked my way up to the head. He had to be holding at least ten inches of meat, and he was thick and curved.

Damn!

I ran the tip of my tongue through the slit and loved his taste. Damon was such a healthy eater and it showed. Either that or I was so enraptured by him that it didn't matter. I took as much of him into my mouth as I could manage without choking and used my hand to cover the rest of his massive dick. I wanted to please him more than I'd ever pleased anyone. This was the man who had risked his life for me, who had become an intricate part of my life, who had become my entire life.

"I want some more of you," Damon whispered—music to my ears.

"My pleasure," I told him as I got resituated on the bed and lay on my side with my feet toward the headboard.

He spread his legs and put his left thigh over my head. I put my left arm behind his back and grabbed the upper part of his thigh with my right as I greedily swallowed more of his dick. He grabbed one of my ass cheeks with his hand, and I moved my hips back and forth, giving in to his desires.

Even though I never thought it was possible, I swear that Damon and I did climax at the same exact time. He exploded in my mouth and some of it trickled out the side of my lips onto the bed. I licked it up—every last drop. Overnight, I'd gone from Ms. Timid to Ms. Porn Star. *What a difference a man makes!*

We took a half-hour break and then made love for the very first time. It was incredible. Damon drilled his dick into me . . . *literally.* I was on my back, gazing into his eyes and kissing him, with my legs wrapped around his back, clamping my pussy on to him like a vise. The heels of my feet were bouncing up and down on his ass as he did a slow grind into me, and it was an amazing feeling of deep penetration. His dick was *huge*! I am surprised Damon didn't go deaf when I screamed during my next orgasm. The people in the next hotel room knocked on the wall, I was so damn loud.

Damon and I both laughed when they banged on the wall.

"They might call security on us," I said.

"Nobody's going to get me out of you," Damon replied, still grinding into me. "Not security, the police, or even the FBI."

"Ooh, I like it when you talk dirty."

Damon picked up his pace and gave me the ride of my life until he climaxed moments later. I found myself shuddering, and I will be damned if my toes didn't curl up.

We made love for the rest of the night, until the sun rose over the horizon. It could have been the first time either of us had ever made love, or it could have been the last time we thought we ever might. It felt like a little bit of each.

My entire life had changed . . . in the span of an evening. I'd have to end things with Patrick, for once and for all. That was a welcome thought. I'd only continued to deal with him because I couldn't have Damon. I was wrong for that, but he'd definitely sensed it—had said as much on more than one occasion—and I could now confess the truth. I never doubted that Damon wouldn't go back to Carleigh. He'd been away from her for three weeks, and if I understood one thing about him, it was that he was a good man and would never go back on his word. It made me feel better to know that she'd constructed the destruction of their marriage. That way, I wasn't the one who destroyed their home life, even though I was sure that many would label me a home wrecker. I was sure that Mrs. Sterling wouldn't be able to wait to throw it up in Patrick's face and make the proverbial "I told you so" statement about what a tramp I was. But I didn't care, not one bit. I had the man of my dreams and I was going to embrace every moment in life. Fate had brought us together, but love would see us through to eternity.

Damon

March 8, 2009

SEVERAL months passed and I'd never been happier. Carleigh had accepted the terms for our divorce, and we were simply waiting for it to be finalized. Brooke and I were purchasing a new home together in Northwest, D.C. She had graduated and obtained her certificate as a pharmaceutical technician and was working at a local drugstore. She was elated to be out of that diner, but still hung out with her friend Tony quite often. I'd never been homophobic, but he took some getting used to. After a while, I understood why Brooke loved him so much. He always gave it to you straight, no chaser. He kept it real, and in a world where people put on so many pretenses, he was a breath of fresh air.

Tony had become such a mainstay around our house that he had convinced me to start yet another dating site for men searching for men exclusively. We were still working on a name for it though. Tony came up with all kinds of raunchy names: Dick4Dick.com; Bottomsup.com; RamMeHard.com; SuckHimGood.com. I tried to explain that all of those names sounded like sex sites. Tony's argument was that it was better to get to the bottom line. He insisted that anyone going on any of those sites is looking to get laid, despite

poetic profiles stating the person is searching for a serious relationship. I didn't agree.

Case in point, Summer. If another couple never made an official
hookup in the history of Able Minded Dating, I would have been
content. Summer had found the love of her life on the site, and I
was elated.

Brooke and I—along with Tony and Destiny—attended
Summer's wedding together.

Summer married Duncan, a lawyer who was also confined to a
wheelchair after a terrible skiing accident in the Poconos. His injury had been temporary though, and he had learned to walk again.
They were the perfect couple and incredibly cute together. When
they exchanged vows at the church, I don't think there was a dry
eye in the place. Why? Because Summer *walked* down the aisle. I
was proud of her. She had been determined to get used to her prosthetic legs before her wedding date. After months of therapy and
learning how to use them, there she was, *walking.*

At the reception, which took place at the Old Ebbitt Grill near
the White House, Destiny and Tony were actually competing over
who could pick up the most men. My, oh my, how times had
changed!

Summer and Duncan shared a first dance together. It was out-
standing as they swirled around the floor to "At Last" by Etta James.
Brooke looked stunning in a sleeveless red gown. I asked her to join
me on the dance floor, halfway through the song. Destiny and Tony
jumped on the floor quickly after we did, both of them having had
a little too much of the champagne punch already.

I shook my head as I approached Duncan and Summer. I tapped
Duncan on the shoulder. "May I cut in?"

He grinned and went to dance with Brooke, not a bad trade-off
in my opinion, and I took Summer into my arms.

"You look so happy," I told her.

"I am happy, and I owe it all to you." She kissed me on the cheek. "I never thought that I would find someone—anyone—to love me, but you told me I could."

"And you did."

"Thanks to you, and your site."

"Oh, you would've found Duncan anyway."

Summer looked confused. I could tell her legs were tiring her some because she held on tightly to my neck. "What do you mean? I wouldn't have found him."

"Yes, you would've. What's for you will be with you, no matter what other circumstances try to intervene." I glanced over at Brooke, who was bantering lightly with Duncan. "Take Brooke and me. We'd seen each other before, but the timing wasn't right. When it was time for us to meet, we did. When it was time for us to love one another, we did."

"I've never seen you happier either," Summer said. "I always thought you belonged with Brooke, but there was that little . . ."

"Marriage?" I chuckled. "Well, things are all good now. In fact, I need to ask you for a favor."

"Anything," Summer said as I began to whisper in her ear.

After the wedding cake was cut, it was time to throw the garter and the bouquet. Summer had a symbolic garter that Duncan was to throw out to the men. Tony ran out onto the floor and wrestled another man down to the ground to get it. After he came back to the table, flailing his arms and breathing all heavy, Brooke glared at him.

"Are you satisfied now? Making a fool out of yourself like that." She tried to suppress a laugh, but couldn't, and we all fell out laughing, even the four other people sitting at the table that we didn't know. "You can't get married anyway," she added jokingly.

"Hey, you never know when the laws in D.C. might change. Besides, my groove is in the heart. I'm ready to meet the man that Candy Land dreams are made of and settle down. I'm sick of all the drama and bullshit out there."

Destiny took another sip of champagne punch. "Amen to that!"

Tony punched her lightly on the arm. "The night's still young. At least your dating pool is thicker than mine up in here. Only slightly though. They're so many down-low men in here trying to pretend like they like women, it's pathetic."

"Well, hell, I can use a little sugar in my bowl," Destiny said. That's when it became obvious that she had consumed too much liquor.

Brooke rolled her eyes at Destiny. "Yeah, right, whatever. Why don't you just hook up with Tony then? You two could take the term *freak* to another level."

Tony and Destiny stared at each other for a moment, like they were contemplating it, then said, "Naw!" in unison.

"Look at all those fish out there waiting to catch the bouquet!" Tony exclaimed. "You'd better get on out there, Miss Destiny." He swirled the garter around on his fingertips. "I've already claimed my destiny, no pun intended."

Destiny was about to get up when I said, "Destiny, why don't you chill! There are so many women out there, you don't stand a chance."

"Plus, she might fall on her ass and make a fool out of herself," Brooke stated sarcastically.

Summer walked out onto the dance floor where all of the

women were positioning themselves to catch the bouquet. She pretended to throw it a couple of times, faking out the women who were ready to pounce.

Then she surprised everyone by walking over to our table and handing the bouquet to Brooke.

Brooke stared up at her. "What's this?"

"You're the next woman to be married."

Brooke was shocked. "What do you mean?"

Summer pointed to the bouquet. "Why don't you smell the flowers?"

Brooke played along and put the bouquet to her nose. She took a long, deep whiff. "They smell great."

Summer sighed, looked at me, and shrugged.

"Brooke, why don't you pin one of the roses on me? It's a tradition," I said, lying.

"I've never heard of that tradition before," Destiny broke in.

"Me either," Tony said. "Not that I hang out at a lot of weddings."

"You're making that up," Brooke said, right on point. "That's not a tradition."

Summer said, "Well, I'm starting a tradition at my wedding." She pointed at the bouquet. "Pin that big, fat yellow one in the middle on Damon."

Brooke seemed reluctant but pulled the rose out, and as she did, she *finally* noticed the four-carat diamond engagement ring on the stem. She gasped. Destiny dropped her champagne flute on the table and it spilled everywhere. Tony let out a slight scream. Summer giggled.

I got down on one knee beside the table. Everyone was watching since Summer had brought the bouquet to our table instead of throwing it.

"Brooke Alexander, will you do me the honor of being my wife?" I asked.

Brooke's eyes almost popped out of her head. Then she whispered, "But your divorce isn't final."

"It will be, and I like to look ahead." I took her hand in mine. "We're already living together, and I don't want to waste any precious time. The second that we can, I want to commit to you for the rest of my natural life. I'm not a perfect man, but . . ."

"I don't need, or *want,* you to be perfect, Damon. I love you for you."

"Then marry me for me."

Brooke started crying as she yelled out, "Yes! Yes! I'll marry you!"

I took the ring off the stem of the flower and placed it on her finger. "I'm going to love you forever . . . and even after forever."

Everyone started clapping as Brooke fell into my arms. It had been a long road, but we had finally arrived at our final destination: *unconditional love.*

Brooke

August 18, 2011

DAMON took me and the kids to the Cayman Islands for a late-summer vacation. Our twins, Judith and Jacob, were playing in the sand, trying to bury Damon, even though their little hands were hardly big enough to scoop enough of it onto him. They were sixteen months old, and I still hadn't recovered from the fifty-eight hours of labor. I almost killed Damon in the delivery room, and the doctor, and the nurses. I was out for blood. But it was all worth it. My family was worth it.

All of Damon's sites were pulling in tons of money, and we were able to purchase an even bigger home once we had the children. We were having an architect make the plans for our dream home, which we planned to build within the next few years. While I refused to give up the job at the pharmacy—I needed to maintain my individuality—I was helping out with everything. Damon now had a large staff, which included Tony, who runs StallionsOnline.com—a compromise between the raunchy and the practical.

Destiny found her a man on the Last Good Men. She had to break a few eggs to make an omelet, but she met a man named Wisdom, who was a local newscaster and sexy as all get-out. She was the godmother of both twins. Bobby was Jacob's godfather, and Steve was Judith's.

My parents were so excited that Damon and I were married. We didn't have a big wedding. We got our license and got married at the courthouse. We were so glad to be together that we didn't need all of that fanfare. We only wanted to get our life together started—and we had.

Damon got up from the sand and walked toward me. I was sitting under the largest beach umbrella that I could find, trying to stay out of the unrelenting sun.

"Your turn," he said, as he plopped down on the huge towel beside me. "They've worn me out."

I was so glad that Damon felt comfortable enough to come out on the beach wearing only swim trunks. Some people stared at his arm, but most people ignored it. He had no reason to feel ashamed.

"I'm not letting them attack me," I said jokingly. "That's Daddy's work."

"Oh, is that in a manual somewhere?"

"Yes, the one that I'm working on now. I'll let you know when it comes out."

"Smart-ass!" Damon sat up and kissed me on the lips, then looked back at the children. "They're so beautiful—a mixture of you and me."

"Yes, they are." Judith and Jacob had curly, medium blond hair, and their skin was the color of cashews. "I hope people don't judge them unfairly because of their racial makeup."

"Oh, please, Brooke. No one cares about interracial couples anymore, so why should they care about what bloodlines our children have running through their veins?"

"Even though Barack Obama is in office, racism is still very prevalent in this country."

"How many people have said anything about you and me?" he asked. "Since we've been together?"

"A few, but they were all ignorant. I don't give a damn what they think, but our kids have to grow up with that ignorance."

Damon took my hand. "I love you, *without limitations,* and no one is going to tell me who to love."

I grinned at him. "Nor me. You couldn't get rid of me now if you became a serial killer."

"Yeah, right. Stop laying it on so thick."

"Okay, maybe not a serial killer." I ran my fingers through his hair. "You could never hurt a flea and you know it."

"I'm so glad that we're together, *married.* We were meant to be."

I looked at the twins and then back at Damon. "Yes, we were."

I got up and ran toward the kids, then dove into the sand and started throwing sand on them.

"Bet you can't bury Mommy," I said.

As they jumped on me and started yelling out, "Mommy," over and over, from the corner of my eye I saw Damon staring out at the ocean. My beautiful, beautiful husband.

Zane's Commentary

HOPE that you enjoyed *Total Eclipse of the Heart* as much as I enjoyed writing it. It evoked many emotions in me, and I gave much thought to constructing the characters and story line, as I do with all of my novels. I wanted to explore many things with this book; some more obvious than others. I have long dreamed of writing a novel with a main character with a disability. Many of my readers are disabled, and they deserve a voice in literature. They love and are loved, like everyone else.

Years ago, I was doing a book signing in Maryland and I was overwhelmed when a group of wheelchair-bound fans came out and requested that we take pictures together. They had never been to a signing before but had asked their caretakers to bring them. We took the photos and had them developed at a one-hour photo shop so that I could sign them. I was extremely moved by that gesture, and I have never forgotten them. So if any of you are reading this, I want you to know how much I love and appreciate you all.

I have never liked shallow people who base a person's value solely on their looks. They do not realize how many positive experiences they miss out on by playing into that mind-set. In this novel, Brooke and Damon were brought together by unlikely circumstances but learned to appreciate and embrace the differences in one another. I did not reveal which of them is African-American and which is Caucasian; it does not matter. What matters is that they found one another amid a sea of toxic situations. I also wanted to prove that a good love story is a good love story. Too much emphasis is put on a book's being an African-American title. Passion and sensuality, love and romance, are universal. So is the story of Brooke and Damon.

Even though Damon literally saved Carleigh's life, she did not truly appreciate it. He was a trophy husband to her. She did not care about his desires to further his dreams or to have children; her only concern was that he looked better than the men any of her friends were attracting. Once he was damaged goods, she had no further use for him. Yet, despite her cheating and lying, when he got ready to leave, she did not want to lose the fight. A lot of people are like Carleigh. Usually men want trophy wives though, and once the wives gain a little weight or do not look like they did before childbirth, the men are ready to toss them aside. But this goes deeper. What would you do if your mate became disabled? Would you stand by his or her side or be ready to move on?

For twelve years I have been giving relationship advice, and never once have I suggested that a person cheat. I attempt to convince people not to, even when they feel justified. While I have written many books about people who do cheat, they generally learn their lesson. In this book, I wanted to show how temptation can creep up without it being the intention of either party. Brooke and Damon's relationship started out innocent enough, but they ended up dating—albeit unofficially. Damon's decision to stay away from Brooke was the only way that he could ensure that they would not end up in bed together. Too many people do not believe that being tied to someone emotionally is a gateway to cheating, but it definitely can be. So if you or your mate spend a lot of time talking to someone else on the internet, chatting with the person daily on the cell phone, or "hanging out as platonic friends," do not be surprised if something else comes of it.

Brooke's relationship with Patrick brought her down in so many ways. Her self-esteem was ripped from her, causing her to bury her pain in comfort foods and to gain weight. Even though he was considered a good man, he was not a good man for her. Nor should she have to accept sharing him with other women. If that was in a memo, I must have missed it. Once she started pulling away from him and allowed Damon to encourage her, instead of put her down, she was able to pursue her dream of bettering her life. I hope that some of you will learn something from that. We should never sacrifice our happiness for someone else, period. Everyone is entitled to happiness, and while many people will be in your life, not all of them are meant to be there. That can be a hard pill to swallow, but it is true. It is also true that you are not meant to be in everyone's life. Your habits and beliefs may not be conducive or advantageous to them. If you are in a toxic relationship, cut ties and begin anew.

I could go on and on about my purpose in writing this story, but, hopefully, that is clear enough and you will think about the messages contained within it long after you close the book. The experience of writing it will last within me forever.

Blessings,
ZANE

The Zane Music Group presents songs inspired by *Total Eclipse of the Heart,* featuring the vibrations of R&B, Soul, Retro, Dance, Latin, and World Rhythms by various hit artists. You have read Zane's books. You have seen Zane's show. Now listen to Zane's stimulating music, designed exclusively for all of the special moments in your life. Executive Produced by Zane and Maxwell Billieon. Available now for digital download on www.PlanetZane.org and www.Zanestore.com.

A Readers Club Guide

TOTAL ECLIPSE OF THE HEART

by Zane

1. Do you believe that Patrick was actually in love with Brooke, or was he with her because he wanted to control her? Do you think he felt that Brooke was beneath him?

2. Why would Patrick cheat even though he made a commitment to Brooke and wanted to marry her? Do you think that people who want multiple lovers should simply stay single?

3. Do you feel that people should do things sexually that make them feel uncomfortable in order to satisfy their lover? How important is it that your lover makes adjustments for you?

4. Was Destiny right when she stated that women need to accept that they will have to share men to have a relationship?

5. Did Carleigh ever view Damon as more than a trophy husband? Do you think she should have ended her friendship with Jordan and her other friends who tried to sleep with Damon?

6. Do you feel that Carleigh was not supportive of Damon's websites because she was jealous?

7. Did the financial strain from the real estate market's falling apart cause Carleigh to treat Damon differently?

8. Was Carleigh right to take birth control behind Damon's back?

9. Would you feel comfortable making love to your mate if he or she suddenly had a disability?

10. Do you think that people with disabilities are just as entitled to find love as everyone else? Would you remain with a mate if he or she suddenly became disabled?

11. How do you think Damon handled his disability? Did he try to hide his true feelings about it?

12. If you had to lose an arm or a leg, which one would you choose and why?

13. How do you feel that Brooke's weight affected her self-esteem? What were Brooke's other self-esteem issues?

14. What were the striking similarities between Brooke's relationship with Patrick and Damon's relationship with Carleigh? Do you think Tony was right when he stated that most men are closet homosexuals?

15. Do you think either Brooke or Damon should have tried to make their current relationship work instead of ending up with each other?

16. Who was your favorite character in the book?

17. In what ways were the characters in this book different from those in the typical romance/erotica novel?

18. After reading this book, do you believe that two people can fall into an extramarital affair without it being intentional?

19. Were you surprised at the end of the book to find out that Brooke and Damon were an interracial couple? Did it affect the way you felt about them or their relationship?
20. Which do you think is African-American, and which do you think is Caucasian? Does it matter?

THE HOT BOX

ZANE

Coming soon in hardcover from Atria Books

Turn the page for a preview of
The Hot Box. . . .

PART ONE: Curveballs

Lydia

I don't know how I got so lucky. Phil and Glenn working two different shifts at the Freightliner factory was like celebrating Christmas
and New Year's every fucking day. And every day was a "fucking
day."

Okay, let me break it down for you. Glenn and I had been in a
committed relationship for the past three years and everything was
copacetic. He was fine, sweet, romantic, and he had a scrumptious
dick. Glenn was the man . . . my man. But here's the thing. No matter how terrific he was, I still needed a little variety and extra spice/
dick in my life.

When I was younger, I believed in the fairy-tale kind of love.
One woman per man and vice versa. Then, by the time I was in the
tenth grade, I realized that shit like that really only did happen in
fairy tales. Men were dogs—straight-up pit bulls, Rottweilers, and
Doberman pinschers. Either they were a new breed, different from
previous generations, or people had swept a ton of shit underneath
the rug back then. Personally, I assumed it was a combination of
the two. Surely women stayed and endured a lot of drama, cheating, and abuse because they were scared, destitute, or ashamed to

have to admit to a failed relationship. A ton of women still did that but a lot of chicks decided to stay single.

I was single—meaning unmarried—by choice. I was so sick of all the articles, blogs, and news stories preaching and whining about how the majority of African-American women would never get married. And? What was the point of getting married? If a man was going to fuck around on you, disrespect you, and possibly bring some incurable shit home to your ass, you were better off running a game on him while he thought he was running one on you. It is going to get to the point when women will have to ask themselves the question: what man would you prefer to die for because he cannot keep his dick in his pants?

The only exception was if the brother was paid—*majorly* paid. Men with money could always get it. Women of all ages, races, and walks of life were willing to drop their drawers and spread them for the right amount of money and prestige. All except for my best friend, Milena. She was on some unrealistic, mind-bending shit.

She had it all in the palm of her hand and ruined it. Well, I kind of facilitated the drama—truth be told. I didn't have a choice. If I'd kept a secret like that from her, and she'd found out that I was privy to it later on, our friendship would've been history. Milena was not the forgiving, or forgetting, type. Those two words were simply not in her vocabulary. So I told her, and the proverbial shit hit the fan.

It was a new day though. Jacour Bryant was back in Kannapolis and Milena needed to wake the fuck up and smell the coffee. She needed to hook back up with him before some other chick pussy whipped him. Jacour was a pro-baller who had recently suffered a knee injury that ended his career, but not his bankroll. He'd decided to move back to the area and the town council was having a big shindig for him the next night. I hadn't seen him yet, but the hoochie grapevine had alerted me that he was finer than ever.

All of us had seen photos of him throughout the years, and I'd even watched several of the Yankees games to see what was up with him. He'd dated all of the top celebrity divas; he'd run through them like they were bases on a diamond. It seemed like he was tied to a different woman every other month. That didn't really surprise me. All of that pussy was being thrown at him, but Jacour wouldn't have settled down with anyone but Milena. Too bad she didn't get that memo.

Those were the very thoughts running through my mind as Phil was sucking the lining out of my pussy—my juicy, delectable pussy. My pussy was like sunshine on a rainy day. Like fireworks in the middle of a snowstorm. Like flowers in the middle of the desert. Like . . . never mind. I'm sure you get the picture. My pussy was off the fucking chain.

"Hmm, your pussy is off the chain," Phil said, reading my mind and coming up for air. "I can't get enough of these cookies."

"You're not done eating the cookies until you drink your milk along with it." I loved talking dirty. "Until I bust in your mouth, you're still on the clock."

"Hell yeah! I'll put in the work!"

Phil went back to "servicing" me and I glanced at the clock. It was a little past noon. Glenn got off at three, the same time that Phil started his shift. I was playing a dangerous game, but it felt so . . . damn . . . good. Did I mention that Phil was one of Glenn's best friends? Oops, guess not. Glenn, Phil, and Jacour were like the three black Musketeers. They could literally fit right into their footprints, even though the novel was written in French nearly 160 years ago and the setting was way back in the seventeenth century.

Phil was definitely Athos. Even though he was the same age as Glenn and Jacour, he acted a lot older than them . . . and looked it.

He hit the whiskey hard, a side effect of living in a small town without shit else to do. Phil was handsome but very secretive and drowned his sorrows in liquor, exactly like Athos. I was glad that he used liquor to cope with his shit. I did not have to listen to his problems, just fuck him.

Glenn was damn near Porthos's twin. He was a bit extroverted, extremely honest, and slightly gullible. He could also eat a sister out of house and home, like Porthos. But instead of being a bit chunky, he worked out religiously to get rid of the excessive calories he inhaled. He never actually ate; he would inhale that shit . . . real talk.

That meant Jacour was Aramis Jr. In the novel, Aramis was portrayed as ambitious and unsatisfied. He was arrogant and loved intrigue and women. If that wasn't Jacour, my name wasn't Lydia Sterling.

I had this way of allowing my mind to wander to the strangest places while I was fucking. Somehow, imagining the Three Musketeers, along with their sidekick, d'Artagnan, fucking me in a barn back in the seventeenth century, made me climax all over Phil's face. Athos had me bent down on my knees slobbering all over his dick as he lay in the hay, while Porthos was hitting it doggie style and slapping my ass like a true swashbuckler. Aramis was standing over us, jerking off and shooting a load on my back, and d'Artagnan was stroking an elephantine dick, moaning and waiting on his turn to ram his billy club up my ass.

"Oh shit!" I screamed out as I exploded. My thighs were shaking with the aftershocks as Phil lapped up all of my juices like a good little doggie.

"Can I pound you with this big cock now?" he asked when he was through.

"A cock is a chicken," I said. "Only dicks can enter my temple of immense sexual pleasure."

"Cock. Dick. Zipper Ripper. My Ramburglar. Whatever you want to call it, I'm 'bout to blow your back out with it."

"Damn, make it bounce, Daddy!"

The nasty talk was really what turned me on the most about Phil. Glenn would not even send me a sexy text message, never mind say that kind of stuff to me in person. Plus, even though Glenn could definitely put a pounding on my pussy, he always wanted to be on top. Fuck that! I loved to ride.

I pushed Phil over onto his back and climbed on my saddle. "Hee haw!" I exclaimed as I started riding him cowgirl fashion.

I didn't give a damn what anyone said. I could cum the hardest when I was on top. A man hitting it from the back could give it a lot of depth, but unless his dick was shaped like a candy cane, he was *not* hitting the G-spot. Sometimes I could get close to the G-spot in the reverse cowgirl position, but I recognized what it felt like when that part of me was touched, and it wasn't happening with a dick.

Now, when I was on top, it was all good. All the right ingredients were there. I was in complete control and, nine times out of ten, he could last longer on his back. Besides, I didn't want dude sweating all over me; hell to the triple no. If anyone was going to drip sweat that day, it was going to be me. It was bad enough that I had to put up with that from Glenn.

A lot of women think that you're supposed to pounce up and down on a dick. Not! That's not riding. Men might be feeling it but that breaks the continuity with the stimulation on my clit. Rocking my hips did the trick every time. I'd imagine myself riding an actual horse bareback, its massive body moving below mine, bouncing me gently as it trots, my clit rubbing up against the leather saddle. The heartbeat of the horse between my legs was the same as the throbbing of a dick while I was riding one. Yes! There wasn't anything like it.

Phil became that horse and took me for a smooth ride. "Um, hell yeah!"

"Work this dick, baby." Phil grabbed my ass and started pounding on my cheeks like an African drum. "Take all this dick."

My cut came on the radio: "My Body's Hungry" by Teena Marie. My body was hungry as hell, too.

"I wonder if I'm a sex addict," I said to Phil, who couldn't have cared less if I was as long as he was getting pussy on the regular. "You think I am?"

"Wha . . . what?" he replied breathlessly.

"Do you think I'm a sex addict?" I asked as I started gyrating my hips like a professional belly dancer . . . or stripper.

"I *think* you're fucking fine, and I *know* your pussy's the best in town."

"How you know all that?" I slapped him playfully on the face. "You done fucked every woman in town?"

"No." He paused to catch his breath and then grinned. "Only half of them."

That motherfucker was lying. I had him so pussy whipped that he couldn't even see straight.

"Yeah? Well, I bet they didn't get it in with you like this."

That's when I fucked that fool into submission. He'd curled up in the fetal position by the time I finished with his Ramburglar, or whatever shit he was poppin'.

"It's after one," I informed Phil a little while later. "You need to bounce."

"I've got two hours left. Let me hit the shower first."

"You know I don't play that."

"How come you don't ever let me take a shower after we fuck? You let me do it before."

"That's because no funky-ass bodies—or balls—hit my sheets. You're not coming up in here, after working an eight-hour factory shift, smelling like a muskrat, and touching me. You can take an after-fucking shower at your own crib."

"You're a trip, Lydia."

"So are you, *Phil*. We're both doing the wrong thing when it comes to Glenn. Don't front like it's only me."

"That's not what I meant. It's not about Glenn. It's about how cold and callous you can be at times."

I propped myself up on my elbow and stared into his eyes. "Look, you're my jump-off and I'm yours. It's as simple as that."

"Jump-offs don't last as long as we have and—"

I pulled the pillow from under his head. "You're getting too damn comfortable. Get going; I still have to change the bedding and air this place out before Glenn gets home."

Oops, I forgot to mention that Glenn and I were actually shacking. Yeah, I was lowdown but Phil had a roommate and there was no way we were getting it in at his place. Briscoe was the biggest gossiper in town; fuck what you heard about women putting business out in the streets. He was the TMZ of Kannapolis.

Phil reluctantly got up and started putting on his clothes. "You want me to come through in the morning?"

"Nope. I got something to do in the morning."

"I don't have to stay long."

"Five minutes would be too long." I paused and wiggled my nose. My bedroom smelled like stone-cold fucking. I was going to have to open up all the windows and spray an entire can of Indian Money up in that bitch before Glenn got home.

"Whatever, Lydia. Like I said, you're a trip."

"Have you seen Jacour since he got back?"

"Yeah, we all hung out last night after I got off work. Glenn didn't tell you?"

"No, but that's cool. I was wondering where he was."

"Humph, you've got a lot of nerve, clocking Glenn's moves."

"Is he cheating on me, Phil?"

Phil looked at me and laughed. "You don't really expect me to respond, do you?"

"Hell yes, I do."

Phil shrugged. "Hell if I know. Maybe, maybe not."

"Well, if I ever find out who the bitch is, I'm cutting her."

Phil smirked. "I'm out of here." He turned to leave. "Call me if you need anything. I'll be home by midnight, as usual."

"Wait, one more question," I said, sitting up in the bed and letting the comforter fall off my bare chest.

"What?" Phil crossed his arms with much attitude.

"It's not about Glenn. What do you think about when we're fucking?"

He shrugged. "I think about us fucking."

"You don't fantasize about other women, or worry about busting a nut too quick, or keeping it up?"

"No, no, and no. I think about how good your pussy feels. I've got to go."

"Oh, now you're in a rush?"

"Damn right. I can't shower here and I have to be at work on time. Plus, you need to do what's good to get this place straight before my boy gets home."

Phil left, and a moment later I heard his car leaving the driveway. The good part about where Glenn and I lived was that it was down a dirt road and no one could spot people coming or going. Otherwise Phil and I would have been busted ages ago.

Glenn got home about four and I had dinner ready for him by five. Lasagna, garlic bread, and salad: his favorite meal. We put in some overtime that night in bed. He must've felt guilty about being out late the night before and not telling me where he'd been. I waited for him to bring it up. Like I said earlier, Glenn was like Porthos: honest.

After I'd sucked him off real slow and lovely, he filled me in on everything that was going on with Jacour, who hadn't been home in years. Glenn had spoken to him on the phone about once a week, but now that Jacour was back, I was hoping they wouldn't be running the streets every night, hitting the bar scene in Charlotte. That was all I fucking needed; my man hanging out with a famous athlete around a bunch of money-hungry hoes. Shit, most of the chicks would fall over a man if he bought them a few drinks. Jacour in a Charlotte nightclub would damn near cause a stampede. My baby wasn't going to be riding shotgun with Jacour when that shit went down. If he brought home even one photo of Jacour and him standing in front of a spray-painted backdrop with a bunch of sluts hanging all over them, I was pulling out my box cutter. There was one surefire way to make sure that wouldn't happen.

"Does Jacour still have the hots for Milena?" I asked Glenn as we were falling asleep in each other's arms.

"Jacour still *loves* Milena but I told him that's a wrap."

I sat up and stared at him. "Why'd you tell him that?"

"Oh, she still feeling him?"

I sighed and lay back down. "She hasn't said that *exactly* but, once they see each other, you never know what might happen."

"I'm gonna call him first thing in the morning and tell him to ask her to his party. You think she'll go?"

I shrugged. "He has a good shot."

"Cool," Glenn said and then turned over. I hated when he did that but he preferred to sleep on his right side and I had this attachment to the left side of the bed.

I stared at the ceiling. Milena couldn't stand Jacour, but I needed her to come to her senses.